Further Comments Not on the Back Cover

"A superb book to relax the business traveller, entertain a holiday-maker, or for the sheer enjoyment of anyone lucky enough to read it! Gripping and funny."
Dave Jarvis – ex-global president, Hilton Hotels International

"A wonderful collection – movies must follow!"
Guy Bellamy

"Trev Hunt's writing harks back to the days when short stories were a real art, when they had to be complete and satisfying, not just an incident we are left to ponder over."
John Hollands, MC – author of the 'The Dead, the Dying, and the Damned' etc

".....I found 'Ibiza Shorts' to be a wonderful companion - far better even than the most gripping of novels! Poignant with a love of life and the author's love of Ibiza."
Anthony J. Pike – hotelier to the stars, Ibiza

"You may, as I did, come away from this book with the distinct impression that you've actually met some of the characters portrayed....."
R. Lawson – English editor of the 'Ibiza Now' society magazine

IBIZA SHORTS

Trev Hunt

Acorn Classics House Ltd

First published in Great Britain in 2005
by Acorn Classics House Ltd

P.O. Box 1565, Wedmore,
Somerset, BS28 4YA

A CIP catalogue record for this book is available from the British Library

ISBN 0–9548058–0–1

Printed and bound in Great Britain by
J.W. Arrowsmith Ltd, Bristol

About the Author

Trev Hunt has recently sold his successful business to enable him to write full time.

A member of Mensa, he holds a private pilot's licence on helicopters, and was once a part-time instructor at an international racing drivers' school, teaching pupils the arts and techniques of safe race driving in Formula 3 single seaters. He is also a past official Liberal parliamentary candidate.

He spends three months every year in Ibiza, and hence is very knowledgeable about his subject island. Back home in England, he lives in an ancient farmhouse in the Cheddar Valley with his wife, Joyce, and their two sons.

Trev Hunt relaxing at his friend's Cesar's Water Sports Centre

Dedications – by Trev Hunt

This book is dedicated to those who, each at the appropriate time, have encouraged and helped me:-

The Late J.W. 'Chinky' Davies – *my brilliant English teacher at the Wells Blue Grammar School, who aided my love of literature, and first encouraged me to write.*

John Hale – *screenplay writer and novelist extraordinaire, whose credits include Ann of the Thousand Days, Mary Queen of Scots, Elizabeth R, The Whistleblower, The Fort etc., who has given me so many hints and pointers when I needed them most, and treated me like his equal, when I am not.*

Guy Bellamy – *considered by many to be the funniest writer in the English language and with eleven comedy novels to his name, Guy has held my hand, and criticised, edited and chivvied me from the birth of this book as an idea right through to publication.*

My wife, Joyce, and son, Andy – *who have both helped whenever and however they could, and think I take them for granted, which I don't.*

Contents

The San Rafael Kidnap

With sophisticated relaxed elegance, thirty-one year old Fiona Newman leaned back in her chair outside 'Bar Don Quixote' in the quiet backwater of San Rafael and drew deeply on a Dunhill cigarette, secure in a long ivory holder, her eyes focused on a point of infinity somewhere high in the blue Ibiza sky. She wore a nicely under-stated floral silk Prada dress, with a matching coat thrown casually over the seat next to her, a simple gold chain necklace with similar styled bracelet, and gentle soft-toned make-up which assisted rather than took over her natural complexion. Parked just a few metres away was her cream Jaguar XKR open sports, a blanket draped over the driver's seat to prevent the leather from burning when she again slipped behind the wheel.

A leopard or panther does not have grace, its movements are slinky. A deer has grace, its movements elegant and energy efficient. Whilst with her come-to-bed dark brown eyes and long black hair Fiona had the hunting instincts of a panther, she moved with the elegant grace of the deer, contriving to make her both attractive to men and dangerous to know.

Of medium height, with a figure to die for, she was so very nearly the real thing, ex-Roedean, randy, and ri – but that was it, she was not rich. Although she did have a rich husband, who gave her a generous allowance, which was nearly the same thing. Nearly, but not quite the same. Fiona Newman was income rich, but capital poor.

So, as she idly watched the few passing vehicles, most of them en-route to or from the Ibiza to San An road, and considered whether to order another Martini, Fiona Newman was fairly content with her life.

With impeccable timing and twirling his exuberant moustache, Felipe, the rather portly waiter, approached and she did order another Martini. Her next port of call was home, and she knew her husband would be there, on-line to San Diego, where he owned an electronics corporation, and from where he also controlled his fuel broking business. Or Philadelphia, where he owned a trucking corporation. It was really quite blissful, she was here enjoying the sun whilst boring old Brad was at home making the money for her to do so.

As he walked away, Felipe turned, an afterthought having struck him, and spoke in his excellent English, his voice made more attractive by its Spanish origins, "Oh, I nearly forgot, Señora, a man left this for you, but instructed me to wait fifteen minutes before I give it to you." Saying which he handed her a plain white envelope.....

* * * * *

Fiona had met her husband, Brad Newman, a couple of years ago when her then friend, Elsie Blunkette, had wangled invitations to the welcoming cocktail party on board an American cruise liner – one of the most luxurious ships afloat.

Tall, slim, elegant, and at just over twice her age, with a fine head of neatly coiffured grey hair, Brad was still grieving over the wife he lost to cancer. Indeed, he had taken the cruise on the advice of his doctor, who was seriously worried about his friend and patient's well being, as he wallowed so deeply in despair and loneliness. Brad Newman was rich beyond the dreams of Croesus, and Fiona showed him a way out of his despair, for after encouraging him with a few American-style dry martinis, she took him to his bed in his 'penthouse' cabin, where she had loved him like he'd never been loved in his whole life before.

The following morning, for the first time in months, Brad found himself ready for a full 'American' breakfast, with hash browns, bacon, beans and three eggs sunny side up. He had stopped grieving, and realised with something of a shock that he had fallen head over heels in love with this classy young English broad, who was totally unlike any other female he had known. But what was even more incredible was that she clearly fancied him, as a man, not for his money – of that he was convinced.

He'd quit the cruise there and then, and booked the best suite at the famous Pikes Hotel. Within a month he had bought a fantastic villa from a newly impoverished German – "Set in a hundred acres of its own ground, and for just a few million bucks!" he confided in his rich Californian accent to a stateside pal called Chuck. And a month after that he married the 'classy young English broad' – Fiona Farnsworth-Jones had become Fiona Newman.

But unfortunately for Brad, Fiona Farnsworth-Jones was not quite the wysiwyg (what you see is what you get) straightforward decent girl he had taken her to be. When still a schoolgirl at Roedean, she had decided that with the single exception of her best friend, mousy little Hazel, who idolised her and was content to act as her school lackey, she didn't like girls, and would never be able to marry one who'd keep her in idle luxury for the rest of her life.

She also decided that she did like boys – they were more fun, had an extra piece of vital equipment to make them more enjoyable in bed, and, at least in her circle, there were many who could keep her in idle luxury, without expecting her to do something horrid, like work.

At the age of twenty-three, she had married Rupert Farnsworth-Jones, a leading light in the Kent county set. A life of private boxes, royal enclosure passes, point-to-points and fox hunting dovetailed deliciously with chartering yachts and private aircraft, soirees with the 'in' crowd, together with hosting and being hosted at the finest restaurants and country house dinner parties – Rupert Farnsworth-Jones enjoyed spending his money as much as she did, and sometimes even faster.

Except, as she discovered soon after a groom found him hanging from a beam in the stable, with a bridle rope round his neck and the best part of a litre of scotch in his belly, it was not his money. For Rupert Farnsworth-Jones had been broke for the best part of two years, had robbed Peter to pay Paul, gambled with money he didn't have, and worked his way through his family inheritance with a vigour which bordered on the heroic. Some may say he chose the easy way out, but all alone in a damp smelly stable, with only a rope and a bottle was not easy, just very, very sad.

Then, at Rupert's funeral, her own father had quietly asked if she could lend him a hundred grand, as he'd 'experienced a bad run on the stock market'. With a sinking heart, Fiona realised that both Plan A, to be born rich, and Plan B, to marry riches, had come to an abrupt end. Leaving her only with Plan C – to try, try, and try again. At the age of twenty-nine, Fiona Farnsworth-Jones was not on the shelf, she was back in the hunt. It was time to search for pastures new – she would chase the money to the sun.

In Nice, Cannes and St Tropez, she nearly struck lucky on two occasions, but both times was beaten to the punch by younger girls. Confiding her financial position over a bar in St

Tropez to François, the aging barman, she had honed in on his suggestion to head for the new 'in' place in the Med, where she could spin out her meagre funds by living in a cheap flat within a few hundred metres of the money crowd in their yachts, and start hunting in earnest.

So Fiona Farnsworth-Jones had come to Ibiza.

With her skilled mannerisms, she had talked her way onto a couple of yachts, been invited to Thailand by an old, and decidedly camp, man, and nearly been raped, though the would-be rapist at least had the good grace to react in the time-honoured way to a well aimed kick between his legs.

She had also been taken under the protective wing of Elsie Blunkette, the most frightful snob she had met in her entire life. Made wealthy by her late husband, Elsie knew everyone who was worth knowing in Ibiza. Or who Elsie Blunkette thought was worth knowing, which was not always the same thing. She was also a rather bitchy gossip and self-appointed moralist.

Fiona Farnsworth-Jones was manna from heaven for her, a girl clearly from the upper drawer, who, Elsie believed, could only add to her own status if she claimed her as a friend – she was therefore pleased to invite Fiona Farnsworth-Jones to accompany her to a cocktail party aboard a visiting American cruise ship.

And that was when Fiona had met Brad.

But her love of sex did not extend to continuing the marathon session of loving with which she'd introduced herself to him – he rapidly found himself reduced to a 'wifely duty' status. Instead, her love of sex and the high life meant she took lovers, many lovers – one-nighters too numerous to remember, and always at least two regulars. Currently, these were her toy-boy, twenty-three year old Tony Smart, and her 'mature man', retired bull fighter Federico Byass. Additionally, there was the possibility of something developing with a French restaurant owner, Michel le Farré.....

As an added bonus, she had also lost the cloying attentions of the awful Elsie Blunkette, who, whilst being a most frightful snob and gossip monger, considered there was a limit to acceptable behaviour, or as she put it, 'a pale beyond which one should not go', and beyond which Fiona most certainly had.

* * * * *

Fiona took the envelope from the waiter, and regarded it with interest. This was delicious – she loved intrigue. There was no name on it, nothing to show it was for her, except of course that Felipé had said so.

Desiring to extend the excitement of wondering which of her lovers had chosen this approach – or was it only a potential lover? - she toyed with the envelope, turning it over and over in her long fingers.

She was still doing so when Felipé returned with the Martini over ice tinkling in her replenished glass, and after the first sip she could resist no longer – she tore open the envelope. To say the least, the contents were not what she was expecting, and having read the short message, her first reaction was to drop it onto the table.

The letter was made up of words cut from various publications. It read "We have your husband. You can have him back for 10 million euros, else in 7 days we kill him. Be at your phone 1800 today for instructions. Signed – The Popular Front for the Independence of Formentera."

Fiona picked it up and re-read the short note three times before letting it again fall to the table, as panic struck her. What it said was obviously nonsense – her husband was safe at the office in their villa, on-line to his business interests in the USA. So what was behind it – was it a prelude to some form of blackmail, or some sort of wind-up in the worst possible taste?

She felt a sudden urge to be at home, to discuss it with Brad. Or did she, for if instead of kidnap it turned out instead to be a form of blackmail, she would not want her husband to be privy to all aspects of her behaviour, would she?

Then on impulse and leaving her glass still half full, she snatched up the letter and ran to her car, pulling aside the blanket as she slid behind the wheel. The powerful V8 engine roared into life, and, with the back wheels spinning, she gunned the Jaguar out of San Rafael in the direction of their villa, two kilometres away.

As she roared along the long track which served as their drive, its surface in the Ibicencan way a mixture of dry dirt and small stones, her eyes failed to take in the beauty of the scene, the citrus trees on their land on both sides, their neighbour's tethered goats grazing, free of charge, beneath the trees, or the low dry stone walls at regular intervals. Instead, her eyes and concentration were applied to keeping the fast car on the loose surface heading in the direction she wanted it to go.

Her husband's carefulness with expenses meant they had no actual live-in servants, and she expected the house to be calm and quiet. What she did not expect as she approached the porticoed front of the magnificent villa she called home was for the main entrance door to be wide open, for Brad was far too cautious for that. Sliding the Jag to a halt, she leapt out and ran into the cool, spacious and largely open-plan house, calling her husband's name as she did so, but in reply hearing only her own voice echoing back from the marble floors and internal stone walls. Two things soon become apparent – her husband was not at home, and there were numerous signs of there having been a violent struggle.

Incredible as it seemed, it would appear that Brad Newman had indeed been kidnapped.

* * * * *

After a stiff gin and tonic she felt more relaxed, and after a second she was actually calm, in the words of the song from 'Oliver', 'reviewing the situation'. Partway through the third gin, her mind moved to the one true friend she had in the world, and, her hand no longer shaking, she reached for the telephone and dialled her mobile number.

"Hazel? Okay to talk?"

The upper-class but less confident tones of her old English schoolfriend came through loud and clear. "Absolutely, darling, I'm having coffee in a McDonalds as it happens."

"Sounds ghastly."

"No – it's actually quite good, although the crockery could stand some improvement. What news – why the call?"

"The most incredible thing's happened, Poppitt – Brad's been kidnapped, and they say they're going to kill him if I don't pay up."

"My God – that's awful!"

"Yes – that is, yes and no. I thought it was awful at first, but you remember what a bore he was when you came to visit us? You said you had to cut short your holiday because you couldn't stand the heat, but I know it was boring old Brad you couldn't stand."

"I wouldn't have said that, Fiona."

"No, because you're too jolly polite. Anyway, Poppitt, I've decided to let them jolly well do it – they can kill him with my blessing. I'll get rid of the boring old fart and get rich all at the same time – and without having to do anything myself."

"You cannot be serious!"

"You sound like John McEnroe, Poppitt, but I assure you I am serious – and I might add that I had expected you to tell me I was doing the right thing, not imply I'm wrong. The kidnappers are due to phone in about an hour, when I'll tell them what they can do, then I'm going to phone my lawyer and get him to pop over from England next week to advise how I can best take charge of all Brad's lovely lolly. Meanwhile, I might just slip out tonight to cheer myself up."

"You've not been drinking, Fiona, have you? You've always had a bit of a ruthless streak in you, but I've never known you like this before."

"Well all I can say, dear little Hazel, is thanks a bunch for your support! Or more honestly, your complete lack of it. I'm sorry to have bothered you, and suggest you get back to your Big Mac or whatever passes for high cuisine in your miserable little world these days."

But in reply all she heard was a 'click' as the phone went dead. Angrily, she replaced the handset, and, although she remained staring at it for nearly a minute, hoping that her long time friend and supporter would ring back, it only returned her stare with the deep purple of absolute silence.

Knocking back the remains of her gin and tonic, she headed for the kitchen to make herself a strong black coffee. As she did so, she checked her watch – just under an hour to go.

"Well Mister bloody kidnapper, we'll soon settle your hash," she said out loud to the kettle as she waited for it to boil.

* * * * *

She had actually fallen asleep when the phone rang, although whether this was a reaction to the excitement or the gin, or both, was not clear. She picked up the phone, but did not speak. After a few seconds, a female voice on the other end of the line broke the silence.

"Señora Newman?"

"Yes – what do you want?"

"I think, Señora, it is more what you want – I assume you want your husband, and we have him."

"Why on earth do you assume I want my husband?" Fiona started to get malicious pleasure from the rather bizarre conversation.

"You received our note?"

"Yes – I thought it was very funny. Who on earth are 'The Popular Front for the Independence of Formentera'?"

"That information is not part of our negotiations, but we hope all the world will soon know who we are. We are demanding independence for Formentera from Spanish fiscal control – to make it a centre of Finance and Insurance. The British have the tax haven of Gibraltar, the Spanish should make Formentera a similar independent low-tax zone – we expect to shortly have support for our plans at the very highest level."

The voice was Spanish, yet not Spanish, almost South American. For a moment, Fiona felt a chill of fear – who *were* these people – drug barons or what?

"So you want the money to finance some publicity – and if I don't pay, you'll kill him?"

"Exactly."

"Ten million euros is an awful lot of money – you'll just have to kill him."

"The price is too high?"

"No, the principle is wrong – you'll have to kill him."

"Is there any price you would pay to get him back alive?"

"No. He is a boring old fart."

"So you want us to kill him?"

"The light dawns! Yes, kill him – you'd be doing me a favour."

"We do not do favours, we offer services. So, instead of rendering you the service of releasing your husband, you want us instead to render you the service of his murder?"

"You're not exactly the sharpest knife in the drawer, are you? But I think you've now got the general idea."

"We charge for our services."

"I see." Fiona paused. Her instinct was to tell the woman to get lost. But pragmatism took over, for she certainly didn't want Brad to be released.

"How much?" she asked.

"To assassinate a multi-millionaire? I should think ten million euros would be fair."

"So the service changes, but the price stays the same?" Again a pause. "One million, that's my final offer."

"Five million."

"Still too much. Half that – and I'll require proof that you've killed him. Evidence and a death certificate so I can inherit his estate."

"Done – two and a half million euros for killing your husband. I shall contact you tomorrow with information as to how you pay. But we always do get paid, or we kill the person who has defaulted." With which the kidnapper hung up.

For the second time that day, Fiona was left staring at a silent telephone. But this time the adrenalin was flowing – she was finally going to be rich.

* * * * *

She stretched out on the settee, and, totally lost in thought, felt like celebrating. 'Don't count your chickens before they're hatched,' her dear old mater had taught her. But nevertheless, she still felt like celebrating. Which to Fiona always meant a man.

But who? Which one? The mature elegance of Federico, her retired bullfighter escort and lover? Or the more vibrant exciting company of her toy-boy – the twenty-three year old Tony Smart?

After lengthy thought, considering the options with anticipatory pleasure, she decided she had had enough excitement for one day, tonight she needed gentling, to lie peacefully in the arms of an older man.

Tonight she needed Federico Byass.

* * * * *

The dawn had passed and become mature morning when the bell called her from slumber. Half awake, half asleep, her hand reached for the bedside phone.

"Yes?" she managed into the mouthpiece. But still the bell rang, and she realised it was the door not the telephone that was calling her.

Throwing the lightest of black robes over her sheer blue see-through nightie, she moved to the stairs, smiling contentedly as her mind went back to last night. Federico had been superb – mature and strong, like the bulls he had once fought. But tender and kind to her as no bull could ever be. Yes, she must certainly see more of her matador, even if he was broke and she always had to pay for their little 'soirees'.

She opened the door to a man of about her age. Of medium height and well groomed, he was dressed in an expensive light-weight pin-stripe suit which screamed 'Savile Row, London', and she recognised him.

"Hello, Fiona, I caught the first flight I could when you phoned – no need for a client like you to wait for a whole week to see me, and I must admit the thought of a spot of sun has its appeal. May I come in?" he said rather than asked with ex-public school confidence.

"Yes – of course Adrian. But I won't actually need you until next week. Anyway, you'd better come in."

Careless of the way her robe swung open, she led her visitor to the lounge. One of the brightest young lawyers in London, Adrian Pincher was well aware of her husband's wealth, but nevertheless, she was rather thrown that he'd reacted so quickly to her cry for help. She'd have to dress her story rather carefully to show she was not anticipating Brad's death with any enthusiasm, or even certainty that it would happen.

She sat down on one of the settees and indicated that he should sit beside her. Then briefly she explained the situation to him, replacing her own instructions to the kidnappers to kill Brad with an alternative version that he had often spoken of his fears, and instructed her to never give in to blackmail, or the demands of a vile kidnapper.

"So you see, Adrian, Poppitt, I can't possibly pay them – which makes it seem that there's a great likelihood that I'm shortly to again be a widow. I asked you to come next week so that if that happened, we could start sorting out the estate – it will be important for dear Brad's memory that I take full control as soon as possible to preserve the assets he worked so hard to create."

"What an awful situation for you to be in, my dear Fiona. Have you contacted the police?"

She shook her head. "The kidnappers said that on the first sniff of police involvement they'd ki . . ." a consummate actress, she managed to sob as she continued, "they said they'd kill him."

"My forté is financial advice, so I can't help with the kidnappers, I'm afraid. But I do think you should consider the police, rather than letting the kidnappers call the shots. Oh dear – that was rather clumsy. I meant call the tune."

"I can't take the chance with the police, so as I also can't pay the kidnappers, all I can do is hope and pray that they'll release him anyway. But," again she managed a sob, "but if they don't, I'm going to need your financial advice, Poppitt."

Adrian Pincher leaned back in his chair, and said, "Oh dear, this is not going to be easy. May I have a drink – water will do?"

She fetched the water – 'Fonter agua congas' – over ice. "What won't be easy?" she asked, continuing the conversation where they'd left off.

"You remember when you were about to marry Mr. Newman, that his lawyer asked you to sign a paper?"

"No – but go on."

"No, I'm not surprised you've forgotten, you were so excited about the prospect of landing a good catch you'd have signed anything. But what you did sign was a pre-nuptial agreement – they're very much the vogue in America."

"And this pre-nuptial agreement says what?"

"That if for any reason whatsoever your marriage ceases to be, you will have no claim on Mr. Newman or his estate, and your allowance will cease forthwith."

"But that was to cover divorce!"

"Or death – a very decisive way in which a marriage might 'cease to be'."

"And you let me sign this, this rubbish?"

Fiona's pulse-rate had doubled, her voice risen an octave, as panic struck her.

"If you're honest, you will recall I advised against it – I even put that advice in writing, and asked you to sign that you'd had the original. Here, I have a copy." He produced a sheet of paper from his pocket, and waved it to her.

For a moment, a bizarre picture of Chamberlain waving the famous 'Peace in our time' paper from the train doorway came to her mind. But, like the original, this was war, not peace. She decided to change tack, to use the skills which God had given her, to get the best out of this man's most astute brain. Letting her robe fall open, she leaned towards him.

"Adrian, there must be a way, something we can do!"

"You have spoken to the kidnappers?"

She nodded, then stood up and moved a pace away.

"I must think, think." He dropped his head into his hands.

"Adrian," she said after a while.

"Yes?" He looked up. The robe lay on the floor, and the see-through nightdress revealed all of this lovely woman's body.

"Did you ever read any Sherlock Holmes stories?"

Unable to keep his eyes off her, his throat had gone dry. "Sherlock Holmes?"

"Yes – he used to describe the complexity of a problem by how many pipes of tobacco he would need to smoke in solving it – a two pipe problem, a three pipe problem, et cetera."

"So?"

"So I don't smoke a pipe. But I often find making love releases the tension and gets the grey cells working. I think we have a three-bonk problem here." She took his hand and pulled him to his feet.

"I miss Brad so much – come to my bed and be nice to me, whilst we talk through our three-bonk problem."

And unprotestingly, Adrian, the hot-shot lawyer from London, allowed himself to be led upstairs to her boudoir.

* * * * *

Incredibly it worked, and whilst he was considering whether to go for what would be for him a record fourth bonk with this incredibly lovely woman, the answer hit him.

"Got it!" he said, "we can't challenge the pre-nuptial agreement – you have no money for legal costs, and we'd lose anyway."

"But what can we do?" Fiona sat up in bed, looked at her companion's crucial part, and realised that physically he was no further use to her – she'd have to instead content herself with his brain. Which was really what she wanted from him anyway.

"When you finally got round to telling me about Brad's terrible violence to you, you said that understandably you didn't really want him back, and anyway he himself would not want you to pay the ten million ransom? That is right, I take it?"

"Absolutely."

"So as they need the cash for their ludicrous scheme, we'll pay them to keep him alive! Say a million a year. But they must keep him imprisoned, and each year produce proof that he is alive. That way both your allowance and life-style will continue, without the burden of your husband's cruel presence."

"Brilliant!"

* * * * *

Two hours later, by which time Adrian had departed to book himself into a hotel, the kidnappers rang again.

"Señora Newman?"

"Si – yes. Oh thank God. Look. Forget what I said yesterday, I have a proposition to put to you. Over time, it will give you much more money. But you must not kill Brad!"

There was a pause before the woman caller replied. "He is already dead. We have killed him as you instructed. Is this an attempt to get out of paying us?"

"Dead? He can't be! No, I want to pay you."

"Good."

"But I want to pay you to keep him alive – not to kill him! Don't you see, if he's dead, I have no money."

"He is, and you owe us two and a half million euros. I shall send his ashes with payment instructions."

With a click, the line went dead.

People hanging up on her was not something Fiona was accustomed to, but for the third time in two days, she found herself staring at a silent telephone, this time with all the colour drained from her cheeks.

* * * * *

She was still sitting, holding the telephone handset, when the doorbell rang. With something of an effort, she dragged herself off her chair and into the spacious entrance hall to answer it.

Yet again it was a man in a suit, although this one was a light fawn, rather than pin-stripe. A tall, older, sun-tanned man who looked as if he'd been hewn out of solid wood, but not without a rugged charm, for even in her distressed state her mind ran automatically to a sexual assessment.

"Ma-am?" The voice American, West American – probably Californian, like Brad.

"'Er, yes. Yes, what is it?" She spoke shortly – she had other things on her mind than itinerant Americans.

"Would you be Mrs. Newman – Mrs. *Fiona* Newman?"

"Yes, what of it?"

"Is your husband in?"

"No he's not in, he's out."

"The latter would surely follow the former, Ma-am. Good, may I come in – it's actually you I came to see? My name is Chuck Davis, and I'm a colleague of your husband's from San Diego." So he *was* Californian.

Without answering, Fiona turned and led the way into the lounge. She was still in a daze from the phonecall telling her Brad was dead.

Unbidden, Chuck Davis sat down, and spoke quietly. "Mrs. Newman, I'm your husband's corporate accountant. But my relationship with him goes back much further than that. I'll be honest – quite simply I idolise him. I met him in Vietnam . . . ."

Still standing, and her mind partly elsewhere, she interrupted him. "Vietnam, what are you talking about?"

"Vietnam was a little war we got ourselves involved in. I was there and Brad was there, neither of us by choice. He saved my life – easy to say, isn't it, just four little words? I was a max of four minutes from being captured by Charlie – the Vietcong – they'd have killed me by torture as they usually did at that time. My situation was hopeless, and the Hueys had been grounded to avoid being shot down." He paused, and sighed with emotion, before continuing, "But Brad was having none of that – I'll never forget the chop-chop sound of his rotors as he flew in through a hail of bullets and lifted me out. You know, I'd do anything for that man – lay down my life, kill for him . . . . Anything. Mrs. Newman, whether you realise it or not, you've got yourself the best goddamned man on planet earth. Which is why I'm here."

Chuck's story was not adding to Fiona's happiness. Suppose he found out that she had ordered his beloved hero Brad to be murdered? Would he really kill for him? Would he kill her for him, in revenge? Assuming the kidnappers didn't do so first, when they found out she couldn't pay them.

"You must love him a great deal."

The sound of the American's voice dragged her back from her thoughts.

"Oh – that. Yes, of course."

"Certainly he idolises you. So many times he's told me about his lovely English rose – how lucky he was to find you."

"Mr. Davis, it's absolutely lovely to meet you and learn of your devotion to Brad. But I am rather busy, and Brad will not be back – that is, Brad will not be back for a few days. What can I do for you?"

"Money, Ma-am, money. No doubt he has been too proud to ask you, or even tell you himself, but the Brad Newman Electronics Corporation is broke. He has often told me about your wealthy family – 'nearly the English aristocracy', he says – and to save his bacon, a cash input from you personally would be mightily appreciated."

"Brad's broke? But that's impossible!"

"I only wish it were, Ma-am, so how soon could you let us have some funds?"

But before she could answer, the doorbell again rang. Without thought, she went to answer it. To a nosy busybody she definitely did not want to see.

Elsie Blunkette was dressed in an odd sort of flower-power sixties outfit with an ill-chosen knitted shawl. She waved a magazine in Fiona's face, and pushed past her into the hall, hitching up her bosoms as she did so in the way some overweight women do.

"There's something here you really must see, Fiona. I say, do you have any gin?"

As they entered the lounge, Elsie saw the American. "I am sorry, Fiona, I see you have a visitor already – not interrupting anything, am I? One can never be sure with you."

Fiona glared at her. "This is a good friend of Brad's, if you don't mind, Elsie."

"Well that's hardly stopped you in the past, has it darling? But company or not, I really think you should see this." Again she waved the magazine, almost triumphantly.

Chuck rose to his feet. "Say, that's no problem, ladies – I'll find the kitchen and make myself a coffee."

* * * * *

"Fiona, I think you should you sit down."

Fiona more slumped than sat on the settee. "What do you want, Elsie, I really can do without your tittle-tattle at the moment?"

"Oh it's rather more than tittle-tattle, darling. You know how friendly you are with Federico Byass?"

"Federico Byass? I might have met him once – I meet so many people."

"You can say that again, darling. But yes, you do know the Señor Byass I'm talking about – the one who's been your escort and lover for the past six months, or should I say one of your escorts and lovers?"

Fiona did her best to look bored. "You actually sound jealous, Poppitt."

"Jealous? Hardly, darling. You see, the word is that your beloved gigolo has Aids. He's long been registered as being HIV positive, as everyone and his aunt knows, but now there is a very definite rumour he actually has the dreaded big 'A'."

"Federico – Aids? I thought it was only gay people who got Aids."

"Alas no. And in any case, many people are AC/DC – they like to bite the cherry at both ends."

"That's a most colourful metaphor, Elsie – but Federico is so masculine!"

Her visitor smiled, and again waved the magazine. "Yet for some bizarre reason, he's rather proud of his notoriety displayed in here."

Elsie passed her the magazine, which was entitled 'Great Gays of Today – Ibiza', before continuing, "The piece about Señor Byass starts on page twenty-seven, and continues, I believe, all the way to page thirty-two," she said sweetly.

In a daze, Fiona turned to page twenty-seven, as Elsie Blunkette explained a little more about her lover, "You see, darling, Federico Byass leads a very simple life, which until today he found extremely pleasurable. He enjoys the company of rich ladies, takes their money, and spends it on young boys."

Almost subconsciously, Fiona flicked through the pages of the magazine, which did indeed show her dear friend Federico in various stages of intimacy with young men – in one photograph, actually with three of them.

"But just because he has Aids doesn't mean I must have it!" she almost cried.

"No, Fiona, though just between friends, tell me, did you have protected sex, or did you take his juices into your body?"

"But I'm on the pill!"

"With any luck the pill will stop you getting pregnant, but it will not stop you getting Aids. Assuming, of course, that the rumours about dear Federico are true."

The doorbell rang. Chuck Davis called from the kitchen, "Don't worry, I'll get it."

A few moments later he showed a rather small man into the room. He was wearing a dark suit, had dark hair, dark eyes, a darkish complexion, and a distinct air of authority about him.

"Capitán Pancho Sanchez of the Guardia Civil to see you, Ma-am. I tried to tell him you were busy, but I guess he kinda pushed past me."

The Capitán carried a briefcase. He was brisk, brusque and business-like.

"Who are you?" he asked Elsie, with the natural arrogance of a senior policeman.

She told him politely, as even for a leading socialite, it paid to be respectful to the Guardia Civil, then added, "I'll go – I can come back later."

"No!" Capitán Sanchez barked. "After I have spoken to her she may need the comfort of a lady friend – for shock."

"I think she's in some shock already," Elsie replied acidly, "but I'll stay if you prefer." Having been reluctantly on the point of rising, and intrigued by what secrets were to come, she sank back gratefully into her chair.

Capitán Sanchez undid his briefcase, extracted a handful of photographs, and laid them on the floor in front of Fiona.

"You recognise the young man – a well known drugs dealer called Tony Smart?" As in two of the photographs Fiona was in somewhat of an intimate clinch with her slim sharp-featured toyboy, she could hardly deny what sounded rather like a charge, the way Capitán Sanchez said it.

"He is a friend of mine, yes," she answered, "is that a problem?"

"A friend – or a business colleague, Señora?" he asked. "You see, if you look at this" – he produced a further photograph from his briefcase – "you will note he is extracting a paper wrapping from your handbag, which same wrapping if you look at that photograph," – he indicated one of the original five shots -"you will also see he actually sells for fifty euros to a middle-aged gentleman. Señora Newman, you have been acting as a carrier for a known drugs dealer."

"But that's nonsense – I hate drugs! Are you saying I'm implicated in some sort of trouble?"

"Very considerable trouble, Señora, and you have implicated yourself. For when we realised your involvement with Tony Smart, we put a tap on your phone. And yesterday we made an excellent recording of you instructing someone to murder your husband – the agreed price being two and a half million euros."

"That's ridiculous! My husband is alive and well."

Yet again the over-worked doorbell made its presence felt. Chuck held up his hands, "I'll get it folks – but hold it right there – this is getting interesting. And if anything's happened to Brad, I'll . . . ." But he was gone to answer the door.

He returned as Fiona was still protesting that her husband was alive and well. In his hands he carried, very reverently, a small casket. Attached to the top of the casket was an audio cassette, and an envelope.

Overcome with emotion, Chuck managed to say, "If my old buddy is alive and well, how come these have arrived by special delivery – the driver says they're Brad's ashes, and the cassette is a recording of his last words?" As gentle as if it were an egg, he laid the casket on the coffee table.

Capitán Sanchez snatched up the envelope, ripped it open, and extracted the single sheet contents. After a brief scan, he passed it to Fiona.

"It is a bill for you, Señora – "To services rendered according to instructions, two and a half million euros. What services would they be, exactly?"

Again the doorbell. This time it was Elsie who said, "My turn, I think, but please no more revelations until I return!"

This she did very shortly, announcing, "A lady to see you, Fiona."

Fearfully Fiona looked up, and broke into tears of joy at the sight of the rather plain-looking newcomer. "Hazel! Thank God! I'm having a terrible day – everyone's being absolutely horrid to me. Golly, but you're a sight for sore eyes. Believe me, I need a good friend like I never did before – I suppose you've come to say you're sorry?"

"No I haven't, you bitch. I've come to tell you exactly what I think of you!"

"Ladies, ladies. Can we first hear the tape?"

"Who is this?" Hazel asked angrily.

"He is Capitán Sanchez of the Guardia Civil. I am Elsie Blunkette, and I understand that gentleman is from America."

"Sure thing, Ma-am. Chuck Davis, at your service."

By the time these introductions had taken place, Capitán Sanchez had inserted the tape into the music centre he had spotted.

"Quiet please," he instructed, and pressed the button.

The unembodied voice spoke with clarity from quad sound speakers around the room – to those who knew him, it was clearly Brad Newman.

"To Fiona, my wife, who I took in holy matrimony just over two years ago. I loved you, and thanked God every night for sending me someone so beautiful and honest to share my life. But pretty soon, God was all there was to talk to, for most nights you were out on the town, spending my money and making a fool of me."

Other than the voice from the quad speaker system, the room was so quiet you could hear a pin drop.

"It's ironic, for the first time in my life I had a situation I could not control – and a cuckold only shares his thoughts with great reluctance. Until now, that is, when I've finally plucked up the courage to tell the world about you. Around a year ago, Fiona, something wonderful happened to me, and if they grant me time, I'll explain in a moment."

The voice gained increased emotion as it stumbled and continued, "They let me hear your instructions Fiona, asking them to kill me for a fee of two and a half million euros. My God, Fiona – how could you? What have I ever given you except love and the life-style you crave? But now to confide in you the wonderful thing that happened about a year ago . . . ."

With a scream, Fiona leapt at the music centre, hit the stop button, took out the tape and threw it across the room.

"No! It's all lies!" she sobbed.

Bizarrely, despite the lack of a cassette, Brad's voice continued, "You see, Fiona, when your best friend, who you treated like dirt I may say, came to visit, we fell in love. By then, I knew about you, your deviousness, your lies, your many infidelities." The voice came from the man himself, not the surround sound speaker system, as Brad Newman entered the room from the direction of the rear of the house.

"But Hazel was good where you are bad," he continued, "decent where you are evil, and honest where you are anything but."

"Brad is too kind in his opinion of me, but despite my feelings for him, I decided out of loyalty to you, Fiona, I must go home, and give your marriage another chance. Though it was not because I found Brad so boring, as you cruelly said – it was because I loved him so much."

Chuck Davis then took centre stage. "Mrs Newman, some of what has happened here today has been a charade to give you the fright of your life as a punishment for your misdeeds. Although it should all stand as a warning, and a considerable part has been the truth," he added. A slight pause before, "Firstly, the arrival of your lawyer was not part of our plans, although we do have a recording of his activities with you, together with his advice which amounted to incitement to kidnap, and for which we shall shortly be reporting him to the English Law Society."

He paused again, this time for dramatic effect, before continuing. "Now it's in the open, perhaps I should properly introduce the people you've only just met. I am indeed Chuck Davis, whose life was saved exactly as I told you when Brad lifted me from the Vietnamese jungle. But Pancho Sanchez is not of the Guardia Civil – in fact he keeps as far away from the police as he can. He lives in Mexico city, and runs the Newman oil business throughout South America. The company and all of Brad's empire is going great guns, by the way – that part was also untrue."

He moved to Pancho's photographs, and picked one up. "The photographs of Tony Smart extracting the heroin he had previously hidden in your bag is genuine – we have had both of you under surveillance."

"And the magazine article and rumours about Federico Byass are also genuine, darling," Elsie interjected. "I always felt guilty because had I not invited you to join me for drinks on the cruise liner, you would never have met Brad, who's such a decent man. When your affairs became so blatant, I felt I really should tip him off."

"Which is when I got involved," Chuck explained, "to repay just a small part of the debt I have owed since Vietnam." He paused before resuming, looking directly into the eyes of the woman who had so betrayed his pal. "But I'm afraid that Federico is indeed very much a careless rather than a properly careful homosexual, and it was when our company doctor saw the magazine photographs that he told Brad he must not sleep with you again. Whether Federico has Aids or is HIV positive we don't know for sure, although it's true that the rumours Elsie related to you are certainly doing the rounds. So for sure, he may well be a victim. As may you, and I can only suggest that you get yourself checked out as soon as you get back to England. Unprotected sex with a homosexual and with a drugs dealer – you must have been out of your mind!"

"So what happens now?" Fiona asked quietly.

"Now you sign this document," Chuck produced it from an inside pocket as he spoke. "It's your agreement to a no maintenance divorce, in return for a one-off payment of one hundred thousand euros. That was Brad's idea, by the way," he added, "I wanted you to get nothing."

"And if I refuse?"

"Then we take our evidence of your drug dealings and conspiracy to commit murder – which was only solved by our involvement, we shall say – to the police. At worst you'll go to prison. At best, your name and good character will be destroyed. We shall then seek a 'no pay' divorce anyway because of your outrageous behaviour, forget all about paying you one hundred thousand, and have you followed in perpetuity, ascertaining your reputation precedes you wherever you go."

Utterly broken, Fiona said quietly, "Do you have a pen?"

Then without further protest she signed the document.

In return, Chuck handed her a package. "One hundred thousand euros, and a ticket on a charter flight to Gatwick tonight. You carry your passport in your bag, I believe?"

She nodded.

"Very well. If you hand over the keys to the Jaguar, you'll find a taxi waiting at the end of the drive. I know it's a long walk, but you have nothing better to do. Mr. Newman will send on your things as soon as you let him have your forwarding address."

"Goodbye, Fiona," said Brad, taking Hazel by the hand.

"Goodbye, bitch," said Hazel, as with her beloved man she left the room.

The room fell silent, all eyes on Fiona.

"Well fuck you! Fuck you all," she said, storming from the room, from the house, and from their lives.

After they'd heard the front door slam, Pancho commented to no-one in particular, "on the contrary, it is you, Fiona, who have been – what was the word?"

"Screwed will do – well and truly screwed," Chuck Davis said with a satisfied smile.

Fair Deal at La Cabeza del Toro

Terri Baker, a pretty twenty-five year old with blue-eyes and medium length auburn hair, disembarked with a song in her heart knowing that she had four weeks' shore leave. She was wearing her favourite off-duty outfit of hipster jeans, a short white top and flat casual soft shoes, whilst over her shoulder she carried her much loved 'kitchen sink' leather bag.

Perhaps May is the most beautiful time in England. Perhaps not. But the light drizzle which greeted her in Portsmouth in no way dampened her spirits, for surely there'd be sunshine tomorrow? And for a period she could forget her chosen career, forget all about a life at sea, and as with ships' crews down through the centuries, enjoy her home-coming.

After ten days of torrential rain, she was not so certain, and loitered with more than casual interest inside the porch of the travel agents in her little home city of Wells, in Somerset. The best offers seemed to centre on The Costa del Sol, Ibiza and Majorca. Why not? Why not – she could kill two birds with one stone, and knew in Ibiza she'd at least be sure of a generous welcome . . . .

* * * * *

Felix Gresham was not really a nice man, although in reality he himself had never even considered the matter. Nevertheless, for those who bothered to look, his character showed clearly in his appearance. A small man, with dark ferrety eyes that were rarely still, thin lips which matched his frame – almost underweight – and with raised bones prominent in his skinny hands. His clothing always drab and well-used, partly due to his meanness, and partly because he feared being thought of as wealthy, lest it was considered his business prospered over much.

An early career working for a bank in his native Zurich had come to an abrupt end when he had been discovered laundering money, the product of a U.S. security van heist, for a substantial back-hander in good ol' American greenback dollars. In the Swiss way, it had of course all been hushed up, but he was left in no doubt that his own career with any Swiss financial institution was over.

His name then, of course, was not the English sounding 'Felix Gresham', but that was many years ago. Now he had his Spanish 'Residencia' and his 'Fiscal', both of which gave evidence that he was a person to be trusted, and officially accepted as a resident of Ibiza.

He ran what he liked to consider a high class antiques and 'objets d'art' shop, based just off the Vara de Rey in Ibiza Town, where, although he had a few larger items of furniture on display, he specialised in small items easily carried home in tourists' suitcases. His most profitable regular line was a range of genuine ancient Ibicencan wooden figures, carved from either olive wood or very hard sabena pine. The fact that they were anything but ancient, volume-produced in an

African village, and came over from Morocco in a rusty Transit van driven by a black Moorish 'Looky-Looky' man called Abdul Amir rested lightly on his conscience but heavily on his ever-growing bank balance.

Some of the articles in his shop were genuine, such as the slightly damaged set of willow-pattern plates on display, the Grandmother clock by the old English makers 'Masons of Rotherham', or the set of porcelain thimbles, and some of these items represented bargains, for in truth he was not an accurate valuer of antiques. His skill lay more in working egg white and cow's urine into brass to instantly age it, or taking a small dark oil painting produced in the style of the Dutch masters by a Belgian artist living in San Miguel, and placing it in the Ibiza sunshine until the oil paint started to crack, creating just that small element of doubt in the mind of a potential buyer as to its true age. Oddly enough, his best line of sales patter with the dark cracked oil paintings was partly honest, "I'm afraid I know nothing about paintings – not my line at all," he'd say truthfully, before adding, "in fact I bought it with some items of furniture from the estate of a very old Dutch lady who'd lived here for many years."

In that way, and taking care to only ever have one of the paintings on display at a time, he averaged a sale of one every two weeks throughout the main holiday season, with the majority of the optimistic purchasers coming from the Netherlands itself.

Every day, he closed his shop early by Ibicencan standards at seven pm, having learnt that the richer tourists would generally be back in their villas or hotels by then, prior to re-emerging to see the sights sometime after ten. In high season, he re-opened at that time for a couple of hours until midnight, finding that people happy with drink and possibly a good meal inside them were apt to spend their money more freely.

He was a man of habit, carefully locking the day's takings in the floor safe, concealed underneath a metre-high carved wooden Indian elephant, before collecting his Renault car from an underground carpark for the twenty minute drive home to Santa Eulalia, where he lived alone in a small house, Casa Tengo, which he always referred to as 'his villa'. Having parked his car at the side of Casa Tengo, he would head for a nearby Spanish bar called 'La Cabeza del Toro' – 'The Bull's Head' – which he liked for its mixed race clientele, its lack of TV or music, and its general ambiance.

La Cabeza del Toro is as typical as a Spanish pub can be – chunky wooden furniture, wooden beams with a few 'jamóns' hanging from them, a selection of beers on tap and a greater selection in the bottle, and probably best of all, an attractive and frequently replenished counter of tasty and reasonably priced 'tapas' produced by the owner's wife, Maria.

Often, for he was not a big eater, two snacks of Maria's tapas was sufficient for an evening meal for Felix Gresham. And of course that meant he'd fed himself without having either to cook or fork out for a proper restaurant dinner.

Entering the pub, and ignoring the Spanish custom of paying for his food and drink only upon leaving, he placed exactly the right change on the bar, picked up the small glass of dry sherry which had been produced without his even asking by the rotund bar owner, Diego, and returned with it to his customary corner seat. Smugly pleased with himself, he had good reason. For was it not less than two hours ago that a fellow dealer had offered €750 for the brooch he carried in his waistcoat pocket? And was it not only last week that he had paid just €20 for the self same brooch?

His thin lips tightened and spread into what he fondly thought was a smile, but would have been described by anyone watching as a smirk. He closed his eyes and recalled the stupid old woman, wearing a traditional black Spanish dress and headscarf, who'd sold it to him. The razor sharp cunning he had developed over a life-time dealing in other people's prized possessions had at once informed him both that the old twit had no idea of the value of the item, and was also desperate for some cash. Expecting to have to go to €50, he'd been pleasantly surprised when she'd accepted his first offer. Then she'd called him 'Señor', and humbly added 'mucho gracias' as she left his shop.

'Silly old bat,' he thought, and sipped his sherry in satisfaction.

A girl, wearing hipster jeans and a short white top, pretty, with blue eyes and auburn hair – although such attributes were lost upon him – was perched on a stool at the bar, and entertaining some of the regulars with card tricks. Or rather, her incompetence at card tricks, for Felix Gresham's quick eyes spotted that money was changing hands. And most of it away from the girl, who was unknown to him.

Intrigued, Gresham joined them. The girl explained that she was trying to learn a new trick that her boyfriend had shown her just before she left England. She fanned out the cards face down. Would Gresham be kind enough to choose one? Gresham would. And kindly replace it? He did.

Gresham noted that the girl was not very dextrous with the cards, and had no hesitation in a friendly wager of twenty cents on her ability to produce the correct card.

She dealt the cards one by one face upwards into a single pile. Just over half the way through the pack, she hesitated in turning over a card. "This was the card you chose," she said with a confident and not uncultured west country accent, turning over the King of Diamonds.

Gresham smirked, again fondly imagining he'd grinned. "Sorry, it was the Ace of Clubs," he replied in his usual whining squeaky voice, as he happily trousered the twenty cents.

The pretty girl smiled wryly. "Give me another chance?" she asked. "Perhaps for a slightly higher stake?"

Warning bells rang in Gresham's head. Was this a set up? "Alright," he agreed, "but only for the twenty cents."

The girl shuffled the pack, a little clumsily, then again fanned them face down for Gresham to select a card. The other locals, watching over his shoulder, saw that he had taken the

Queen of Spades. He returned the card, still face down, to the pack, which the girl then cut. Next, and just as she had done before, she started dealing out the cards, one by one and face up, into a single pile.

Gresham watched, subconsciously counting the cards. 21, 22, 23, 24 – the Queen of Spades. The girl had missed it, continued dealing. 25, 26, 27, 28. Gresham watched, said nothing. Then she hesitated over the 29th card.

"I know I'm right this time," she said. "Are you sure you wouldn't like to raise the stake a little?"

Gresham, secure in his knowledge of the girl's error, had no hesitation. "I'm a sporting man" – the greed shone from his eyes – "make it a euro if you like. Even five."

The girl eyed him confidently. "I come from a long line of gamblers myself – Dad was a bookie, before he went broke. I'll make it as high as you like. What say a hundred euros?"

Gresham could hardly believe his luck – after the brooch, this was too much. "A hundred – five hundred! Whatever you like." He had difficulty keeping the tremor from his voice, which had suddenly moved an octave higher.

Then caution entered. Supposing the girl didn't pay up? "I trust you have that sort of money?" he added.

Without a word, she withdrew from her enormous leather bag a sealed polythene bank packet, bearing the legend '€1000 – 20 x €50'.

"You're prepared to bet that?" Gresham squeaked.

The girl nodded.

Gresham was by now sweating with excitement, his hands hot and moist. He produced his wallet and counted out the contents – €400, and this he placed it on the bar.

"You want to bet the €400?" asked the girl.

Gresham could hardly get his breath. "No, no – the full thousand. Eagerly he pulled out the brooch. "Only today I was offered €750 for this – I'll put it in instead of the €600."

The girl picked up the brooch and examined it. "I'll accept that in the pot instead of €500, but not €600." Gresham wasn't really bothered – he wasn't going to lose anyway. "Alright, I'll put in a cheque for €100."

"No cheques."

Gresham was stumped. Should he reduce the bet to €900? That would be throwing a hundred away. He called the barman.

"Diego, will you cash a cheque for a hundred euros, drawn on Banca March?" He tried to keep calm.

The bar owner nodded. "I should think you're okay for that, Señor Gresham."

Eagerly, Gresham's scrabbling fingers wrote the cheque, then grabbed the two fifty euro notes as the barman handed them over.

"There, €1,000 – now let's see the card!"

The girl held up his hand. "First in view of the amount of the bet, I think you should write down your card on a piece of paper."

The barman ripped the top sheet from his pad, and passed it to Gresham. Gresham wrote 'Queen of Spades', unseen of course by the girl.

The girl looked at the others. "Has he written down the correct card?"

Gresham coloured. "What are you. . . ."

The girl cut him short. "No offence meant, of course."

The locals nodded.

Gresham folded the piece of paper, and placed it with the brooch and the little pile of money.

"Now show me my card!" he demanded.

The girl ignored him. "Before I accept the bet," she said, "let's be certain that we both agree what it is." She paused. "I bet you one thousand euros to your five hundred and that brooch, that the next card I show you will be the card you chose, and have written down on the piece of paper. Is that correct?"

"Yes, yes, that's correct. Now show me the card."

"If you insist," the girl murmured. She picked up the pack. Then she smiled, and put it down again. Instead, she picked up the discarded pile, and flipped quickly back through the top few cards until she came to the Queen of Spades. She turned the other cards over, face down, leaving only the Queen of Spades face up.

"This is the next card I'm showing you, and I believe it's the card you chose." She picked up the piece of paper, and unfolded it. "Yes, I had an idea I was right." She then allowed her pretty face to break into a lovely smile as she scooped up the cash and pushed it into her bag.

Felix Gresham had heard the expression 'speechless', but never quite believed it. Until now. His eyes had popped nearly out of their sockets, and his strangled voice wouldn't come. He was actually speechless.

The girl picked up the brooch. "Nice to have this back again."

Gresham found his voice. "You – you cheated me! And what do you mean, 'nice to have this back again'?"

"I did not cheat you, Mr. Gresham – you thought I had made a mistake and sought to take my money because of it. But then, you're used to taking other people's money, aren't you?"

"You cheated me – you know I thought you were going to the other pile!"

"Mr. Gresham, I have no idea how or what a mean and greedy person like you thinks, but I suggest you mind your tongue – I'm getting a little tired of being called a cheat when I'm not, and might just lose my temper. I should perhaps warn you that I'm a karate black belt, by the way." The girl's voice had gained steel. "It was a fair bet, and had you not been greedy, you wouldn't now be five grand poorer."

"Five grand – what on earth are you talking about?"

The girl eyed the brooch lovingly. "This brooch – it's only a month ago that I paid four and a half thousand U.S. dollars for it in Singapore. It has to be worth at least that in euros here. And then of course there's the cash."

She could see that Gresham didn't understand.

"I suppose you'd like me to explain?"

Gresham nodded.

"I'm an entertainer on a cruise liner – mainly magic and cards – though I make more money from poker than in wages," she added happily. "I thought that brooch would make a nice present for my old Spanish Gran, so I bought it and sent it to her only four weeks ago. I'd no idea that she was so hard up, of course, or I'd have given her the cash. She'd just been too proud to tell me."

The light dawned on Gresham. "The old . . ."

"'Fool'? 'Bat'? Or more likely, 'Sucker'?" the girl interjected. "What exactly was the word you were searching for, Mr. Gresham?"

Gresham's eyes dropped, and he didn't answer.

"Anyway," the girl continued, "I've got it back now, and with a bit of interest."

She dropped the brooch in her bag to join the cash, slapped Felix Gresham on the back, and her tight bum wiggling jauntily, walked happily from the pub.

Juan-Miguel and The Film Stars

"My nipples are sore!" Jane, young, well spoken, blonde, blue eyed and beautiful, reached for her factor twelve Nivea sun lotion and started to gently massage the offending items.

"What do you expect," responded Vicky with a grin, "most of the time since we arrived you've spent flashing your tits at the Mediterranean sun, or any boy who glanced your way. Why don't you turn over, and give your back a chance?" This time the speaker clearly from Birmingham.

"Vicky, you know it wouldn't be natural for Jane to lie on her front."

"Now now, Sandra, don't get sarky, just 'cause blondes are statistically more likely to pull," Jane retorted as she continued with her massage.

"But blokes go for big boobs, and in that department I'm the winner!" Sandra, from the Welsh Valleys, responded happily.

"I've heard that freckles are the biggest turn-on," this from the freckle-faced Vicky. "And surely, we're all three, how shall I put it, fairly attractive to the opposite, er, sex"

"But none of us have had any luck so far – have we?" Jane commented absently, as she replaced the top on the Nivea.

"Give us a chance," Sandra objected, "my hormones tell me my luck's soon going to change. And we did only arrive in Ibiza yesterday morning . . . ."

"And were in bed – our own beds – by midnight, rather than hitting Pasha's or Space," Vicky commented disconsolately.

Relating the above conversation in print, the words look hard, even bitchy. But none of them were spoken with malice, the three girls being firm friends. In fact, Jane the blonde, auburn-haired Vicky, and short dark-haired, and slightly plump Sandra had been room mates for three years at Cardiff University, from which august establishment they had all graduated with honours, Jane and Vicky in English, and Sandra in philosophy. The Ibiza holiday to the package tour paradise of Playa d'en Bossa in the south west of the island was their self-awarded reward for three years of effort.

"When we do pull, I bet I draw the short straw," Jane said, continuing the conversation.

"You mean a plonker?" Sandra asked absently.

"No – I mean the one with the short straw."

The other two burst out laughing at Jane's obvious concern about biological logistics.

"There's a greasy looking chap over there ogling us" – this from Vicky.

Trying hard not to look as if they were looking, the other two looked.

"The one with a pony tail? Nearly six foot, with the expensive-looking club shorts? He's not greasy, he's Spanish, and the sun tan's for real."

"And in fact he's quite good looking."

"Nice body and pecs, too."

The object of their attention appeared embarrassed to be the object of their attention. But despite that, and somewhat hesitantly, he started to walk towards them. Clearly this was no 'I'm God's gift to women' macho approach.

"English?" The accent good, but the word, like the walk, spoken hesitantly. "Please forgive me, ladies, but are you actresses?"

As one, the three girls burst out laughing. Was this a corny approach – or what? Probably the oldest in the book . . . .

But the man's obvious embarrassment only seemed to increase at the response. "I sorry, I not mean to joke, but I am looking for three actresses."

"Most men are" – this from Sandra.

"We'd quite like three actors," interjected Vicky, "film stars, if possible."

The Spaniard grinned, and when he did so his face lit up with a natural happiness as only the Mediterranean Latins can do. And the grin only added to his good looks, giving him a boyish charm that belied his actual thirty-three years.

"Allow me to explain." Magically his English had improved as he fished in his pocket and took out an embossed business card, which he passed to Jane, the blonde one.

"My name is Juan-Miguel Torres de Cantabria." And according to his card, it certainly was.

Jane passed it to Vicky, who passed it on to Sandra, who read it aloud. "Juan-Miguel Torres de Cantabria, Presidente, Triple-E-Films de Ibiza."

"We don't want any film, our camera's a digital."

"No, no, no – you misunderstand. May I?" Without waiting for an answer, he sat down next to them. "And my name is pronounced 'Wan' – Miguel, not with the 'j' hard, in the English manner."

Jane grinned at him. She quite liked this Spaniard, who suddenly seemed more confident, no longer embarrassed. "So what don't we understand?"

"I do not sell film for cameras – I am film director – best known and best skilled in the whole of Ibiza." He paused to allow his words to sink in. "I was expecting three actresses to arrive this morning from England on the Iberia flight from Heathrow. But they weren't on the flight. I'd booked them into the Hotel Club Playa d'en Bossa because they wanted to be near Space, the big disco club, but so far they've also failed to arrive there. I thought they might by mistake have gone to the Hotel Playa d'en Bossa instead of the Hotel Club, but they're not there either," he added disconsolately.

"I suppose you've checked with London for your actresses?" this time from Sandra, ever practical.

"Yes, yes, yes – but my London agent cannot find them! In fact he is what you might call a load of bollocks."

The word, spoken out loud with a Spanish accent, sounded somewhat incongruous, and Sandra and Jane both had to choke back a laugh. But Vicky, slightly pompous, would not let him get away with it. "I most certainly would not call him that – neither I nor my two friends use such words."

The Spaniard smiled, and the sun shone from his face. "I sorry. I no wish offence. But I now have big problem, you see." The quality of his English appeared to alternate from good to fair each time he spoke.

"What sort of a problem?"

"We start shooting on location next week. The German financier flies in from Hamburg in two days time, with the scriptwriter to write changes, and full team of cameramen, editors, prompters – and tea lady because the three female leads are English. They're all booked and ready to roll next week. When that happens, we start to spend money like a Las Vegas fruit machine paying out the jackpot . . . ."

". . . And you're three actresses short?" cut in Jane, thoughtfully.

"You have it in one, my English lovely," Juan-Miguel replied sorrowfully, and suddenly in remarkably good colloquial English.

"What sort of money would the three actresses be paid?" This again from Jane.

"Twenty thousand euros each," whined the Spaniard, "for just four weeks' work. And if we over-run, a daily retainer of a thousand."

Sandra twigged the reason for Jane's interest. "As it happens, we are in fact actresses . . . ." A vision of their three rather amateurish productions of the Christmas pantomime at uni swam before her eyes, ". . . although most of our work has been stage, rather than film."

"What sort of film?" from Vicky, ever proper, ever cautious.

"Oh – an adult film," Juan-Miguel tried to be off-hand.

"Do you mean 'adult' as in not for children, or 'adult' as in 'blue movie'?"

Far from being further embarrassed by this, yet again Juan-Miguel grinned. "I suppose adult as in blue movie is the most honest." He held up his hand to stop Vicky interrupting him. "But please, our films are of taste – we are 'Triple-E-Films of Ibiza' because our films are entertaining, exciting and erotic, not 'Triple-P-Films' because they're perverted, poor and pornographic."

"There's a difference?" asked Jane with rather more than a slight hint of scepticism.

"Oh yes! Our films are genuinely proper movies, with a good story, some romance and humour, and always a twist in the tail. But . . . ."

"But what?"

"But unlike our colleagues in Hollywood, we don't stop at the bedroom door, and when we move inside the bedroom, the covers are off the bed. Although more often it is in God's wonderful fresh air, rather than the bedroom," he added.

"So they're pornographic!" Vicky was not about to let him get away with it.

But the Spaniard became angry. "No, they are not pornographic!" He started to get up. "We have no butcher's shop shots."

"Butcher's shop shots?" With some difficulty, Jane repeated the words. "What are they?"

Juan-Miguel Torres de Cantabria sat back down. "Let me explain. A pornographic blue movie is aimed at sick people – mainly sick men – who just want to see close up pictures of people doing unnatural things to each other. An erotic movie on the other hand appeals equally to men and women and merely shows nature in its true gentleness." He paused, before continuing, "I sorry I lose my temper, but I proud of my work, and . . . ."

"And what?" again from Jane.

"And for a moment, just a moment, I thought you might consider helping me." There – it was out now, on the table, or at least on the beach.

Silence for several seconds, before "Twenty thousand euros?" from Sandra.

"Each?" added Jane.

"Where do your films get shown – I'm sure they wouldn't be legal in England – or Wales?" from Vicky.

"In England?" Again Juan-Miguel grinned. "No, we source the best looking actresses from England, and show their beauty in Germany and Holland. But England – never."

"So supposing – just supposing, that is – we considered, er, helping you, no one back home would get to know?"

"No – definitely no." A pause, before, "You're not, are you – considering you might help? You would be wonderful for the three leading roles."

"No butcher's shop?"

"A film of taste and decorum?"

Yet again the Latin grin – he'd won them round! "Yes, there'll be no butcher's shop, and yes, the film will be in good taste. But I think we go too fast."

"Too fast?"

"Yes – how do I know you can act – can you be uninhibited without clothes? And how do you know you can trust me?"

"I'd been thinking the same thing – about trusting you," commented Vicky.

The other two nodded in agreement.

"Look – I have idea," the Spaniard said suddenly. This time he did get up. "Why don't we take day off tomorrow, and sail to Formentera – or perhaps s'Espalmador – in my motor yacht? Just the four of us. That way I can give you screen tests with no spectators, and you can decide whether you want to work for me."

"On your yacht?"

"Yes," replied the Spaniard, "I'll anchor in the bay, and pick you up from the beach here in the rib – say about ten o'clock?"

"The rib?"

"Yes – the rigid inflatable boat I carry on the yacht. I use it for water skiing and a shore tender." He made to move away, suddenly in a hurry. "Just bring yourselves, your costumes and a sarong – I'll have food and drink on board."

Then with a wave, and before they could answer, he was gone.

"So what do we do?"

"A day on a yacht sounds quite acceptable, thank you," Jane commented.

"And twenty thousand euros would pay off my student loan, and leave some change," added Sandra practically.

"So another early night – we want to look good for him?" chipped in Vicky.

The others nodded in agreement. "But not too early . . ." the words spoken by both girls together, as they sometimes are.

* * * * *

"Space", the brainchild of Pepe Rosello, and only a couple of hundred metres from the girls' hotel, is entered past purple railings followed by three steps protected by a red-trimmed awning, which somehow has the appearance of an old jousting tent. The club enjoyed the company of the three graduate girls for most of the late afternoon and evening, to be followed by "Amnesia" on the Ibiza Town to San Antonio road. That establishment saw them party on into the small hours, although the hour was indeed still quite small – four is not a large number – when they tumbled into their beds back at their package tour paradise.

But the incessant beat and Ibiza spirit measures had certainly had an effect, as they made their way onto the beach at quarter to ten the following morning, and stood looking out to sea.

"Bet he doesn't come – it was just a wind up," the ever sceptical Vicky said as she morosely kicked a small sea shell, causing sand to rise with it, and catch in the sea breeze to re-settle behind her. Despite her tight finances, like her companions she had bought a couple of new bikinis for the holiday, and was wearing a smart denim outfit from River Island, over which she also wore a matching buckled min-skirt from the same establishment. Sandra had entrusted her dwindling funds to Dorothy Perkins to hopefully disguise her plumpness with a camouflage pattern, whilst Jane had relied upon a grey and black number from good old Marks and Sparks. They also wore their new sarongs, bought that very morning for €4 each from a shop fronting onto the beach.

The beach at Playa d'en Bossa is the longest on Ibiza, running all the way through to Figueretas. Away from the water, the sand is soft, and by mid-day in summer, unbearably hot to bare feet, although realising that, the authorities have thoughtfully provided walkways of wooden planking. Not far out to sea there are numerous and rather picturesque small rocky islets, whilst closer to the shore and to both sides of their vista, intrepid early morning types were already out on pedaloes. In front of them, some small children in flotation rings played ball in the shallow water, and just off to their right, a father and son team set about building a sand castle, with the father the self-appointed builder, and the son the carrier of water, as Will Shakespeare might have called him.

Already hot, with the thermometer ticking up over ninety and towards a hundred, the clock also ticked – onto and past ten o'clock. Away to their left, and somewhat impressively, the hydrofoil ferry known as the 'Rápido' accelerated out of the old Ibiza Town harbour and up 'onto the step' as it departed for the ten mile journey to Formentera.

Further out to sea, just below the horizon, a rather larger ship was crossing more sedately from their right to left – unbeknown to the girls, a ferry from Alicante bound for the Ibiza Ferry Port. It is a fact that whilst they obviously realise Ibiza's an island, most visitors give no thought whatsoever to the sheer logistics involved in transporting to that small holiday Mecca, where no straight line measurement is more than thirty miles, everything they and their hundreds of thousands of fellow pleasure seekers need to sustain life.

Hence Ibiza and ships literally go together like bread and jam, or possibly gin and tonic is nearer the mark, with Spanish distilled Larios being the brand of choice at €8.99 a litre. And wherever you look off whatever coast, there are always ships, and boats, and yes, in the skies overhead, the planes bringing the happy ones starting their holidays, or taking the sad ones home to finish them.

What looked like a white speed boat appeared away to the left, bouncing a bit as it crossed the wake of the Rápido. But as it drew closer, it grew in size, until, despite its speed, it was quite obviously a motor yacht. Without in any way slowing, it headed in towards the shore, before, when still about a hundred metres out to sea, it executed what Jenson Button might call "a little tail slide", bringing it to a rather dashing halt. At that range, the figure on board was not recognisable, but he did wave, and somewhat hesitantly, and certainly hopefully, the three girls waved back.

It took about five minutes for a dinghy to be slung out and lowered onto the sea, the person on the yacht – more accurately a motor cruiser – jumped into it, and headed straight in towards the shore.

"Told you he'd come – I think he's a regular guy," from Sandra.

"Well he's certainly got a regular motor yacht," added Jane.

By which time the dinghy had slowed, Juan-Miguel jumped from it into the shallows, and started to pull it onto the beach. The three bikini clad girls, unable to hide their enthusiasm, ran towards him, their beach bags bouncing at their sides.

"Hola – buenos días," he greeted them. "I sorry I late – bloody tourist blocked my exit from the marina." Then he slapped his hand over his mouth. "Oh, I also sorry – I forget you not like swearing."

At that very moment, with everyone on the beach looking at them with envy, they would have forgiven him anything.

"I no ask your names yesterday," he added, as he helped them into the dinghy, or rib, as they now knew it was called. So they introduced themselves, he pushed the rib away from the beach, spun it round with a practised hand, jumped in and fired the engine.

"How will we get on board – we won't have to climb a rope ladder will we?" asked Jane, as they approached the bow of the yacht.

The Spaniard laughed as he trickled the dinghy round to the stern, "No my little English angels – here, you see, there is a low level after deck for diving from, or accessing the rib. The girls started to stand, but he held up his hand to stop them. "No, please stay seated until I tie on, then I'll step onto the yacht, and pull you on board one at a time."

And this he did, very efficiently and with little wasted effort. The girls passed through a little sort of gate to a small open deck, set with a table and four canvas 'director' type chairs.

"Please to excuse while I stow the rib," as he operated the electric davits. Again, with little effort he did as he said, hoisting the rib out of the sea before joining them.

"So – this is my Astondoa. You like?"

"Your what?" from Sandra.

"My Astondoa – the make of my boat. First, I show you over it, then we have bucks fizz – okay?"

The happy nods and comments indicated that this was, indeed, okay.

"You can climb ladder?"

The ladder with broad wooden steps was fixed to a bulkhead, and gave access to an upper deck. "This is the flying bridge, where we sunbathe and I can also drive from – there are controls up here as well as in main cabin for if we have raining."

The girls looked up at the blue sky – it looked like it would never rain again.

Back down the ladder, he opened a sort of patio door into an immaculately fitted dining area, with two L-shaped couches opposite each other, rather than individual chairs. Forward of that area, and up three steps on the right, was the main control deck, with wood and leather and enough instruments to rival the Starship Enterprise. To the left, and down a few steps, was the tiny galley, complete with fridge, sink and gas cooker.

"The gas cooker is my idea, to allow for cooking when not in the marina – standard fitting is electric," he explained.

Vicky pointed towards another cooker, "That looks like a microwave," she said, "surely that's not gas?"

Juan-Miguel laughed. "No, the microwave *is* for use in the marina, although the fridge will run on gas or 12 volt or from the mains."

He continued moving towards the bow. "On the right we have the two-berth cabin," he explained, "with two full size single beds, a wardrobe and two overhead lockers".

Then he opened a door on the other side of the boat. "Here are the heads – the servicios – loo, shower and wash basin." And then in the bows, or the front, we have," here he paused to throw open the door with a flourish, "the master bedroom!

Or these days, should I say the mistress bedroom?" he added mischievously.

The cabin was beautifully fitted with high quality polished wood, overhead lockers, double wardrobes each side, a small dressing table, and dominating all this splendour, a double bed that at the very least was super king-size.

He tapped the roof of the cabin. "Up above there is another sun-bathing place for two people, with nice leather cushions – but please be careful and use your sarongs or a towel, because the leather can get very hot!"

He started to return to the stern. "Now, I will get the juice and champagne and glasses – actually we use plastic, but still call them glasses. Whilst you take off your clothes."

The girls started to move towards the stern, before they realised what he had said.

"Whilst you take off your clothes," he confirmed and smiled before continuing, "that is what we'd said, and in Ibiza it is nothing special – people do it all the time. Especially on boats," he added.

And, in somewhat of a daze, the three girls moved to the aft deck, where they took off their bikinis, and sat at the table to await their bucks fizz.

"It actually feels quite nice," commented Jane after a few moments.

"You're right," confirmed Sandra, "and my knicks *were* a bit tight – look, they've left a line across my tummy."

The others dutifully looked, and sympathetically observed the line caused by Sandra's tight knicks.

Meanwhile, Juan-Miguel had slipped out of his shorts, but was still wearing a brief covering in the form of a thong. The champagne was in an ice bucket, the orange juice in a jug, and the glasses, although plastic, were at least shaped like proper flutes. He poured a small amount of juice into each glass, then turned his attention to the bottle of Cordonui – not strictly champagne, but a sort of Spanish equivalent. The cork made a pop and flew out, as champagne corks should, and with something of a flourish, the Spaniard poured the bubbles into the glasses. He raised his towards them, "Salud, my English angels – here's to an enjoyable day."

And, naked as the day they were born, the three girls joined him in the toast.

"Salud."

* * * * *

The Cordonui gone, the Spaniard announced it was time they set sail, which in the case of his Astondoa comprised firing up the two Volvo 370 horsepower engines.

"Now we go to s'Espalmador – is a beautiful island with a blue lagoon bay where we can anchor and swim."

Jane joined him at the controls on the upper, or fly, deck, whilst Sandra and Vicky went for'ard to sunbathe their way across a short stretch of the Mediterranean. The sun shone, God was in his heaven, and all was well with the world. With the sea calm and unruffled – no 'white horses' in the waves – an easy twenty knot cruise all too soon brought them to the picturesque bay of s'Alga on the little island north of Formentera. It was just as Juan-Miguel had described it, although such knowledge could not be kept to him alone, and a few other boats already rode at anchor at varying distances from the golden sands. Furthest out were a couple of seaman-like sailing yachts, their deeper draught dictating they should not venture too close to the shore. One other motor cruiser, a Sunseeker speed boat and a rather larger 'serious money' yacht completed the list of the five neighbours.

Although the 'serious money' yacht was a trifle old-fashioned to her eyes, Jane stared at it in admiration, "It looks like it could sail to America," she said in awe.

Juan-Miguel laughed. "It's called a 'Grand Banks'," he said, "a boat for very rich people. But its twin Caterpillar engines drink a lot of diesel, so part way across the Atlantic, you would run out of fuel and find yourself in a luxurious rowing boat. And does one really wish to exchange where we are for New York harbour?"

One didn't – one was quite happy here, thank-you very much.

Looking across to the other boats, the girls were re-assured they were not alone in their nudity, and indeed, they had already started to feel it was the natural state which of course it is.

Juan-Miguel produced a second bottle of Cordonui, and with it a plate of thinly sliced cured ham, with a side plate of gherkins.

"Jamón Serrano," he proclaimed proudly, pronouncing 'jamón' as 'hamon', "the pride of Spain, and for the privileged only. The food will soak up the alcohol," he assured them.

The girls tasted the ham, and found it really was delicious, helped down very easily by the Cordonui. Then Sandra, who had been looking longingly at the cool blue sea asked if they could swim.

"I think first you should let the champagne settle," Juan-Miguel replied, "then we can all swim ashore and refresh ourselves with a mudbath – the island is famous for the therapeutic qualities it endows. Why don't you and Vicky have a short siesta on the sunbathing deck, whilst Jane and I do the same below decks, and I give her a little screen-test?"

Which is what they did, with Jane's 'screen-test' taking place on the king-size double bed in the main cabin. Whether it was the champagne, the sun or the surroundings, or simply the man himself, who was quite the best endowed she had ever known, but she had never in her young life had such a strong and passionate loving, and almost screamed with ecstasy when eventually he slipped into her with the ease of a slim foot into a well-oiled boot. Girls from a previous generation and a bygone age would have known it, if they were lucky, as 'a thorough rogering', although the phrase itself and its origins are now lost in the mists of time.

She would willingly have continued the 'screen-test' for ever, and certainly Juan-Miguel seemed capable of doing so, but all too soon he announced, “Now we join the others for our swim ashore.”

* * * * *

“Why can’t we take the dinghy?” from the slightly plump Sandra, “I’d much prefer it.”

“Don’t be such a wimp,” retorted Vicky, “it’s only about a quarter of a mile, and with your boobs you’ve got built-in water-wings anyway. Isn’t that right, Juan-Miguel?”

She turned to face the Spaniard, and couldn’t help noticing that following the screen-test, he’d neglected to replace his thong. Involuntarily, her eyes flicked downwards, and her face registered her approval of a truly magnificent organ – then went red as she saw that he’d watched her brief survey.

“It’s like a muscle – the more you use it the bigger it gets,” he explained easily.

To save her embarrassment, instead of replying, she turned, climbed onto the rail, and executed a perfect dive into the blue waters of the lagoon. Knowing her dive had been a good one, she trod water and turned to wave to those still on board, and was a little miffed when Juan-Miguel rebuked her.

“You must not do that again – the water isn’t deep, and there are many rocks. The swimming platform is at the stern, where you came aboard.”

Which indeed it was, and it was from there that Jane and Juan-Miguel dived, and Sandra slipped down the sea ladder, to join them.

The swim ashore was a doddle, the sea warm, and of course with a higher salt content than the mighty oceans, the Mediterranean offers a buoyant platform to assist the swimmer should they need a rest.

But as they walked ashore, the red hot sand was a shock to their feet, so they found it easier to walk in the shallows. After a short distance, they came across the famed mud pools, with others already enjoying themselves and frolicking about in the foul-smelling mud.

The girls were adamant, "Not us," they said with one accord.

But as Juan-Miguel threw himself into the mud, he laughed at them. "There is an English saying, I think, don't knock it 'til you've tried it."

Which of course they did, and afterwards as they washed the mud off in the Med, admitted that their bodies tingled all over, and they felt better for the experience.

* * * * *

Back on board, Juan-Miguel produced a plate of bocadillos – the rather odd word literally meaning 'snack' which the Spanish use mainly for baguette, or club, sandwiches – comprising queso curado de Manchega (a tasty cheese from La Mancha), chorizos (slices of red spicy sausages) and tomatoes.

"I'm a little thirsty," said Sandra, "I don't suppose you've any more champagne?"

"Sandra, my Angel from England, I have many, many more bottles, but I suggest that instead we try a little of my own Sangria – it's mainly lemonade, and in this heat you should not have too much alcohol."

In the English county of Somerset, back in the days when every farm made cyder, local lads would offer tourist girls a glass, which was usually enjoyed. But if the local lad was after his oats, and wanted to, well, speed things along a bit, the second glass might contain a goodly sized slug of gin, a spirit that blends most happily with scrumpy cyder and is untastable to the initiate cyder drinker . . . .

Many Spanish bars toss a few slices of fruit in a jug, pour in some cheap red wine, and then fill the jug mainly with lemonade. But a proper Sangria is made preferably twenty-four hours before consumption with generous proportions of roughish red wine, sherry and Spanish brandy. Juan-Miguel was nothing if not generous with his portions, the lemonade being added almost as an afterthought just before serving.

And so the sun, the scene and the alcohol took its effect, and the three English girls relaxed even more.

"I think it is now time for Vicky and Sandra to have their screen-test," Juan-Miguel said quietly with the confident smile they had come to admire, "Jane did very well, and I believe could be uninhibited in front of the cameras."

"Together?" asked Sandra, and Juan-Miguel noted that she had not objected to the principle of the 'screen-test'.

"Surely you're not a prude?" he replied easily, "if so, it is no problem . . . ."

"I'm game," said Vicky, leaving the issue in no doubt, "but can we use the sun beds – I've never made love in the open air?"

And so Sandra and Vicky and Juan-Miguel went for'ard on deck, whilst Jane took a short siesta underneath them in the cabin.

Juan-Miguel proved he could handle two girls in the masterful way he had loved Jane earlier, and bodies slippery with sweat and sun-tan oil and female excitement intertwined happily in what the French call a ménage à trois, as he skilfully brought both of them to the edge of their climax almost simultaneously, before releasing them over the edge into orgasm in tidal waves of rolling tumbling pleasure, first one then the other.

Later they were joined by Jane, who was feeling rather left out, and by which time the three girls had lost all their inhibitions, and happily participated in a gentle orgy which hurt no-one. Indeed, Juan-Miguel had left them several minutes before they realised his absence as the twin Volvos burst into life. The anchor chain rattled aboard, hauled in by its electric winch, Juan-Miguel backed out of s'Alga bay, and turned the prow away from s'Espalmador for a quiet trip back to Playa d'en Bossa.

"So do we get the job?" Jane asked as she stepped ashore from the dinghy.

Juan-Miguel smiled, "You did well today – I'll phone my associate in Germany, and if I can persuade him you're okay actresses, I'll pick you up here at ten tomorrow morning."

Then with a grin and a wave, he was gone, the dinghy aquaplaning back to the yacht.

* * * * *

"Is that his boat?" asked Sandra.

"That's the high-speed ferry to Formentera," replied Vicky, "your eyesight's appalling."

"It is only quarter to ten – he's not due for another fifteen minutes," Jane commented, as she slipped off her sandals to paddle in the sea, before continuing over her shoulder with a grin, "After the time I gave him yesterday, believe me, he'll come."

"I think he proved he can do that – several times!" countered Vicky, grinning at the memory.

Time passed. They all paddled. They joked, they recalled every moment of the previous day, and they spoke of their forthcoming roles as filmstars.

Again Jane checked her watch, "Well it's now quarter past ten, so where is he?"

"I shouldn't think Spaniards are renowned for their promptness – they're too laid back. Just relax – I'm sure he enjoyed our, er, company enough to want us for the film."

More time passed, the mood changing gradually to despondency.

"Suppose he's forgotten?"

"I don't think he'll forget me in a hurry – we kinda gelled."

"So where is he – it's nearly eleven?"

By eleven-thirty, they reluctantly accepted the truth – their great lover, Juan-Miguel Torres de Cantabria, was not coming.

And of course, they never saw him again.

In later life, they would each change elements of the story as they boastfully related to friends the day that a handsome Spanish millionaire film director fell in love with them, and talk about the dreamy fairytale time they had on his yacht. Alone of course, just Jane, or Sandra, or Vicky, as the case may be, alone with their handsome Spanish lover.

* * * * *

The lovely bay of Portinatx is in the north east of Ibiza, affording a vista many consider the most beautiful on the island. To the right are low level rocky cliffs, whilst the view to the left takes the visitor back in time, with a collection of ancient fishermen's boat houses. In the height of summer, the beach is an obvious honey pot for sun worshippers, whilst the sea itself plays host to many bathers, as well as numerous craft at anchor – some impressive, some less so. Whilst more actively, a speedboat races across the water towing a large inflated banana upon which happy young men bounce up and down, before a quick flick of the boat's rudder turns their rubber craft over to deposit them squealing and laughing into the water.

Across the road from the beach is the aptly named 'Pedro's Buenavista Restaurante', with a large open covered terrace enjoying the twin benefits of a cooling breeze, and the wonderful view from which the establishment takes its name. The two pretty German girls paid for their meal, and made their way across the road and down the sloping path to the beach. They had arrived the day before on their first trip to the island, and were still a little awestruck by the beauty of their surroundings. Coming from Bremerhaven, that was of course understandable.

As they searched for an unoccupied sun brollie, a handsome man with a pony tail approached them. "English?" he asked them pleasantly.

"Nein – Deutsche," they replied together.

"Ar so. Gut. Sind sie schauspielerinnen?" The German word for 'actresses' slipping easily off the man's tongue. "Ich habe ein kleine problem," he added by way of starting his explanation, as well-rehearsed in German as English.

It had been nearly a week now, and Juan-Miguel fancied another day out on his boat, living close to nature, in pleasant surroundings, with attractive and amenable company, such as the two lovely German girls . . . .

A Victimless Crime

"I think, sir, that you must actually live on Ibiza?"

The old man turned in surprise to the young girl on the adjacent table, to confirm that the question had indeed been addressed to him. He was seated at his favourite place in the relaxed elegance of La Casagrande terrace, directly overlooking the Marina in Santa Eulalia.

La Casagrande is a classy bar-restaurante created on two levels, the lower of which consists of chairs and small tables unprotected from the sun. A few steps up brings the visitor to the smart covered terrace, with the featured fawn colour carried through from the awning, or 'toldo', to the coverings on the round and oblong tables and their matching chairs. Marble pillars are each set in an ornamental flower basin, from which vines climb lazily to encircle them, whilst the quiet and gentle background music intrudes not at all on the general ambiance. Should the visitor venture further inside, to the building itself, they would find bamboo barstools matched by similar chairs grouped around the various dining tables. And lest it be thought that the more basic needs were not cared for, immaculate 'servicios' with automatic lighting and washing water are gender denoted by original paintings, the whole worthy of the London Savoy or Ritz . . . .

Though old – he himself preferred the term 'elderly' – he was still enough of the male animal to appreciate the beauty of the questioner. She was in her early twenties, with a naturally pretty, rather than made up, face, brown eyes and short auburn hair cut into a sort of pixie look in the manner of Brigitte Bardot when she was eighteen. She wore, instead of the modern young person's denim in its various forms, a simple floral dress which emphasised her youthful figure without in any way exaggerating it.

Politely, as was the habit of his age group and class, the old man raised his immaculate panama hat before replying, "Yes – yes I do, and have for a great many years. But how did you know?"

The girl shrugged her shoulders before replying. "That is easy. Your suntan is deep, real, not from just a few days on holiday. The waiter clearly knows you and what you like – your coffee arrived without the necessity of an order. And you spoke to him in what I imagine is very good fluent Spanish – at least good enough to enjoy a little joke, for he laughed at your words."

The old man smiled and removed his panama, placing it neatly at the back of his table, behind his coffee and the newspaper he had been about to read. Although he himself would not even notice the fact, he was truly a picture of sartorial elegance – tall and slim, wearing an immaculate hand-tailored linen suit, a pale maroon shirt, and the famous 'egg and tomato' tie of the MCC. At his feet, a metre long brown paper parcel indicated that prior to his arrival at La Casagrande, he had been shopping.

"You are indeed a good detective," he said with a kindly smile, "may I now attempt my own appraisal, although it will doubtless be a very poor effort compared to the powers of observation you have just demonstrated, Mademoiselle."

Again he smiled, this time at her surprise at being identified as French. "Oh yes, your English is very good," he said, "but your soft pronunciation cannot hide the proud country of your birth. So where in that great land do you come from? Not the north – again the softness is too great. Nor, I think, Paris, for whilst I am sure Parisians are perfectly charming people, they do have a certain capital city arrogance about them." He paused for a moment before continuing, "It would of course have been easier had you spoken in French, which I suspect would have been in the accent of the south west – Bordeaux, Biarritz – perhaps even as far east as Toulouse."

She was visibly shaken by his accuracy, and talk of her own country made her slip back just for a moment into her native tongue. "C'est incroyable! That is incredible – I live in the wine shipping town of Libourne, and a few months ago, graduated from the University of Bordeaux!"

"So what do you do, my confident Mademoiselle?" The old man posed the question as much to himself as to the girl. "The obvious answer is that you will become an English teacher – your pronunciation really is very good indeed. But then the way you were watching me, observing and deducing as would, for instance, a detective. But somehow I don't think you are with the gendarmerie – there would not be the need for such excellent English. I think you might just be a writer – possibly a reporter, with an ambition to move on into television."

"I am a trainee journalist with the 'Sud-Ouest'," she replied flatly, bemused. What she didn't say was that in her first day's training, she had been taught there was no such thing as a 'newsworthy story' – a newsworthy story was merely a collection of facts presented in an interesting way by a skilled reporter. Although of course, if the facts themselves were interesting, then half of the reporter's job was done for them . . . .

And another thing she had been taught is that there was a collection of facts sufficient to create a 'story' anywhere and everywhere – the paper had to be filled with copy even if no-one had got out of bed that day, which of course itself would be a story. And in the quest for the ability to conjure a story from nowhere, she had also been taught to not ignore the older generation, for most of them had one if not several stories to tell which could make good feature articles on a slow news day. Instinctively she had thought that the elegant Englishman had something to tell her that she could turn into copy.

There followed an amiable silence before the girl posed her next question, or really two questions. "How long have you lived here, and why Ibiza?" she asked.

The old man smiled before answering. "I suppose I've been here nearly fifty years now. But why Ibiza, you ask? Ibiza for me represented the end of a long journey."

"Would you like to tell me about it?"

Again the smile, before, "Tell my life's story to an ambitious young journalist, so it can be plastered all over the front page of her newspaper? No, I think not, Mademoiselle. You see, it has and could become again a matter of life or death – and in the latter event it might so easily involve myself."

The words were spoken in such a matter-of-fact way that at first the girl thought she had not heard correctly, or if she had, then mis-translated a crucial word.

For a while, she found herself stunned into silence, before she managed, "A dramatic answer, Monsieur, but in reality is there much crime on Ibiza?" She asked the question, groping for a way forward, although to use the generic word 'crime' when he had been much more specific was, she thought, rather lame.

"Crime, Mademoiselle? I think you must first explain your concept of crime."

She thought for a while before replying, "I suppose I see crime as where someone physically hurts another or steals something that doesn't belong to them."

But the old man shook his head. "That's far too simplistic," he said. "Let me put it to you that there is victimless crime and victim led crime."

"Victimless crime? I do not understand – how can you have victim*less* crime?"

He smiled and laughed gently. "I think that many would argue that victimless crime is not really crime at all, although technically of course it is. Take for example a bank or insurance company, both with wealth beyond the dreams of avarice, the morals of the gutter, and such a diversity of owners – mainly other similar institutions to themselves. Allow me to suggest they do not suffer in any measurable sense if an individual manages to slightly get the better of them, whether by something as simple as an exaggerated insurance claim, or defaulting on a loan, or a more calculated and comprehensive scam."

He paused to allow the girl to comment, which she did. "I *think* I see what you mean," she said, "though if everyone . . . ."

". . . Then there is the biggest institution of all," the old man added, preventing further objection, "the government, whether it is French or British, or that of any other country. A government, Mademoiselle, will steal as tax with the full weight of the law ten units of currency to return just one in value."

"But surely, if everybody refused to pay tax, a government would have no money for old people, or hospitals or . . . ."

Again the old man cut her short. ". . . Oh quite so. But the major crime, the theft, is actually *by* the government, with their criminal inefficiency, yet in law, administered by the self-same government, it is the individual who tries to retain his or her wealth to obtain ten currency units of value for a cost of ten who is deemed to be the wrong-doer. But I affirm that obtaining money from, or not paying money to, a government is a victimless crime – or no real crime at all."

The girl was becoming convinced that there was a story here, a hidden agenda behind the old man's words, if only she could keep him talking.

"And a victim *led* crime, Monsieur," she asked, "what is that?"

"What ordinary people such as you and I understand by the word 'crime'. A home broken into and personal possessions stolen, either to fuel a drug habit or by an illegal immigrant without the papers to acquire genuine employment. An old lady mugged in the street, a handbag snatched from the arm of a girl by a motor-cycle pillion rider, gratuitous violence on the innocent, or damage caused by those crazy from too much alcohol."

Again he paused, before adding, "You see the difference? We should in fact judge crime by the suffering caused, not by the sums involved. Here on Ibiza, as far as I am aware there is little victimless crime, although no doubt many of the beneficiaries from elsewhere live here in luxurious houses with yachts in the marina. But victim *led* crime, that I fear is on the increase on Ibiza, as it is all over Europe, and will continue to increase until the forces of law and order revert to being servants of the individual citizen, rather than the state."

She nodded wisely, lost in thought. Even in her young life, the gendarmerie had become more alienated from the ordinary people, usually coming into contact only in deliberately antagonistic road blocks, where those stopped were treated with arrogant disdain by those who should in fact serve them.

"Would you care to join me for a coffee and croissant – they're jolly good here? Then we can continue our conversation more quietly – I fear we have attracted attention from other tables," he asked.

"That would be most kind, Monsieur," she said, moving to do as he suggested. As she sat down she put out her hand, "Yvette Landreau, Monsieur, I am very pleased to meet you."

He shook her hand, which was soft and cool, and bowed his head for a moment in old-fashioned formality. "And I you, Mademoiselle Landreau. My name is Peter Sheridan."

He beckoned the waiter and ordered croissants for two, together with two large black coffees – known as 'Americanos' in Ibiza.

"Are you an honest girl, Yvette?" he asked her suddenly, his gentle voice belying the almost brutal directness of his question. "If you make a promise, do you keep it – do you *always* keep it?"

"I was brought up to be a good Catholic, Mr. Sheridan," she replied, using his English title rather than her previous French form of address.

"A great many people have been brought up as good Catholics, Yvette, and around half the confessions they make each week concern duties not performed properly, and broken promises!" But he smiled to take the malice from his words. "You see," he continued, "I have in mind being very cruel to you, but I can only do so if I can be sure you can and will keep a promise."

"Cruel, Monsieur, I do not follow . . . ." – back to the French form of address.

"Yes, if you will give me your absolute promise that you will never ever divulge it to anybody, I *will* tell you my story – it would help to unburden myself, to share with someone the knowledge of what happened so long ago."

"But the cruelty, Monsieur?"

"The cruelty will come from a young ambitious journalist having a great story she cannot publish." A pause before, "So, do you promise?"

This time it was her turn to smile. "Oui – yes, yes I promise that whatever you tell me will remain secret between us." For some reason her heart was suddenly pounding with excitement.

"I believe you," he said, "but here unless I'm very much mistaken are our croissants."

Impatiently, she started into her croissant, before, with her mouth full, she begged him to start. "Your story, Mr. Sheridan, where does it begin?"

* * * * *

"Let us say that the relevant part begins when I was a young man of twenty-six. I had progressed from prep school via public school to Oxford, where I had been honoured with a first, and from whence I was fast-streamed into the Foreign Office. At the F.O., it seemed I was soon thought of as a rising star, and after a few years I gained early promotion with a fairly major second-stream posting to Buenos Aires, possibly aided by the fact that I spoke reasonable Spanish. To me at that time, life appeared so easy, for although we had the serious side of supposedly representing British interests and making assessments of the Argentinean economic and political situation, much of my time was spent in diplomatic socialising. I say," he commented, "I do hope you like your croissant – you must try the marmalade with it, it's jolly good."

"The croissant is indeed excellent, Mr. Sheridan, but do please continue."

"Yes, quite. Now where was I? Oh yes, the socialising. It was at an Embassy ball – just one look and I was hooked. Her name was Antonia de Montaña, she was twenty-two, and the epitome of a Spanish beauty – long black hair, flashing eyes, and a figure to die for. Such was the grace of her movements that unbidden the other dancers fell back to yield the floor to her alone, as she progressed from a rumba to a traditional flamenco. Eventually we were all applauding, egging her on to yet greater brilliance with her clicking heels and the fan and castanets which had appeared as if by magic.

"In those brief moments I fell deeply and completely in love – it was as if my very soul was hers. And, dare I say it, before the night was over, she had fallen in love with me. Within two months we were married, and very shortly thereafter I was posted back to London, for an extended briefing on problems HMG had in various parts of the world."

"HMG?" she asked, "who is that?"

"Sorry, my dear – 'Her Majesty's Government', then only recently changed from 'His Majesty's Government', following the death of King George VI.

"In London, I was granted the privilege of my own trainee to act as my assistant – a brilliant young man from my old Oxford college. David Ponsonby rapidly became like a younger brother to me, and the odd thing is, he even looked like me, could even have *been* my younger brother, although he had what we then called beatnik tendencies, the forerunners of the hippy movement, and wore his hair considerably longer than could have been considered smart. You can well imagine how pleased I was that he and Antonia also became good friends.

"He had a most inventive mind, and was always dreaming up radical and novel solutions to problems, solutions which no-one else would have thought of. And as he was my protégé, dare I say it I received quite a few accolades for ideas that in reality were really his.

"For five wonderful months, the three of us were inseparable. We enjoyed a truly fantastic social life in London and the home counties, with invitations to the finest balls and weekend country parties. But of course, such happiness can never last for ever, and to us the end of happiness came with a single word, the name of my next posting."

"Which was?" Yvette prompted gently.

"Cyprus. Cyprus in 1956 at a time when Britain administered it, and Greece sought what it called 'enosis' – union with Greece. Which of course the Turks, who also lived there and made up about twenty percent of the population, wanted none of. The Greeks had two flamboyant figures in their cause – the commander of EOKA, their terrorist group, who was known as General Grivas, and the supposed rubber stamp of respectability, a Greek Orthodox Archbishop called Makarios, who we would eventually exile to the Seychelles, before in our usual manner bringing him back to become president. Stuck in the middle of all this mayhem were several thousand unfortunate British national servicemen, and a few diplomats, whose ranks were about to be swelled by one – me."

"And Antonia?"

"Ah, thereby hangs a tale. Because it was deemed to be a war zone, Antonia was not allowed to accompany me to Cyprus, and I counted myself fortunate to have such a good and trustworthy friend as David Ponsonby, who was the same age as my wife, to look after her in my enforced absence. At David's wise suggestion, I insured my life on a government sponsored scheme for a quarter of a million pounds, and the following day climbed the steps onto an RAF transport bound for that troubled paradise in the eastern Mediterranean. I remember being touched that David and Antonia turned up to see me off, and the warm feeling I had seeing them standing side by side waving as my plane taxied out – little did I then guess what would be the circumstance of our next meeting."

* * * * *

"So – what was Cyprus like in those days?" he continued. "Basically a nightmare. Nicosia was a fortress town, and we knew our lives were in danger at all times – or as they quaintly say nowadays, twenty-four seven. My one consolation was Antonia. She wrote three or four times every week proclaiming her undying love, and I of course did likewise. Also, because our letters were conveyed in the diplomatic bag by military transport, they were not only regular, but prompt. If she wrote on a Tuesday, I would be reading her words on Wednesday, or at the very latest, Thursday morning.

"Gradually of course reality set in. For myself I began to question what we were actually doing in Cyprus – why had our little country deemed it necessary to go out and conquer over half the world? And what value did it now give to us, as we fought terrorists in Africa and Cyprus, having recently lost control of the second most populated country on earth – the supposed jewel in the British crown which we called India? Is this what my life was to be – a succession of embassies and consulates in the world's trouble spots, as we gradually gave back that which was never really ours in the first place?

"Antonia's letters also began to change, to complain that she didn't marry me so we could live over two thousand miles apart. But even so, I'll never forget the shock of opening the letter which arrived from her six months and one day after our separation."

* * * * *

He paused to sip his coffee and finish his croissant. For a moment the girl thought he was not going to continue, but she need not have worried, for he was just getting into the swing, his mind far away in both kilometres and years.

"That letter was different in both style and content, and whilst I did eventually obey the instruction in the first line, I nevertheless remembered every word of it, and indeed, do so today."

"What *did* it say, Monsieur?" she prompted.

"It said '*My Darling, you must burn this letter when you have read it. I cannot go on like this, living apart, and have had an idea. I want you to get killed by the terrorists – that way I can claim the life insurance, and because you will have died in service, will even continue to receive most of your pay as a widow's pension. Of course, my darling, I don't really want you to die, but it would be so easy for you to issue a passport and documents in a false name, and simply disappear. After a few months I would meet up with you in a far away country, and we could spend the rest of our lives in luxury, with no requirement to work or ever be separated again. Please think about it, your loving wife, Antonia.*'

"I remember dropping the letter as if it was already on fire. But then I read it and re-read it, and then I did indeed burn it.

"It was madness, of course, complete and utter madness. But I could not get the idea out of my head – and back then a quarter of a million pounds was a great deal of money, possibly the equivalent of fifteen million euros today.

"So our exchange of letters continued, but now with more purpose behind them. I was to become Peter Sheridan, for that was not my name then. I issued my own passport and driving licence in that name, with even a birth certificate to back them up. It was agreed that we would meet eight weeks to the day after I disappeared – that would give her time for my memorial service, to collect the insurance money, endure a suitable period of mourning, and then make the natural decision to take a holiday to start to re-build her life.

"For our chosen rendezvous, I selected a country on the far side of the world – Australia. Taking care to be far away from any possible diplomatic service colleagues, we were to meet in a small town by the name of Mandurah, about sixty kilometres to the south of Perth, the capital of West Australia. And in that town I chose from a map a bridge over the Peel River Inlet.

"In the event, our plan went off like a dream. I disappeared one day, and after about twenty-four hours it was assumed I had been kidnapped by EOKA, with EOKA itself finally deciding to grab the available publicity by announcing they had shot me – an unexpected bonus, and truly a gift from the gods.

"By then, under the name of Peter Sheridan, and having for several days hopped on and off a considerable variety of aircraft – giving my custom to nearly as many airlines, including for the last leg 'Queensland and Northern Territories' – I was safely in Australia. I stayed for a few weeks in the growing city of Perth, which not many years before had been known as 'The Swan River Colony', where I found the climate very much to my liking. Nowadays, Perth has a claim to being the most beautiful city on earth, but back then it was not so, although with many of the houses built of wooden shingling, it had a certain amount of rustic charm – and a cheap and sunny way of life. I had managed to accumulate a fair amount of cash, and led a comfortable if simple existence enjoying the extensive beaches and the tang of the Indian Ocean. After three weeks in Perth, I caught a bus down to Mandurah, and checked into a small but adequate hotel, where I passed the time awaiting the arrival of my wife. The Peel Inlet proved to be a beautiful area, with the deep blue waters a haven for fishermen, and the local Swan lager quite acceptable to my palate."

The girl smiled, as she chipped in, "A perfect example of what you have called 'a victimless crime', Monsieur, although others might think differently."

The old man returned her smile. "Exactly, my dear – a victimless crime. At least it was so for a while."

* * * * *

"You can imagine my excitement," the old man continued, "as the day of our re-union approached. I realised of course that it was not an exact science, as 'eight weeks from the day I disappeared' depended upon when Antonia had been advised that had happened. However, I was greatly disappointed when she was not there on the first possible day. I exchanged a few pleasantries with the men fishing for crayfish off a lower footpath attached to the bridge over the Peel Inlet – it really was an idyllic spot. Then I had a few beers at the nearby pub, and eventually went back to my hotel feeling rather dejected.

"Still, there was always tomorrow, and I eventually fell asleep with hope in my heart.

"But unfortunately, the second day was a repeat of the first, with somehow my disappointment greater. And so sadly it went on. Every day for ten days I went to the bridge, outliving my welcome with the cray fishermen, who I am sure had concluded I was a basket case, as I patrolled up and down, looking, always looking. I added the post office into my list of duties – she would have no knowledge of my hotel, but may well have telegrammed a message to me there. I gave the pub a fair bit of business as well, with many of what they call 'midis' of beer to replenish the fluids I sweated off.

"Clearly something had gone wrong, and I was in the most awful predicament. On the far side of the world from my homeland, I was a man who didn't exist, was officially dead except for my false persona. And whilst I had funds for perhaps seven months, if I spent money on travel, there was clearly going to be less to keep body and soul together.

"Eventually, I decided I had no option but to take a chance, and do what we had agreed I would not do under any circumstances – I would phone Antonia at our little rented flat in Chelsea. In those days, of course, to phone England from a small town in Australia was far from easy. I used a public phone box near the blue waters of the Peel Inlet, and it took the operator fifteen minutes to establish all the necessary connections. All except the last one, that is.

"'I'm sorry, sir, that number is not available – it's a disconnected line. Can you re-check?' I did so, and had of course given her the correct London number.

"Something was very definitely wrong, for we had agreed that Antonia would keep the flat for at least six months, when she was then due to inform everyone that she was returning to Argentina.

"By the following day, I decided to take an even bigger chance, and this did make me sweat at the thought of it. I would phone my protégé, David Ponsonby. As I told you, my Spanish was fairly proficient, and also I have always been pretty good at mimicry – I thought I could fool him by pretending to be a family relative of Antonia's from Argentina trying to locate her, speaking in heavily accented English. Also, with it being David, if God forbid he did rumble it was me, I hoped our friendship was close enough that he'd keep quiet about it.

"Again there was an interminable delay with me perspiring in the little phone box as I waited to be connected to the

Foreign Office in London. When the PBX girl answered, in what I hoped was English with a flawless Spanish accent, I asked to be put through to David.

" 'I'm sorry sir, Mr. Ponsonby no longer works here – he has resigned from the service,' she said.

"Stunned, I asked if she knew why, for switchboard operators are a great source of knowledge.

" 'In confidence he was very upset by the murder of a close friend in Cyprus, and in his own words has decided to drop out – in the office the thought is that he's hit the hippy trail.'

"Feeling numb, I thanked her and hung up. But the odd thing is it took me two days of tortured thinking, with my mind going round in circles, before the truth hit me with the force of an express train – David and Antonia had run off together! I was the poor dumb cuckold, officially dead, and on the far side of the world, whilst they had my quarter of a million life cover – I did think of it as mine – and the widow's 'death in service' pension as well. Gradually, further realisation came, for of course, the ever-inventive David had dreamed up the whole plan! I should have realised that Antonia's mind, whilst fairly astute, could never have come up with anything so devious. It was always going to be a double-cross, and I was the sucker to be sacrificed."

"So that which you called a victimless crime now had a victim, Monsieur?"

The old man nodded vigorously, "Quite so, my dear, quite so – a poor and rather stupid victim. I knew I *must* find them – it was my only hope. But where should I look? The earth may be a small dot in the cosmos, but it's an awfully big place to search for two people who could be anywhere on its surface.

"I had just two clues – Antonia was never comfortable speaking English, and the girl at the Foreign Office said that she thought David had joined the hippy trail. Although I was well aware of his beatnik tendencies, he wouldn't, of course, want to do so in the guise of an impoverished traveller, nor would Antonia – no VW micro-van decked out with flower-power murals for them. They would prefer to put down roots in some quiet backwater, where they could safely invest their ill-gotten gains and enjoy the good life.

"But where? Where would they both be happy? The whole hippy movement was still in its embryonic stage, although the trail itself led to the east, India and Afghanistan – but as I said, I doubted they'd be on it. In America, there was a presence in California – especially San Francisco – and Spanish has long been a second language on the west coast of the USA, which of course would help Antonia. Whilst in Europe, St Tropez in the south of France seemed to draw them in large quantities, and more recently, Ibiza, remote and undeveloped, reached only by boat or an ancient DC3 tail-dragger plane.

"So – I had to start somewhere, although I realised it was hopeless. My thinking was no doubt flawed somewhere – for after all, it had been so far – and the sheer logistics of my search would compare to giving short odds on finding a needle in a haystack.

"Paying only in cash, with many connections and overnight stops, it was seven days later that the DC3 touched down with a well-executed three point landing on the dirt strip which was then this island's only runway. My global search had begun, and I had opted for Ibiza, Spanish speaking and popular with those seeking to drop out from a conventional western lifestyle.

"I had read my tourist guides, and told the taxi driver to take me to what was a sort of outpost for the English – Santa Eulalia del Rio, which boasted the only river in the Balearics. Although to this day, I have only seen it flow with water on three occasions. On arriving in Santa Eulalia, I asked the driver to find me an hotel, and he dropped me at a most admirable one very close to where we are now seated – although it was of course so different back then, and the building itself is now much altered. I recall there was a most magnificent swimming pool, and rather incredibly, nothing whatsoever between the hotel and the sea – just a dirt track and a few rocks.

"I did my best to make myself at home, although of course I was desperately unhappy, expecting to spend a forlorn five or six weeks exploring Ibiza, asking questions, searching – always searching for the two who had betrayed me, and for the money I considered was rightfully mine. Then I would head off somewhere else, in what I was convinced was a wild goose chase, for in reality I doubted I would ever find them. Possibly I would make San Francisco my next port of call, a city named for the patron saint of dumb animals. Perhaps he would bring me luck, for that was surely what I was.

"That is what I had expected. But the very next day, my first on Ibiza, my luck changed. I had wandered along the rocky foreshore from my hotel, for in those days there was no Paseo Maritimo, and no beach, when I nearly tripped over them! Their heads were close together in the manner of lovers, as they shared a table and laughed over their coffees outside a bar near the bottom of the Rambla.

"Fortunately, they were so wrapped up in each other they hadn't seen me, so I withdrew to a safe distance to watch them, without myself being seen. That sounds very calm, cool and collected, but of course, I was anything but. In my heart I had never expected to find them, yet fate had intervened and I had done so at the first throw of the dice – perhaps by working so closely with David, sub-consciously I had learnt to think like him, so perhaps I had had the most fantastic luck, perhaps not. I broke into a cold sweat which soon became a hot sweat. My heart was hammering against my ribs, and I simply didn't know what to do. I was so sure of failure in my search, I had not even considered what I would do in the event of success.

"Obviously I had to confront them, but what then? What did I want? Would we sit down amicably and discuss things, or just have a blazing row? Would they agree to a two-way split, in return for my silence? Or insist on me only having a third?

"But of one thing I was certain – I could not confront them where they were. Eventually the immediate decision was taken from me, for they finished their coffees, and hand in hand started to walk up the Rambla towards the taxis – you have no idea how much it hurt to see my wife and best friend so obviously in love with each other. I watched as they got into a taxi, and it headed off in the direction of Ibiza town.

"On the spur of the moment, I made a note of the taxi's number, and headed across the main road for a drink to wait and pray that it returned to the rank. I recall that I needed a strong drink, and unusually for me, had a scotch on the rocks.

"I did not have long to wait, for after only half an hour or so I saw the taxi turn into the Rambla to loop round and join the end of the rank, so the driver could take his turn and await his next fare. Affecting casualness, I approached him, and said that I thought I recognised two friends get into his cab a while ago – could he tell me where he'd taken them?

"'Si, Señor,' he said, 'to an old finca off the road to Cala Llonga. You can't miss it,' he added, 'there is a blue painted rock at the side of the road about half a kilometre before you reach the bay. I'd take you myself, but it's not my turn, and besides, I'm about to have my lunch in Yebisah's, which as you can guess, will take a couple of hours or so at least.'

"I thanked him for the information, and pretending no haste, headed for the taxi at the head of the rank, asking only that I be taken to Cala Llonga. After we passed a turn-off to a village called Siesta, the road became a very rough dirt track – I had no idea that Ibiza would be *quite* so backward – and as we approached Cala Llonga, I spotted a picturesque solitary finca on my right, with a blue painted rock where the rough track over to it joined the road.

"The driver dropped me in the bay, I paid the fare, and wondered what to do, for there was not a soul in sight, and nor was there even any building. Eventually, I spotted a sort of bar-kiosk, and headed for it – my earlier whisky and the heat of the day had given me quite a thirst. When I got there, it was open, but lacked the most important ingredient of a barman. There was, however, a notice, written of course in Spanish, which I translated as 'Please help yourself, and leave the money behind the bar'.

"Wonderful! Not only that, but opening a gas-powered fridge revealed a good supply of San Miguel. God was in his heaven, and suddenly all was well with the world – at least compared to what had passed recently. I opened a bottle of San Miguel, and sat at a small table where I was protected from the sun by a large bamboo shade. There, I enjoyed the beautiful tranquillity of Cala Llonga as it then was, and contemplated my next move. But little did I suspect what would in fact happen.

* * * * *

"God knows how long I sat there all alone on the beach, except for the company of San Miguel, but by the time I decided to head for the finca, there were five empty bottles lined up neatly on the table. I left the money for the beers, and started to walk back along the dirt road towards the blue rock.

"Thinking about it even now, I suppose my betrayal and predicament, the heat, and the San Miguels had all played their part. I reached the blue-painted rock, and found my hurt and anger now combined with fear, at least a sort of trepidation, for what lay ahead of me.

"The finca really was idyllic, the house being set on level ground in pine woods, which rose to cover the hillside behind. Whilst on either side of the track to it, and protected by signs saying 'Coto Priva de Casa' there were citrus orchards, laden with both lemons and oranges. At the side of the house, a pile of cordwood had been partly chopped into logs, indicating that it was not always hot on Ibiza, and by the logs an axe showed that some of the work had been done recently.

"Still I had not been seen – no challenge had come from the house, and I wondered whether the lovers were still at home – perhaps I had delayed too long on the beach. Then I heard a noise from around the back – it was Antonia's giggling laugh, and with a sick feeling in my stomach, I recalled the usual activity she was engaged in when she uttered it. I crept along the side of the house, peeped round the corner – and there they were. A large double bed, presumably intended for outside siestas, had been placed under the pine trees, a little way from a Heath Robinson sort of barbecue affair. They were, of course, both on it, as naked as the day they were born, and busily exploring that which they obviously saw as the delights of each others' bodies.

"That was the moment I flipped. What had I ever done to either of them that they should treat me this way? I moved to the wood pile and picked up the axe, then whirling it round my head I charged round the corner, screaming vengeance like a Viking berserker.

"To say they were surprised to see me is an understatement, as it is to say there was sudden terror on their treacherous faces. It only took one mighty slash at each to kill them, but at least I had the satisfaction of knowing that before they died, they knew who was sending them to another world. Perhaps it would have been better if they had had longer to consider the matter, to realise exactly where their betrayal had brought them – but the deed was done. Still the madness was upon me, and recalling the allotted traitor's death in olde England, I deliberately hacked each of them into four pieces – I had killed them by drawing, and although it was too late for the preliminary partial hanging, they had now been quartered as the fitting reward for their crimes.

"It was a couple of hours before I had calmed down and realised my predicament. There was blood everywhere, including me, and I had eight chunks of human being to dispose of."

In the calm tranquillity of La Casagrande, Yvette Landreau had gone very pale, her face a picture of shock.

Eventually she managed to stammer, "Monsieur, you have just admitted to a very brutal double murder – I *must* inform the Guardia Civil."

Resignedly, the old man smiled. "And break your word? I think not. Besides, what I have related happened nearly fifty years ago – does it really matter? Remember the sequence of events – I was the supposed beneficiary of a victimless crime. Then that which I considered mine, my money and my lovely wife, Antonia – oh she was such a Spanish beauty – were both stolen from me. It had become a victim *led* crime. If there were such a court as a court of moral ethics, then I am sure Antonia and David would have been found guilty. Bearing in mind the whole affair started with my own supposed death, the capital penalty was the only fair punishment, and I had carried it out promptly and efficiently.

"I say, the croissants were very good – would you like another, with a coffee, of course?"

"C'est bizarre, Monsieur! In the same breath you can quietly talk of croissants and hacking people to death. Incroyable!"

"I take that to mean 'yes' to the croissant." Peter Sheridan caught the waiter's eye, and placed his order before continuing.

"Now are you going to be quiet and sensible and keep your word, in which case I shall tell you the remainder of my story, or are you going to be dishonest and silly and break your word?"

Despite the intensity of her horror, the French girl did want to hear the rest of this incredible man's story, so with her conscience tugging both ways between her word and her public duty, she nodded. The coffee and croissants arrived, and she absently stirred some sugar into the strong black liquid before answering.

"I shall keep my word, Monsieur, and wish to hear the remainder of your story."

"Good. Jolly good. Now where was I? That was it – I had eight pieces of human torso to dispose of, a blood soaked mattress, and my own blood splattered clothing, which I'm afraid did rather give me the appearance of one who works in a slaughterhouse.

"Using some brushwood for kindling, and some of the logs from the pile, I soon had a good-sized bonfire going. I threw onto it the mattress, which fortunately was of the foam rubber type, and my own clothes. Inside the finca I found a primitive sort of shower, gravity fed from a tank on the roof, and I washed and scrubbed myself clean. Although I still had a messy job to do, to temporarily hide the eight quarters, I recall that I did feel considerably better after that shower.

"I found an old pair of shorts belonging to David, and as he and I were, or perhaps I should say, had been, the same size, I slipped them on. Finding a pick and a spade in a tumbledown outhouse, I soon dug a makeshift grave a little way into the wood. I tossed in the bits, and collected some sizeable rocks to go on the top to prevent dogs from digging them up.

"After that, I recall I felt safer – I could now dispose of my eight pieces at leisure, and in a manner I had already decided.

"Then, David's shorts joined the rest of my clothing on the bonfire, together, reluctantly, with the axe, for it really was a very good tool, with the keenest of blades. When I think of how it had . . . that is, it was just like a knife through butter. I pulled on a pair of jeans I found in the bedroom, and set about searching through the finca. An ancient desk revealed the neatly ordered files I had hoped for – David Ponsonby had always been the most meticulous of men, and whilst Antonia had little interest in such matters, it was his sure touch which made my task much easier.

"The quarter of a million pounds insurance money was untouched as a very large deposit in Antonia's name at a bank in Santa Eulalia. There was an unsigned contract to buy the finca and three hectares from a man called Manolo Lopez, with the buyer's name not yet detailed – so hopefully I could take that over.

"What I needed was a bank account in my own name – that is my own new name – at a different bank, into which by the simple expedient of forging Antonia's signature on cheques I could gradually transfer the funds. And also as a matter of urgency I needed what I believe nowadays is sometimes referred to as a set of wheels.

"Suddenly my heart stopped, for I heard a sound from outside. My heart in my mouth, I went to see what it was. In reality, it was a 'who it was', for a small man stood there grinning. He wore an ancient and rather battered straw hat, baggy trousers held up by leather braces, a dirty blue collarless shirt, and open but practical leather sandals. He was grinning happily, showing mainly gum, but with a few gold crowns to lend a bit of colour, and I took to him immediately.

"He greeted me with 'Hola, David, qué t'el?' – so obviously had taken me for my great, now late, rival. He nodded towards the mattress, still burning merrily on the bonfire, and by scratching himself vigorously and nodding, indicated that he thought I was doing the right thing to get rid of the fleas. But then his next 'words' – they were actually a mime of someone writing their signature – followed by 'Si? No?' was obviously asking if I had signed the contract – he *must* be Manolo Lopez.

"Fortunately I remembered that David did not speak much Spanish, so we were set to continue by pigeon talk and sign language. However, I greeted him by name as a long-lost friend, and as he did not correct me, knew I was right in my hunch. I also decided to bite the bullet about my name, and in pigeon Spanish explained that whilst David was my name for work, my real friends called me 'Peter'. As I now considered him a good friend, he too must now call me 'Peter'. Again the almost toothless grin, as he indicated he would be delighted to do so, repeating the name several times to make certain he had it right.

"I then indicated to him that 'el contrato' would be signed 'mañana' if I could find a 'notario', and hoped that we could soon conclude our business, which obviously pleased him.

"But he nearly stopped my heart with his next question, 'Antonia?' he asked, looking towards the finca, clearly disappointed that she had not come out to greet him. It was on the spur of that moment that I came up with an idea, and it was one that worked so well, I was to stick with it through the years to come. I explained that my lovely wife had family problems, and had returned to Argentina to look after her old and very sick mother.

"He nodded approvingly, for he too was old, shook my hand, and departed happily. My first rather large hurdle had been crossed very successfully, but I must not be complacent, for there would be many traps ahead which I must avoid if I was to start to enjoy, albeit alone, the life Antonia had described to me so graphically in her first letter on the subject. I recall that at that moment my mind drifted back to another moment – the day I received that letter at my digs in Nicosia, a seeming lifetime ago, though in reality it was of course only a few months.

"The following day, I walked into Santa Eulalia with something of a spring in my step. The dirt road was quiet and pretty, the cicadas sang in the pine trees, and the sun shone brightly but without too much heat from a clear blue sky. This latter was a bonus, for I was wearing some of David's smarter clothes for my interview to open a bank account.

"On entering Santa Eulalia, and just over the now-famous bridge, I spotted on the right a small and rather ancient bar. And alongside the bar, with a 'Se Vende' sign on the windscreen, was a Seat 600 car. A dirty sand in colour, its glory days, if indeed it ever had any, were clearly behind it. It was, however, ideal for my purpose, with the model being so common on Ibiza it would be nearly invisible.

"I turned into the bar and ordered a coffee. As the barman produced it, I enquired about the car, and learnt that it belonged to his brother, who only lived fifty metres away – would I like to see him?

"Indeed I would. The brother duly arrived, middle-aged, balding and running to fat, he had what I was to eventually call 'the Ibiza grin' – they really are a happy, friendly people.

"He assured me the car was 'muy bueno', that he would be sorry to sell it, but needed the money. He then wrote on a piece of paper the number of pesetas which would need to change hands for this magnificent 'coche' to become mine. I looked at the figure, drew a neat line through it, and wrote out a figure exactly half. Excitedly he shook his head, but I could see he was pleased to actually have an offer. He wrote down a figure midway between both, I increased my original one by ten percent, we shook hands and I took out a roll of notes to pay him. Then I wandered over to inspect my purchase.

"I was pleased to see that the manufacturers had thoughtfully provided a spare engine in the boot, but then rather disconcerted to discover that the original one in the front had apparently been removed. I was destined to drive the little Seat many thousands of kilometres round my adopted island, but would always regret the absence of the second engine to give it a little more 'oomph'.

"After paying my bill and collecting my things from my hotel, I next opened an account at a small but friendly bank just round the corner from Antonia's own chosen financial repository with a cash injection in pesetas of around five hundred pounds and a cheque in my favour signed by Antonia – I had regularly signed her name in our previous existence, as she had no interest in business matters – then in the little Seat, which I had already christened 'Sandy' both because of its colour and the sandy dust which covered it, I headed back down the road to Cala Llonga, to plan my future. The visit to the notario to sign the purchase contract for the finca could wait until tomorrow.

"But I was already clear about two things, I liked Ibiza and I was sure others would come to do so as well – my capital would be safest invested here in real estate, mainly in land, as I awaited the time when the rest of the world would discover this beautiful island, and I would be able to build my hotels, villas and apartments to accommodate them. I had no immediate need of much capital, for I could, after all, live on the pension provided to keep my late widow alive, as it were.

"So, overcoming a perhaps natural urge to run far away from what I thought of as the scene of a joint traitors' execution, I decided to remain here and take my ease – to enjoy the good life in such amiable surroundings.

"And as I sit here so many years later, still taking my ease, I can tell you in confidence that I don't regret it for a moment, and also I am wealthy beyond my wildest dreams – certainly far, far richer than when Antonia first suggested the scheme to me."

The old man leaned back in his seat and smiled at the pretty French girl. "So there it is, Yvette – the perfect victimless crime."

But Yvette Landreau was having none of it – she could contain herself no longer. "Mr. Sheridan, by your own admission you are a double axe-murderer, and had you not extracted what now appears as a rather macabre promise from me, I would have gone straight to the police. How can what you did possibly be a victim*less* crime?" The French girl was almost beside herself with anger.

Unruffled, the old man turned to answer her. "But I was not a murderer, Yvette, surely you must see that? I was merely the executioner for the non-existent court of moral ethics."

"Moral ethics, Monsieur? You had committed an immense fraud and violently murdered two people – and you still haven't explained how you disposed of the bodies you'd hacked into eight pieces, that is four pieces per body!" The girl was having difficulty putting her emotions into words.

"Yes – the disposal of the bits. As they had contrived to leave me as far away as possible, in Australia, and mindful that the body parts of old-time traitors were displayed at the cardinal point entries to London, I thought it appropriate to treat them likewise. With a map and a compass, and taking Santa Gertrudis as near enough the centre of the island, I plotted lines to the four cardinal points, north, south, east and west. Then as far as possible, and starting at the coast, I would travel inland along my plotted lines, selecting on each the most remote and well concealed area I could find. Then, as my first job upon waking, with my trusty spade and pick and a goodly quantity of quicklime, each day for the next four days I buried one bit of each of them in the same hole – they had wanted each other, they could have each other.

"You can well imagine that after such hard physical work, I was ready for a jolly good English breakfast – even today I remember how good they tasted, with the smell of sizzling bacon the perfect antidote to the odour of rotting flesh."

"Mr. Sheridan – you are the most evil man I have ever met! You have tricked me into a vow of silence, but I know that for the rest of my life I shall have nightmares about you!"

As the venom poured out, an aristocratic looking Spanish lady ascended the steps of La Casagrande and headed towards them. She was dressed with great elegance, still beautiful despite her advanced years, and her eyes and jewellery flashed in unison.

The waiter bowed his head in respectful greeting, and smiled with pleasure. "Senora Sheridan," he said, "buenos días".

The Senora Sheridan nodded to him, and spoke to her husband. "I'm sorry I'm late, Peter, the charity morning just went on and on – now we're going to also be late for lunch with David at the consulate, and you know he especially asked us to be on time. But I see that as usual you've found yourself some attractive company."

She put out her hand to introduce herself to the French girl, "Antonia Sheridan, my dear. I do hope my husband hasn't been boring you with one of his stories – that's the problem with writers, they have great difficulty telling the truth from fiction."

"Yvette Landreau," the French girl responded in rather a daze, "and no, he's certainly not been boring me – in fact quite the opposite." She still had not quite taken in the fact that Antonia was clearly still alive, and the whole tale had been an elaborate fiction.

"I had no idea David Ponsonby had 'especially asked us to be on time', Antonia," the old man replied to his wife, "I haven't seen him for weeks – though I'm reliably informed that you have."

"Yes, we bump into each other occasionally."

"Appropriately put, no doubt."

He clipped a twenty euro note to the tray containing his bill, rose to his feet, and stooped to pick up his parcel. Then he put on his panama hat, picked up his newspaper, and smiled at the French girl.

"Thank you for your company, Yvette, it's been most pleasant meeting you."

As they headed towards the steps, Antonia noticed the parcel. "You've been shopping again, Peter – what have you bought this time?"

"I've been to the ferretería, Antonia, and bought an axe – a nice sharp new axe."

And, for once lost for words, all the French girl could do was watch them go.

An Ibicencan Meal

The young German and his English girlfriend sat down at a small square red table in the shady open-fronted porch at Can Lluch, the well-known Spanish restaurante and bar on the right of the road from Santa Eulalia to Cala Llonga. The area was set out with many similar tables and matching red chairs, some paying homage to the saint of Estrella Damm beer, whilst others urged the user to 'beba Coca Cola'. To the front of the building, and partly hidden by palms and carob trees, an extensive gravelled parking area was already host to a Honda Trail Bike, an ancient Vespa, a Renault Clio, a rather well preserved English Nissan Maxima, a Peugeot 406 taxi, a Renault Kangoo, and a Suzuki jeep.

The German was medium – medium height, medium weight, medium brown hair, medium brown eyes, but with a smile that had broken the English girl's heart the first time she saw him. She was shortish, with long black hair and dark eyes, her face attractive without being overtly pretty. Below the neck, her figure was such that appreciative glances from the male of the species was her regular lot in life. They ordered two 'cañas' – small draught beers – and studied the menu.

"Try el plato del día, Señor – at only seven euros for three courses and wine, it's the best value meal on Ibiza."

Hans and Becky both looked in surprise at the man on the next table, who had indeed spoken to them.

"Thank-you," said Hans, "we shall take your advice."

Other vehicles – vans, pick-ups, four-wheel drives, cars – arrived, their occupants mainly, but not exclusively, local workmen looking forward to their lunch, taken late in the Ibicencan way. Most greeted the young couple's new friend by name.

"Hola, Pedro."

"Qué t'el, amigo?"

And one, a rather more formal gentleman wearing a neat shirt and tie, even offered, "Buenas tardes, Señor Sanchez."

The use of his family name was somewhat unusual, because to nearly all his many friends and acquaintances, the sixty-seven-year-old was known as Pedro el Pescador – Pedro the Fisherman.

Shortly, Pedro was joined at his table by another, almost a lookalike – not really surprising, as it was indeed his brother, Pepe, younger by four years. Their stocky frames, sun-tanned skins and thick-muscled arms bespoke for them both of a lifetime's toil under the Spanish sun, with their happy faces showing that this perhaps had not been such a bad thing either. Their English friend, Brian Smith, puns that Pepe and Pedro are alike as two 'P's' in a pod – a new take on an old saying – with even their voices being hard to distinguish if you didn't actually see the brother who was speaking.

Pepe Sanchez was not a fisherman, he was more a 'deportista', a sportsman. If he went in a boat it was to see how fast it would go, or perhaps how quickly it could pull him on water skis as he held the tow handle with one hand to lean back flamboyantly and wave to any girl within a hundred metres. If he dropped a sea anchor, it was not to fish, but for himself to descend into the depths of the Mediterranean, wearing scuba gear.

He was also a huntsman, being a good shot with his Castellani 'over and under' twelve bore, and since his puberty, now many years ago, had enjoyed chasing both woodland wildlife and women. Indeed, it was not known whether he frightened the women or the rabbits most, although of late he had married, and quietened down a little, chasing fewer of each.

Since his marriage, he had also taken pride in his vegetable garden, and if this was perhaps out of kilter with his 'deportivo', sporting, image, his love of good food meant it nevertheless tied in well with his gourmet life-style.

"So, Pedro, how goes it?" he greeted his brother in Spanish.

"Like a whore's mother," Pedro replied, using the rather odd and ribald response well known in Ibiza as meaning something along the lines of 'Actually rather well, old chap'.

At the adjacent table, Hans and Becky, who both spoke Spanish, exchanged looks of astonishment, for neither of them had heard the phrase before, and as stated it didn't even make sense.

"How's the fishing?" Pepe asked his brother.

"Fantastic – yesterday I caught my biggest fish ever – a monster, a veritable prince – no a *king* – of fishes. An emperador, at least five and a half, no six metres long."

Pepe nearly choked over his newly arrived beer. "Nearly six metres long – are we allowed to see this leviathan of the deep?"

"No – I let it go."

"Let it go before or after you caught it?"

"After – I fought it for over two hours, and when I finally got it into the boat, it was so magnificent I let it go."

"Tell me, brother, how do you get a six metre fish into a boat which including the cabin measures only five metres?"

"With great difficulty."

Pepe nodded sceptically.

"And a lot of skill," his brother added.

"Was Jordi with you – or any other witnesses?"

Pedro shook his head. "No, I achieved it all by myself. Have you done anything exciting this week?"

Pepe nodded. "I went scuba diving to find the ferry boat that sank off Roca Lisa in 1870."

"You found it?"

"Oh yes, and I actually swam into it."

"That must have felt weird, and a little eerie."

"It was, but the *most* eerie part was when I swam into the captain's cabin, only to find above the chart table . . . ."

"Yes – go on!"

"That the lantern remained hanging from the cabin roof, swinging with the flow of the water, and . . . ."

"And what?"

"And the candle was still alight!"

This time it was Pedro who had a problem choking on his beer. "You say the candle was still burning in a boat that sank in 1870?"

Pepe grinned. "Okay, Pedro – you cut three metres off your fish, and I'll blow out the candle."

As the two brothers burst out laughing, they were joined in merriment by Hans and Becky, who had been listening incredulously to the brothers' tales.

"You like our Spanish joking, then?" Pedro asked Hans, "We enjoy funny stories, but I thought Germans do not have any humour."

"Hummer is German for lobster – what is funny about a lobster?" Hans asked innocently, his voice soft, gentle, to a girl, sexy.

Becky leapt to her boyfriend's defence. "It's simply not true that Germans have no sense of humour – it's just that their humour is different, and they take work more seriously – that's why they build such good cars," she added.

"So what work do you do?" Pepe asked Hans.

"I am a chef."

"If you like good food, you've certainly come to a good place for your holiday – Ibiza is famous for its excellent local cooking."

"I'm sure that's so, but we're not here on holiday," Becky explained, her accent clearly indicating her English south east origins, "we're going to open a restaurante."

"That's good news – and it's great that you're here at Can Lluch to learn about traditional cooking," Pedro said enthusiastically, before a thought suddenly struck him. "You're not going to open a *German* restaurante? I ate in one once – they gave souvenir T-shirts to the survivors!"

"No, it will not be German food – it will be Eastern cuisine, a blend of Thai, Vietnamese and Chinese dishes, with a few inventions of my own."

Pedro put his hand to his forehead in mock horror. "Not another stickchop restaurante!" he said.

"Chopstick," his brother corrected him, "you said stickchop, and the word is chopstick."

"No matter – we have too many of them. If they gave you only one stickchop at least you wouldn't be able to eat the food, but they insist on giving you two, making it just about possible. But tell me – what is wrong with local Ibicencan cooking . . . .?"

". . . With good local ingredients . . . ." interjected Pepe.

". . . Like our mother used to produce."

"Do you remember her setas silvestres, her cazuelas . . . .?"

". . . Her graixoneras?"

Pepe turned to the young couple. "You cannot open another chopstick restaurante! You must learn to prepare proper Ibicencan food – that is what people want."

"But Hans is very inventive – his cooking will not be like any others!" Becky protested. "Tell them about some of your specialities, Hans, about the beef . . . ."

Hans laughed. "I don't think they'd be interested in my beef and prawn pouches, or red curry fishcakes, or . . ."

". . . or your baked duck with sliced baby oranges, or your pork in spicy caramel?" Becky interjected. "Of course they would!"

But Hans shook his head. "If people enjoy a particular style of cooking, Becky, they often don't want to even *try* another. Would *you* eat mealy-meal – ground and boiled maize served with gravy – it's the staple diet of millions of black South Africans? And remember, the whole world knows the native Australian always cooks on a barbie, the French eat frogs legs by the ton, the American always eats at McDonalds and the English eat only chicken tikka masala."

"You infuriate me when you joke like that!" Becky said angrily, "Why can't you be serious?"

"I am a German – I am always serious."

But the two brothers shook their hands sadly. "That all sounds even worse than stickchop food," Pedro said. "We must convince you about Spanish cooking." Suddenly he snapped his fingers, "I've got an idea, Pepe! Let you and I prepare a meal – no, prepare a *feast* for these two – a proper Ibicencan long luncheon . . . ."

". . . .That goes on into the evening and continues into the night?"

"Exactly."

"With all local ingredients – we could start with an emperador, what you call a swordfish," Pedro explained to Becky "- I could catch that fresh off Tagomago."

"My brother is a very good fisherman," Pepe confirmed, "you see, he treats the fish as his intellectual equal – which I suppose they are."

"Thank-you, my brother the mighty hunter – what will you cook?"

"Your emperador will be followed by a rabbit casserole – I will shoot fresh rabbits in the woods, and we'll have the finest organic vegetables from my garden – no E-numbers or monosodium glutamate." Pepe said confidently.

"We'll cook for you on Sunday, the day after tomorrow . . . ."

". . . All local ingredients, prepared in the traditional local manner . . . ."

"Certainly," Pedro confirmed, "now you must tell us where you are living – we will cook at your home."

* * * * *

It was shortly after eight o'clock the following morning that Pedro stowed his hamper, and with a nimbleness that belied his age, jumped aboard his beloved 'el Rey del Mar' – the 'King of the sea' – tied up at his berth in Santa Eulalia Marina. The wooden boat was five metres long, very seaworthy, had a small cabin, and was powered by a sixty horsepower Yanmar diesel, which gave it a surprising turn of speed if ever he desired to fish off another part of the island, and get there quickly.

Today, however, he planned to go only a short distance to the area around the small island of Tagomago, not far north of Santa Eulalia. He was well equipped for his day out, with various fishing tackle and baits, together with a selection of 'bocadillos' – lovely crisp baguette style sandwiches – 'queso' – a selection of cheese from all of Spain, but with an emphasis on his beloved Manchegan, and of course olives, jamón Serrano and crisps for nibbles. A six-pack of Mahou Classica beer, two bottles of Faustino VII vino tinto, two litres of frozen agua 'sin gas' – still water – which would gradually defrost into refreshing cool water through the day – and a flask of his beloved strong coffee completed the iron rations to which he would be restricted through his arduous day.

Pedro 'Pescador' anticipated it with pleasure, as he pressed the button to start the Yanmar, and slipped the mooring rope.

As ever, he allowed his boat to chug out of the marina with the engine on little more than tick-over, leaving behind the restaurantes and bars awaiting their first customers in a few hours time, and took in the familiar scene with an almost un-seeing pleasure – the long high hill to the south covered with pine trees, and fronted by steep cliffs, with nevertheless the odd house clinging precariously to them, before he opened the throttle to about sixty percent power to give him the twelve to fifteen knots which was his preferred speed.

'Life has its little compensations' he thought, as he pointed the prow north-east to Tagomago.

* * * * *

Pepe Sanchez loaded his Castellani 'over and under' into his ancient four-wheel drive Seat Panda. This was followed by his cartridge belt containing a mix of number five and number six shot – to allow for shooting both furred and feathered game – his old and much-used game bag, his own slightly smaller version of his brother's picnic lunch, and the last important item – 'Pedro', his Podenco hunting hound. With his rather exaggerated sense of humour, it gave him a perverse pleasure to name his dog after his brother, and to have trained it to obey his orders, something he had abjectly failed to achieve with the human original.

He slammed the boot of the car, long used only as a two-seater with ample space behind the seats for dogs, guns, food, shopping, and on occasions, tools, and jumped behind the wheel. In his garage he had an immaculate five-year old BMW 320 Dti, but his day to day transport was his much used and abused Panda.

He gunned the engine, and set off towards the hills and the pine woods, with Pedro barking excitedly behind him.

* * * * *

It was late in the day when the Seat Panda turned off the top, bypass, road to park at the side of the hill close by the entrance to 'Es Marcat' – the covered market in Santa Eulalia. Pepe quickly, almost furtively, slipped out of the car and down the steps into the air-conditioned market. He knew what he wanted, and where to get it, and headed to his favourite butchers. There he had a choice of lamb and pork hanging from overhead bars, and under the glass display counter, beef, liver, mince, various sausages including chorizos, black pudding, home-made beef burgers, and the wonderful yellow fleshed chicken – pollo pages.

"Pepe Sanchez, the hunter!" asked the butcher, "you've brought me some rabbits – I certainly can do with them?"

"'Er no, I'm not selling, I'm here to buy."

"That is excellent news – I need the trade as well. What is it to be – I have some very tender Argentinean beef entrecote, or a very good shoulder of lamb? Or perhaps a small suckling pig for Francisca to pop in the oven – I know that 'lechon al horno' is a favourite of yours?"

The words came with difficulty, quietly, his tongue almost tripping over them. "Please may I have two, no, perhaps three, rabbits?" he asked.

The butcher grinned broadly. "You joke, eh, Pepe?"

Grimly Pepe shook his head. "No joke."

"But surely if you want rabbits you can shoot them?"

"If you must know, I tried, but in five and a half hours hunting, the only rabbits I saw were when I was having my lunch, the gun was unloaded, and the dog was tied up."

The butcher had difficulty in restraining a laugh. "So now you come to me, not to sell, but to buy! To you, Señor, a special price – fourteen euros for the three," as gleefully he reached down his last rabbits from the overhead hooks.

Pepe took out his money clip. "I suppose they are *Ibicencan* rabbits?"

The butcher shook his head. "They might not even be Spanish – possibly French or Italian. Do you know, Señor," he said in a conspiratorial tone, "sometimes we even get them from China."

Pepe slammed down his money and picked up the bag containing the rabbits – he did not need a geography lesson on the origin of them.

"Please tell no-one about my purchase," he implored, then more quietly as he moved away from the counter, "I bet they *are* Ibicencan rabbits . . . ."

The lack of rabbits was not his only problem, because he had just learnt that the previous day his wife had exchanged his wonderful crop of tomatoes for a sack of Portuguese onions. "The tomatoes will grow again by next week, and your onions had long since finished," she explained.

"But why Portuguese?" he'd moaned. "The whole world knows Spain is famous for its onions!" And to add insult to injury, she had used his last three cucumbers to make a pickle.

Pepe moved on to his preferred greengrocer's, a stall with a wonderful display offering bananas, plums, giant red peppers, green peppers, apples, ugly fruit, melons, tomatoes, broccoli, lettuce, radish, string beans, peas, carrots, mushrooms, potatoes, and celery. Hoping no-one he knew was watching, he hand-picked three kilos of tomatoes.

"A wise choice, Señor, finest Italian," the greengrocer commented as she bagged the purchase.

"Cucumber?" Pepe asked miserably.

"Si, Señor – from the Dordogne. And as you know, the best cucumber is a French cucumber."

Pepe was almost on the point of telling her where she could stick her 'best French cucumber', when a firm hand descended on his shoulder.

"Buying vegetables, Brother – not cheating, are we?"

For the first time in many years, Pepe blushed bright red. "It's, it's not my fault, Pedro," he wailed, "Francisca has cleared my garden." Then he turned to the greengrocer, "Two kilos of mushrooms, please, and no, I do not want to know where they come from."

"I didn't know you grew mushrooms, Pepe, did naughty Francisca clear those as well?"

"No, Pedro, it has perhaps been too dry, but I couldn't find any 'setas' in the woods."

"So what else have you bought – what's in the bag?" Pedro asked him.

"What bag?"

"The bag you're trying to hide behind your back," saying which, Pedro grabbed for it, and snatched a glance inside. "My, my – you shot so many rabbits that you've also brought some to sell, have you?" he asked mischievously. "Do you want me to deliver them to the butcher's for you?"

"Okay, okay, Pedro, very funny." Then a thought struck him as flash of inspiration. "But why are *you* here? After fishing you usually go to Casa Piedra for a few beers." There was possibly more to his brother's presence than mere coincidence . . . .

"I thought tonight I'd have a change."

"And go shopping – you *hate* shopping?"

"I just thought that today I'd have a change."

But Pepe was now hot on the scent. "How was the fishing?" he asked quietly.

"I had a very pleasant day, thank-you," his brother replied.

"And the emperador? You caught one of sufficient size to impress our young friends?"

No answer.

"So what *did* you catch?"

The answer took some time in coming, like teeth being pulled. "If you must know, a few sardinas, a small lenguado, and two calamares."

"In a whole day?"

Pedro Pescador nodded miserably.

"And you're here to actually *buy* an emperador?"

Again a nod.

Pepe the renowned hunter paid the greengrocer, and slapped his brother on the back.

"I think we'll keep quiet about our shopping expeditions, and tomorrow we'll cook a good Ibicencan meal for our young friends, eh? I'll pick you up around eleven."

And, laughing so much that tears ran down his cheeks, Pepe the great hunter left his brother, the great fisherman, to return home to his wife.

"Good luck with catching, sorry, with *buying* an emperador," he called over his shoulder as he walked away.

* * * * *

Laden with flagons, beer, flasks, food, and two happy brothers, the battered old Seat Panda picked its way slowly along the rocky dirt-surfaced track.

"You got the emperador alright?" Pepe asked.

There was a slight pause before Pedro answered. "Eventually, yes."

"Eventually? Where from?"

"A frozen food shop in Ibiza."

"Not from the market in Santa Eulalia?"

"No. They had emperador, of course, but only in slices from a very big fish – I wanted to produce a whole fish to show the young people what it is like."

"So you bought a frozen one, which is now, I hope, fully defrosted. Where did it come from?"

"I told you, a frozen food shop in Ibiza."

"But that was after it had stopped swimming, that was when it was dead. Where was it when it was alive and flapping – Ibiza, Mallorca, off the mainland . . . .?"

"Australia."

"Australia? You're joking."

"No, the shopkeeper said that Australian fish is very good as there are fewer waste chemicals flowing into the South Pacific than into the Mediterranean."

"So our local Ibicencan ingredients include an Australian fish, rabbits that might have come from China, Portuguese onions, French cucumber, and Italian tomatoes."

"But good Spanish Rioja wine and Mahou beer! Is it much further, Pepe, you said you thought you knew the place?"

"I *think* I do, but if I'm right it's not a finca or a casa, as they said, but what we would call a 'chabola' – a shack," Pepe replied, "Anyway, I believe it's just around the next bend."

And so it was.

Hans and Becky were sitting outside at a rather rustic table, and waved a happy smiling welcome. But in truth the 'finca' they had rented was little more than the chabola Pepe had remembered. No matter, some sort of stove to cook on, and most of their day would be spent outside, sheltered from the worst of the sun's heat by the pine trees which grew close up to the small patch of land the chabola occupied.

* * * * *

Thirty minutes later, Pedro and Pepe were already on their third beers, drunk straight from the ice cold cans.

"Hans and I are very much looking forward to your 'typical Ibicencan meal', when do we begin?" Becky asked, as so far all their visitors seemed to want to do was drink beer.

"It already has," Pedro replied, "it's the Northern Europeans who make the mistake of separating drinks from food . . . ."

". . . You see," Pepe interjected to a glare from his brother, "a good meal requires a balance between drinking and eating, with each dish complimented by, not fought against by, the drink taken at the time . . . ."

". . . With the third, most important element being the ambience – the location, the people, and the mood."

"But we are not eating, so the meal has not yet begun!" Hans objected.

"But it has!" Pepe countered. "We are sitting round having a pleasant chat and a thirst-quenching drink – if I were in a restaurante I would not yet want to even *see* a menu, let alone start choosing my meal."

"But as we're not in a restaurante, can you break the suspense and tell us what we are to have?" asked Becky.

Pepe laughed. "Okay, but as the eating is to last all day, we shall have two full-size main courses, rather than a small fish course – in between we can take a break of an hour or so, and have an enjoyable chat as we are now."

"Or even a small siesta!" Pedro continued. "Anyway, to business. It is so pleasant sitting here that I suggest our thirst-quenching aperitifs continue with a crisp dry white wine – we have a few bottles of a very cold Marques de Riscal. With the wine we can of course enjoy some olives, followed by bread and alioli. This will eventually be followed by an excellent gazpacho, made for us last night by Pepe's wife, Francisca .

"A good gazpacho has to be made well in advance so the flavours can properly blend together, and of course should be served very well chilled," Pepe explained.

"I have heard of gazpacho," Hans said "- it's a sort of iced vegetable soup, isn't it?"

Pepe laughed. "Some say the name actually means bread and water, which it certainly contains, but a good gazpacho is a little more than either of our descriptions. Here," he put his hand into his pocket and withdrew a crumpled piece of paper, which he passed to the young German, "Francisca wrote out her own recipé for you, and with the help of our Dutch neighbour, translated it into English. I'm sorry," he added, "we could not find a German translator, and I forgot to tell her you speak Spanish. Also, Francisca says if your restaurante is to be for tourists, they might prefer less garlic!"

Hans unfolded the recipé, and was surprised at the detail; he was also genuinely touched by the kindness of the lady unknown to him as he read:-

~ ~ ~ ~ ~

Francisca's Gazpacho – for Señor Hans

List 'A'

Juice of 2 Lemons (or 5 tablespoons wine vinegar)
1 kilo skinned ripe Tomatoes
2 cored and chunked Green Peppers
(or other colour if no green)
1/2 chunked Cucumber

6 cloves Garlic
1/2 small chopped Onion
List 'B'
2 slices (50 gm) de-crusted bread soaked in water
List 'C'
100 ml Extra Virgin Olive Oil
1/4 diced Cucumber (additional to list 'A')
2 teaspoons Salt
1 teaspoon chopped Basil
1/4 litre Water
Method.
Put List 'A' ingredients through processor until pureed then strain into large bowl.
Squeeze water from bread in List 'B' then puree in processor, keep motor running,
As the Olive oil from List 'C' is slowly added to incorporate with the bread,
add other List 'C' ingredients + some of the sediment from List 'A'.
Add pureed List 'A', then the Water
Taste, season then refrigerate.
Garnishes:-
Baby Croutons, Onion, Red Pepper, Hard-boiled Eggs, Cucumber, Apple, Melon

~ ~ ~ ~ ~

"Wow – that looks good," he said as he read the recipé. "You also mentioned sangria, Pepe – when do we have that?"

"Not yet," Pedro chuckled, "after the gazpacho, and whilst we are still enjoying the vino blanco, we shall have my magnificent emperador."

Pepe coughed to hide a grin, and received a glare from Pedro for his trouble.

"I often cook an emperador as a kebab – the flesh is firm like tuna, but with more flavour and just a few more bones. But I thought if instead of kebabs I cut it into steaks, and lightly marinate them in a mixture of oil, vinegar, garlic, lemon and tomato juice, I will barbecue them for you. The barbecue flavour will contrast nicely with Pepe's cazuela a couple of hours or so later . . . ."

"I suppose you have a barbecue?" Pepe asked.

The German chef grinned. "Yes, of course, but I thought you'd probably prefer to make one with a few stones and bits of wire."

"When you go fishing, that is often the best sort!" Pedro retorted, "Build a barbecue and cook your fish on the beach when it has only moments before popped out of the sea."

"Just like your emperador," Pepe commented innocently.

"Do you prefer charcoal or wood?" Hans asked, as he rose to build and light the ancient Heath-Robinson barbecue just a few metres away.

"Charcoal, if you have it," Pedro said, "and yes, if you light it now, it should be ready for when we need it in about an hour and a half."

"And after the fish?" asked Becky, "What then?"

"Then we relax and drink sangria and possibly enjoy a snooze to allow our food to digest," said Pepe.

"And after that?"

"We shall greet the onset of evening with my 'cazuela de conejo con setas' – rabbit casserole with wild mushrooms."

"Do people really eat rabbit in Ibiza?" the girl asked, "I'm sure they don't in England."

Hans nodded. "People are frightened of myxomatosis, which is actually harmless to humans – but I think you'll find country people in England and Germany still enjoy rabbit. And it's certainly popular in France and other Mediterranean countries. Do many restaurantes here have it on the menu?" he asked with interest.

Pepe nodded. "My favourite restaurante is 'The Wild Esparragos' at Cala Llonga – they have the ideal mix of what we discussed earlier, a great ambience, good wine and cocktails, and excellent food – including a traditional cazuela de conejo similar to the one I am going to make for you. Which reminds me, I'd like to start it now, for it is best cooked long and slow."

* * * * *

That was how the 'typical Ibicencan meal' went, long and slow. Long and slow through the late morning (mainly drinks), the afternoon, then the early and late evening. Several jugs of sangria had followed the four bottles of Marques de Riscal and the barbecued emperador, and preceded the cazuela. The cazuela and the cheese which followed had been accompanied by 'just a few' bottles of Marques de Caceres Tinto Gran Reserva, and to round off the food, a goodly portion for each of them of Francisca Sanchez' graixonera pudding.

The drinking had been rounded off with black coffee, of course, and a choice of a dark Soberano brandy, or the lighter '103' which Pedro preferred.

By the young people's standards it was quite late – past midnight – when the brothers finally loaded their utensils into the car, and set off happily and blotto down the forest track.

But by the standards of Pepe and Pedro, the night was still young, and as the little Seat bumped its unsteady route back to the tarmac road, Pedro asked his brother, "A small beer on the way home?"

"It's still very early – with luck they might still be open. We could probably manage two! Do you think we convinced Hans and Becky about traditional cooking?"

Unseen in the dark, Pedro nodded. "I'm certain," he said, "there will not be another stickchop restaurante."

Amiably, this time his brother did not correct him.

* * * * *

In the little finca, or chabola, the young lovers retired to bed, their tiny room lit only by a solitary candle.

"What did you think?" Becky asked.

"I thought the meal was excellent, and they have also given me our advertising slogan – 'Nice People – Nice Ambience – Nice Food – Nice Drinks'."

"That's nice," Becky murmured, as she cuddled up like a spoon to the man she loved. "Any ideas from the food?"

"Lots! Mostly I have learnt how really excellent the local ingredients of this wonderful island are! Just like Pepe and Pedro, I shall always use them, and tell everyone. No imported rubbish, my food shall all come from Ibiza or the sea that surrounds it."

"Good healthy food," she replied.

"If I thicken the gazpacho a little with more oil, and sweeten it with balsamic," he continued enthusiastically, "it will make a superb salad dressing, and the baby croutons will add a crunchiness to the salad as well. Also gazpacho would make a rather wonderful adaptation of a Bloody Mary – we could call it our house cocktail – an 'Ibicencan Mary'. Then the rabbit . . . small chunks flavoured with a light soy sauce, or perhaps hoi-sin might be better, and tossed in a wok – I must experiment."

"And the swordfish?"

"A great find! Lovely firm flesh like Pedro said, and a strong enough flavour to take an exciting marinade – I can try cutting slim julian strips for wok cooking, or even dipped in tempura batter for deep fat frying might . . . ."

She reached around him, her hand moving to his groin. "Hans, it all sounds wonderful. But for now, please don't cut anything off your long fish, and I'll blow out the candle . . . ."

With which the little chabola deep in the woodlands lapsed contentedly into darkness.

The Teenage Pop Star of Figueretas

Penny d'Arcy languidly stretched her petite young body, her famous blue-green eyes flicking to check the time on the bedside clock. It was only about eight-thirty pm, but with the high tech shutters on her cabin windows closed, it could have been the middle of the night. She turned back to the book she was reading, then, on impulse, threw it as far as she could across the cabin, putting into action the oft-quoted Dorothy Parker advice, "This is not a novel to be tossed aside lightly. It should be thrown with great force."

How many times had she read the naffin' love story before, only of course with a different title and different named characters? Girl goes out with mates, girl meets boy, boy and girl fall in love, girl loses boy, girl gets boy back.

If only it happened like that in real life! Again she stretched out on the enormous round double bed – a feature of the owner's suite on her multi-million pound yacht. *Why* couldn't she get to sleep? Last night she hadn't slept a wink, nor the night before. She *must* be tired. She flicked a button, the cabin lights dimmed, and then a solitary one lit automatically, gradually moving across the ceiling to descend down the wall, copying the setting of the sun. As the 'sun' went down, 'stars' came out in the ceiling, twinkling like a night-time summer sky – the whole system a kindly meant present from her manager. Said to be therapeutic if you're alone, romantic if you're not. She was alone, so had to make do with the therapy.

"When you're worried and you can't sleep, then count your blessings instead of sheep" the old, old song went. Not that she was worried, just a desperately unhappy twenty-two year old multi-millionaire pop star who had gained the whole world, but lost the boy she loved. And that love had started right here, in Ibiza, not far from where her luxury yacht was now anchored. Her mind drifted – was it really only six years ago that, as ordinary Penny Brown, she had come to Ibiza with five mates, all aged sixteen, to celebrate their recent release for ever from the tyranny called school?

* * * * *

Some people are catalysts, they make things happen without even realising it. They become popular, and are usually the centre of attention. Frequently but not always they are fun people, but above all it is their charisma that makes them a catalyst.

Certainly little auburn haired Penny Brown was one, and had been for many years. When Helen, one of her best mates, hit on the idea of having a school leavers' holiday to Ibiza, and started drawing up a shortlist of those she would like to come along, inevitably Penny had been top of that list. When you were with Penny, things, well, just happened, fun things, different things. When she danced, she commanded the floor with her lithesome grace and energy. When she sang, like the pop star she dreamed of being, she sang with power, rhythm and range. Nor was there any need to chase boys when you were with Penny – although her figure had yet to fully develop, boys were never far away. So it was now with the group of six girls who had arrived in Ibiza the previous day. They had much in common, they were all sixteen, they had all done various part time jobs to save the money for their holiday, and they had all talked their parents into subsidising those savings. Also they had just escaped from the awfulness of the school they had been forced to attend for what seemed to them most of their lives. And they were all off the leash for the first time, to enjoy a holiday without parental control.

"No drugs, mind, Charlotte."

"No, Mum."

"If you date a boy, Emily, remember there's a little present you should save for your eventual husband."

"Yes, Mum." No point in telling Mum that 'the little present' had been given some two years ago to 'that nice boy who lives next door and wants to become a vicar'.

"Just remember, Helen, you are not allowed to buy alcohol until you're eighteen."

"That's in England, Dad, I don't think it's like that everywhere."

"It is for my daughter – no alcohol."

"No, Dad."

Helen thought of her stern faced father now as she sipped her vodka Red Bull. He once told her she was like the brown girl in an old Boney-M song, whoever they were, brown hair, brown eyes, and a decidedly brownish skin. Although she noted he made no reference to the big boobs of which she was so proud. Not that he was a bad dad – she giggled as she realised she had thought in rhyme – but he was just so un-with it. Was there such a phrase as un-with it? No matter, for if there was, it certainly applied to her dad.

They were in the bar of their holiday hotel in San Antoni – still called 'San Antonio' by most of the world despite the Ibicencan government officially changing it back to its original name. With its pool and gardens and palm trees, the hotel, situated just a hundred metres from the sea and three minutes from the town centre, was luxurious beyond their wildest dreams or youthful experience, also what they expected for the money. And now they were involved in that most happy of activities, planning a programme for their holiday. In an ideal world, it would be simple. They would spend everyday on the beach, showing off their lovely and nearly naked young bodies to any boy who wanted to look.

Then every night, with inexhaustible funds and no requirement for sleep whatsoever, they would go clubbing. They knew all the clubs by reputation, but had never yet actually been inside one; Eden and Es Paradis, both in San An itself, the giant Privilege (which had once been called 'Ku's') and the famous Amnesia, both on the road to Ibiza, which the girls had yet to travel. Pacha, founded by Ricardo Urgell and actually in Ibiza, was of course the one that started it all, and Space, at Playa d'en Bossa, which was goodness knows where.

But the clubs were expensive, and their funds were not inexhaustible.

"Supposing we do three clubs?" said the slim dark haired freckle-faced Brenda, her accent, like the others, the rather pleasant sound of her native Essex. "If we don't drink much, and fill our glasses at the taps in the loos, we should be able to afford that."

"But the clubs are what we're mainly here for!" from Dawn. She was blonde and blue eyed, but unfortunately rather tubby, claiming to anyone who'd listen that it was merely puppy fat that was slow to disperse.

"And boys!" Emily reminded her. Like Dawn, she was also blonde, but unlike her friend was slim and tall, a fact she tried to disguise as much as possible by such devices as sitting on chair backs, or leaning on walls. "We want to pull whilst we're here!"

In this latter they were about to be successful, for a group of six teenage lads at the bar had been eyeing the group of girls with interest. Without realising it, the girls all looked to Penny to make a decision.

"Brenda's right that we could easily run out of money, but Dawn's also right – we want to go clubbing."

"And chase some talent," Emily again chipped in.

Penny laughed. "Wrong! Let the talent chase us." She paused and sipped her Red Bull, before telling them what they would do.

"Let's draw up a list of clubs in our order of preference, then it's just a matter of how far down the list we can get before the money runs out." The nodding heads indicated agreement, as, just for a moment, Penny's eyes met those of one of the boys at the bar; he had dark hair and was watching her intently. Oddly, a tingle ran down her spine, before she continued. "I suggest we start with Amnesia, because it sounds the most fun. Then Privilege for a Manumission show. We could do a day-time visit to Space for some funky garage stuff – Saturday would be best for that. Then Es Paradis if we're still in funds."

"What about Pacha?" from raven-haired Charlotte.

"It's supposed to be very stylish, and they do have Ministry of Sound there quite a bit," said Helen.

"I know – it's the one favoured by the older Yuppie crowd."

"So?"

"So we put it after Es Paradis, which we can walk to – I think it's somewhere on the waterfront."

"A-ho – they're coming," said Emily, nodding her head towards the group of lads.

And so they were. Or at least five of the six were, for one had stayed at the bar, quietly sipping his pint of beer.

The boys had the greatest chat-up line in the world, "Can we buy you ladies a drink?" one of them asked. He had lightish hair and a slight build, and his accent was almost London, but not quite, a kind of semi-posh London.

"With six straws, I suppose?" Charlotte replied, her brown eyes flashing in the way she had practised in front of her bedroom mirror.

But the boy smiled, "My my, aren't you the sharp one? OK can we buy you six drinks – provided you tell me your name."

"Charlotte."

"Brian."

"Pleased to meet you, Brian. I'll have a vodka Red Bull, but can I have it in a glass with ice and a straw – it looks so much cooler."

"That's what you are, is it – cool?" Brian asked.

"That's for us to know and you to find out," Penny chipped in, but her eyes were on the boy at the bar, not Brian. Penny never chased boys, they came to her. Only this one didn't. This one, handsome, tall and confident, sat at the bar watching her.

It was then that Penny did something totally out of character – she actually went towards a boy.

"Hello," he said gently, "thank you for coming over, Penny – my name's Shaun."

"Penny," she said, "how do you know my name – you psychic or something?"

The boy laughed, and for Penny the sun shone from his eyes. "Hardly – but I do have good hearing, and I heard one of your mates call you 'Penny'."

He paused, before continuing, "From your accent, I'd say you're from the East Coast – but somehow you don't seem like a country girl."

"Alright, Sherlock," she said , "at least you didn't say 'you sound like an Essex girl'. My name's Penny and I'm from Colchester. But where are *you* from – surely not Ireland, with a name like Shaun?"

"Ha-ha! No, not Ireland – try Guildford. And to save you asking, just because my name's Shaun I'm also not a barber."

"No? So, clever clogs, what do you call a girl on the horizon?"

He thought for a moment, then said, "Don't know – what *would* I call a girl on the horizon?"

"Dot. As in she was only . . . ."

". . . . She was only a Dot on the horizon!"

They both burst out laughing. And that was it, with Shaun things were to instantly prove so easy, so much fun. Whatever they did, whatever they said from that first time they met, Penny Brown and Shaun Miles would seem to think as one. Sitting at the bar away from the others, they talked about their families and their dreams. Penny confessed to him her ambition to be a pop star – not a casual ambition, as with many young people, but a well thought out, deeply burning ambition – something she was determined to do. Although he clearly liked a laugh, in a way Shaun was more serious than other boys she had known – two years older than her, the A-Level results he was awaiting were destined to take him to his chosen university of Bath to study Computer Sciences, following which he wanted to further train as an accountant.

"You see," he explained to the girl hoping for a maximum of four or five middling GCSEs, "with company accounts being so much computer based, if I have a knowledge of both programming *and* accountancy, I should be able to walk into any top job I choose."

"Don't you like clubbing?" she'd asked in response, nodding at the group she had left.

"Clubbing – yeah, that's fab, but there's so much more to Ibiza than rap and over-priced booze."

"You speak like you know the place."

He nodded. "My parents first brought me here when I was ten."

"So you must know *all* the clubs!"

"Yeah, I suppose so. They're pretty much as you've described them – sorry I *was* listening to you earlier. I suppose my favourite's Space, because they hold parties right through Saturdays and into Sunday. That means you can dance outside and enjoy the sun instead of flashing lights. Then Amnesia's a fun place – but heck, so are they all."

"So what else is there to do, besides clubbing – pick oranges?"

He laughed, "Don't knock it 'til you've tried it. Ibiza, well it's a real fun place to explore. I like cooking, and enjoy good food. But do you know, there are a great many lovely little bays, with beach bars and cafes that do wonderful seafood, where the bill for a whole meal will set you back less than you'd pay for a vodka Red Bull in a place like this? And provide a meal for two," he added pointedly, "for the price of the same drink in Pacha."

She laughed. "So when we've run out of dosh, you can take me to a beach bar."

But he turned the tables. "If you're asking me for a date, my sweet Lady Penelope, I guess the answer's 'yes'."

"You cheeky monkey – I wasn't . . .," but then she hesitated, and realised that was exactly what she had been doing. She, Penny Brown, the champion boy magnet of Essex, had actually asked one for a date, and she blushed at the realisation.

* * * * *

The twelve young people seemed to hit it off, and stuck together as they enjoyed the rap, house and garage music at the various clubs. At first, the sheer size, spectacle and noise they found awesome, but rapidly became blasé so they could talk knowledgeably about Manumission, Ministry of Sound and all the top DJs. Emily and Brian had seemed to establish some sort of relationship, as did Penny and Shaun, but although they got on famously, the rest of the group seemed fairly interchangeable in their friendships.

On a couple of occasions, Penny surprised her new boyfriend, for that was how she'd come to think of him, with the extent of her ability in front of the microphone. The first time was karaoke night at their own hotel, when she was clearly on a different planet from the other contestants.

But the second was at a large bar near the seafront, where they'd gone for a cheaper evening as their funds started to run low. When the resident five piece band took their break, she stepped up onto the stage, picked up the mike, and looked at the MC. Taking his shrug for a 'yes' she burst into a Tina Turner number, throwing herself around the stage in time with her own unaccompanied voice. As the applause died down, she switched to a Madonna song, and this too met with noisy appreciation from the audience. Then, to show her versatility, she moved to a slow country and Western ballad, 'Old Flames', and magically got her, mainly young, audience to sing along with her. When she'd finished, and bowed her way off stage, it was not only the audience who applauded, the band too joined in to show their appreciation.

* * * * *

The following day, Shaun borrowed an elderly Nissan Micra from a Spanish friend he had known since boyhood, and he and Penny set off to explore the island. She felt very grown up about this, it being the first time she had been out for a date with a boy in a car. Small and elderly the Nissan may have been, but Penny Brown could not have been happier had they been in a Ferrari.

Starting from San Antoni, they had turned off the main road to Ibiza at San Rafael, heading east across country on a picturesque winding route, passing by citrus orchards and ancient fincas to Santa Eulalia, where they'd parked by the marina. There they had a lot of fun walking the jetties, eyeing the yachts, and pretending to decide which one to buy. The jetties were named south to north alphabetically, whilst the vessels tied up to them ranged from thousand horsepower plus speed boats costing hundreds of thousands to six-metre sail boats, motor cruisers, boats for charter, traditional day fishing boats, diving boats, yacht tenders and even one row-boat. Lending much colour to the marina were the bars and restaurantes such as The Tavernetta or Bistro Mariposa, as did the yachting service companies like V. Mari Nautica's ships' chandlers, or the world-leading UK boat companies of Sunseeker, Fairline and Guilford Marine

Then walking south from the marina, past the water bus terminal, she'd felt oddly jealous when Shaun set himself the task of finding the best boobs on display on the beach, but then realised he was only doing it to tease her. She considered Santa Eulalia 'a bit posh but nice' after San Antoni, but nevertheless enjoyed herself when they went to the elegant sea-front restaurant called 'The Atenea' for coffee and cakes.

Over coffee, Shaun told her about a water-sports centre at S'Argamassa, near Es Canar, "It's called 'César's', after the owner, César Jerez" he explained, "you can para-glide whilst I jet-ski".

"Para-glide – is that what I think it is?"

"That depends on what you think, but basically they strap you into a parachute, take you out on a speed boat, then, attaching you to a rope winch, you sort of take off and fly."

"That sounds fab," the girl said enthusiastically "- can I really try it?"

Forty minutes later, looking down from a height of around fifty feet at the numerous national flags, flying from poles situated along a largish rock, which with the help of some concrete was used as the landing stage, she was not so certain about 'sounding fab', and for a while was so frightened she thought she'd wet herself. Then she relaxed, and really did enjoy the ride. When it was time to let her down, the man controlling the boat winched in the rope and gradually slowed, bringing her with care onto the little platform at the back. The grin on her face said it all – she'd enjoyed her ride.

After a quick check on their finances, Shaun elected to forgo his ride on the mighty 750cc Kawasaki Jet-Ski he loved so much, to instead buy a lunch of sardines and salad with a few 'patatas fritos' at César's beach bar for the girl with whom he admitted to himself he had fallen in love.

In the afternoon, they explored the town of Ibiza, both the old harbour side town of Sa Penya and the high town of the citadel, the D'alt Vila.

Emboldened, Shaun asked if she would like to go to Es Cavalettes 'for a swim and sunbathe'.

"What is it, and where is it?"

"It's a beach with sand dunes and a fantastic Hawaii style bar-cafe, where people swim and sunbathe without wearing an abundance of clothes."

"An abundance of clothes? Do you mean it's a nudist beach?"

He coloured. "Er, yes."

"Okay."

"Okay? You mean we can go?"

"If you reckon it's alright."

So for the first time in her life, Penny Brown took her clothes off in front of a boy, and just as importantly, he reciprocated. 'God, he's beautiful', she thought.

They swam in the sea – 'hey ho,' she thought, 'at least I won't get my cossie wet'. Afterwards, they found a private spot behind a sand dune to stretch out on their towels and languidly allow the sun to dry them.

Then she lost her virginity to Shaun Miles. Lost? In all honesty, she gave it willingly.

* * * * *

Later, happy, content and wrapped in the girl's arms, as the sun started its descent, Shaun checked his watch – eight-thirty. Again they counted their combined wealth, an operation that did not take a great deal of time.

"I know just the spot to round off the day," Shaun said, when they realised they were not exactly Euro millionaires. "There's a bar-restaurante in Figueretas, this side of Ibiza town, where you can get a good square meal for just a few euros, and later . . . ."

" . . . .And later, what?"

"Well, around ten-thirty, they stop serving food, and the restaurant becomes something else."

"Not lap dancing? You've surely had enough excitement for one day!"

He laughed. "No – a really trendy karaoke bar, so you can again impress me with your brilliance!"

* * * * *

'Mike's Kitchen' in Figueretas is one of several smaller establishments which over the years has become an institution of Ibiza. It opens prompt at six pm, and, with probably the most rapid service on the island, serves a vast number of English-style meals, early evening to those with young children, later to the middle aged, then later still to the young and young at heart who want to stay and sing the night away to karaoke.

Outside there is a spacious terrace in front of and to the right of the bar-restaurante, with tables and seating for many diners, whilst inside along the right hand side are five brown-painted concrete alcoves with bench seats, and above them for decoration three truly giant Budweiser bottles.

Closing time tends to be a flexible friend, being more akin to the economics of the number of late night revellers spending money than anything to do with the hands on the clock.

Above the main karaoke 'stage' area is an illuminated Budweiser sign, and for the better enjoyment of the enthusiastic participants, throughout the establishment there are multiple TVs to display the words currently being enjoyed, or sometimes, murdered. The exceptionally well-stocked bar has numerous beers on draft, including Caffrey's, Estrella, Carling and Becks, as well as less alcoholic drinks such as Pepsi, 7up and various Kas fruit flavours.

Penny and Shaun enjoyed their meal, both choosing entrecote steak, hers well done and his rare. As they kept holding, and squeezing hands, Penny looked around at the other diners, and wondered. Could they tell? Did she look different? Was there something about her that screamed, "I'm no longer a schoolgirl – today I became a woman!"

After the steaks, they had wedges of the most delicious pineapple ice cream called 'piña helado', and then quietly and efficiently around ten-thirty, the restaurante stopped serving food to become a karaoke bar. This, of course, is not good news everywhere, at least not one hundred per cent of the time, although to the youngsters' amusement a middle aged Mum from Reading had a fair stab at the all-time karaoke favourite, beloved of the tuneless and drunks, 'My Achy Breaky Heart' and an elderly couple created much interest with a take-off of Dolly Parton and Kenny Rogers singing 'Islands in the Stream' – the interest coming from their lack of regard for conventions such as sticking to a particular key, to such an extent that had it not been for his beard and her more than ample bosom it would have been unclear who was supposed to be Dolly and who was supposed to be Kenny.

They were followed by a younger man, who gave a reasonable rendition of the late, great Buddy Holly's 'Everyday', whilst his wife proved his chief barracker saying that if he didn't stop making a damned fool of himself, she was going home and taking the car.

Then Penny moved to pick up the microphone, and the atmosphere changed as she moved into the Tina Turner number she had performed in the seafront bar in San An. But when she tried to put down the mike, cries of 'more, more' prevented her from doing so – karaoke night became cabaret night, and to the delight of her audience, she performed four more numbers before returning to her seat and a very proud boyfriend.

Almost immediately, a man in his thirties slid into the couch seat next to them. He was quite tall, round-faced, dark-haired, and running to fat in a not unpleasant kind of way.

"You know, you're good," he said, "really good."

Penny laughed, flattered. "Thank-you," she said.

"You look plenty young enough," the newcomer continued, "do you want to make it in the pop business, or do you have other ambitions?"

Again Penny laughed. "Oh yes, I want to make it as a pop star – and I suppose you're going to offer me a contract?" she joked.

The man smiled. "That's exactly what I expect to do – after hearing you in a recording studio of course. Here's my card." From the back pocket of his jeans he produced a wad of business cards, and passed her one.

She and Shaun read it together. It said simply 'Red Sky, DJ' followed by an email address and the number of his mobile.

"*You're* Red Sky?" Shaun asked in wonder.

"The DJ we saw in Amnesia?" Penny added.

"With long red dreadlocks, big dark shades and the jump suit featuring the setting sun?" Shaun continued.

This time the man did laugh. "Yeah – great outfit, isn't it?" Then he quoted his 'signature' patter, "*Red Sky at night, virgin's delight!* I'm famous all over the world, but the moment I take off my stage gear, I'm invisible – it gives me the best of both worlds, I've got the glam life of a celeb and an ordinary life when I want it – so I can often come to great places like this for straightforward English cooking and the like."

"This contract," from Shaun, "you play rap and garage kind of stuff, but Penny's voice is definitely pop material."

"In Ibiza I do indeed play what you say, but in the UK, if you've ever listened to it, you must know my radio show is far more across the board."

Shaun nodded thoughtfully. "And you could get her a recording contract, although you're not a producer?"

"Actually I do get involved on the production side, but tend to keep it quiet in case I'm accused of favouring my own numbers on the turntable. As if I would! But believe me, if tonight is anything to go by, and she can re-produce it in a studio and on stage, with my contacts and her talent, there's no doubt I can get her a recording contract. Then of course all the additional paraphernalia like guest appearances, and media coverage par excellence."

"Wow!" from Penny.

* * * * *

And so the deal had been done. For Penny, the next three years was like living a fairy tale, with herself as the principal character. 'Reds', as she had come to know him, had been as good as his word, and aided rather than hindered by her great youth, she had leapt to stardom. Chat shows, TV spectaculars, videos, she was rarely out of the public limelight, taking to her new lifestyle like a duck to water.

Only one thing intruded to keep her less than totally happy, for she saw less and less of Shaun. As expected, he got great 'A's , and enrolled at Bath University for a three year course on Maths and Computer Sciences. For a while they'd kept in touch, but she knew he was miffed at all the hangers on who perpetually surrounded her. She also suspected he was a bit jealous when she spoke so easily of her friendship with the A-List celebrities he knew only through the media.

Then suddenly one day he wasn't even there. He'd gained a two-one honours degree, whatever that was, and dropped out of sight. Even a firm of private detectives failed to find him, and for Penny, the absence of the boy she loved made the dream world in which she lived so artificial. But where was he? The world is a big place, and she knew that with his intelligence and c.v., Shaun could get a job in any part of it.

* * * * *

Penny d'Arcy looked at the twinkling stars on the cabin ceiling, and rubbed her eyes. It had been three years since she had tried the detective agency, three further years of a career in which she had enjoyed ever increasing fame and good fortune, but failed to find either hide nor hair of Shaun Miles.

This was hopeless – she'd never get to sleep. She may just as well stick on her wig and shades, and with Terry trailing her, find a bar somewhere where she could drown her sorrows. She flipped a switch on the intercom, "Terry, be ready in fifteen minutes – I want to go walkabout. Say jeans and smart casual, you never know where we might end up."

A pause, then, "Yes, I know it's dodgier for me on Saturday night, but if I don't get off this boat, I'll go crazy."

She slipped into her version of Red Sky's 'incognito' disguise – a wig, big shades and a hippie style one piece flower-power dress usually saw her through. Terry was waiting for her by the gangplank. She'd christened him 'Terry' when he'd first entered her employment as personal bodyguard, her own 'Minder', named after the wonderful character, Terry McCann, played by Dennis Waterman in the TV series. Hailing from the West Indies, her Terry was about the size of Lennox Lewis, but where Lennox was not bad looking, Terry certainly was. Not just bad looking, he was really ugly, which made things a little difficult sometimes, for part of their disguise was to pretend to be on a date. But one real look at Terry, and folk tended to not ask questions.

Because of its size, her yacht was anchored in the old harbour near the ferry port offices, rather than the Marina, so that after a gentle stroll of only a few hundred metres they reached the palm-covered terrace of the trendy 'Mar y Sol', where everyone who is anyone meets to chew the fat, talk about friends and put the world to rights. They sat on aluminium chairs with mock wicker plastic webbing at a small round table, and surveyed the scene. Beyond the terrace they could glimpse the port road entrance post and barrier, and beyond that the numerous ferry boats, now at rest after the hard labours of the day.

She felt better after two swift G and T's, then told Terry she just wanted to walk.

"Where to Miss d'Arcy?"

"I don't know – anywhere, I just want to walk, okay?"

So they walked, aimlessly. Through the Vara de Rey and onto the long stretch of the Avenida de España. At the top, by McDonald's, they turned left, back towards the sea. Suddenly, Penny stopped.

"My God – we're in Figueretas. Terry – for God's sake, we're in Figueretas!"

"Are we, honey?" Sometimes polite, sometimes informal, but always watchful, always minding, was Terry.

"Terry – it was here that I met Reds – here he discovered me! I must find it – what was it called?"

"I don't know Miss d'Arcy, honey, but I'll sure help you look." His voice belying his physique, soft and gentle – a deliberately cultivated mix of his native West Indies and the American Southland.

They walked along, looking at bars, shops, takeaways, until suddenly Penny stopped. "My God, this is it – Mike's Kitchen! Terry, come on, you can buy me a drink from that roll I gave you."

Two more G and Ts slipped down rather easily, as again she sat in one of the alcoves and watched the restaurante metamorphosise into a karaoke bar. People started to drift in in anticipation, as the music started. For the first time in many months, Penny felt herself relax. Her seat was a sort of curved couch, in such a way she was unable to see the people who sat down behind her in the next alcove, but instinctively she listened to their conversation, as a young girl spoke.

"So you actually live here – not just on holiday?"

"My – aren't you lucky – I'd just die to live in Ibiza," from a different female voice.

"What do you do – drive speedboats or run discos or something?" from the first voice.

A man answered. "No, it's a bit more boring, I'm afraid. I'm an accountant at a firm in Santa Eulalia." The voice, more mature, a little older, but definitely his voice!

Penny had heard the phrase 'being turned to jelly' and never quite believed it. But she was, first a shiver ran down her spine and her skin tingled all over, then she became like jelly, then her very vitals seemed to turn liquid.

"Gosh that is boring! Why Ibiza – you could do that anywhere?" the second female asked.

The man laughed. Oh that laugh – just hearing it again gave Penny goose pimples.

"If you must know, I lost my heart once in Ibiza, and I've come to live here hoping that one day I'll find someone to give it back to me again."

"That's so romantic."

Unsteadily, being certain to keep her back to the group behind her, Penny headed for the stage area and took the microphone. A quick word to select the right tune and she burst into song, still with her back to the audience, deliberately choosing the old karaoke number, the one they had laughed at when the middle-aged housewife had sung it in this very bar a seeming lifetime ago. But nevertheless, in her adapted female version, the words so truly expressed her thoughts . . . .

". . . Don't tell my heart, my achy breaky heart – I just don't think she'd understand . . . ."

At that moment, Shaun did something he'd never done in his whole life before – he dropped his pint of beer. They both turned round, and across the crowded bar-room, their eyes met, as Penny d'Arcy tossed away her wig and shades and sang her own version of the old karaoke number to the man she loved.

". . . and if you tell my heart, my achy breaky heart, she might blow up and kill this gal."

As the song ended, and realising that for some incredible reason they really had heard the famous Penny d'Arcy singing a karaoke number to them, the audience rose to their feet to applaud.

But there was no press photographer on hand to take the million dollar picture, as, crying tears of joy, she fell into the arms of the man she loved, and whispered 'yes' when he asked her to marry him . . . .

The Man from Santa Gertrudis

The young Englishman was sweating. This was partly due to the Ibicencan August sun, to which he was not accustomed, and partly to the oddly behaving scooter he had rented just an hour before. Back home in his native Birmingham, Dave Walker, a physically stocky and mentally bright twenty-five year old, handled his Honda 650 motor bike with skill and confidence, but here in Ibiza, with no tank or engine between his knees, and the freckle-faced auburn haired girl he loved jumping around behind him as if she had ants in her pants, things were not so easy. And it was made worse by her absolute confidence in him.

To be fair, she'd never yet even ridden on the back of his Honda, or indeed anything else with two wheels other than her own bicycle, so he didn't blame her – though it did make the little machine really difficult to control.

They were headed for the village in the centre of the island – or for the argumentative, at least as near to the centre as makes no difference. Within living and indeed post war memory, the dirt road that wound its way from Ibiza Town up to San Miguel passed through Santa Gertrudis, or to give the village its full title, Santa Gertrudis de Fruitera. Here, in days gone by, the traveller – often a local farmer – might park his donkey cart in the small square, and perhaps then slip inside the beautiful old church for a moment's peace and reflection, as well as to escape from the sun. Then he'd move on to Bar Ulivans or Bar Costa for a tapas – maybe even splash out on a jamon serrano if he felt rich – washed down with a sherry or perhaps a beer.

Enough of this still remains for a sensitive visitor to imagine what it used to be like, but the tarmac road between Ibiza and San Miguel now bypasses the village, and a turn-off to the left is necessary to enter the little square, which is still there, in front of the church and near to the bars.

But the tranquillity is no longer, replaced by a vibrant sense of affluence, the growing village a magnet for tourists, ex-pats and indigenous locals alike.

It was with some relief that Dave Walker parked the scooter in the little square, and looked across at the wonderful archway of the old church. Not at all religious, the two young lovers felt they just had to see inside. But the girl, younger and considerably shorter than her not over-tall companion, watched as the dark oak double doors, held together with giant ancient nails, refused to yield to the well-made Brummie's attempts to open them, for – a sign of the times – they were firmly locked to protect against thieves, and presumably would remain so until Sunday masses to be held, according to the notice, at mid-day and eight-thirty. Sadly, progress is not universal, some aspects of life deteriorate in its wake.

Instead, they made their way to Bar Costa, not knowing that unwittingly they were lucky enough to have picked one of the institutions of Ibiza, a seemingly small bar-restaurante which inside is extremely picturesque, with hams suspended from the ceiling in the old traditional manner, and grows in size like the Tardis the further that the visitor explores. Not only that, but as they approached, a group of three friendly middle-aged Germans vacated an outside shady table, and with mock over-politeness offered them their seats. Thus they found themselves in a prime position to relax and check out the scene, and of course enjoy a beer and tapas. Just as the farmer transported by his donkey cart would have done only a few years before.

Nearby was another Ibiza institution – or at least it had become so since it was founded in 1973 – Casi Todo, 'The House of Everything', famous for its regular auctions of antique, and sometimes not so antique, furniture and bric-a-brac. Whilst they waited for their beers, Dave briefly checked it out, and found for sale an incredible selection of pottery, bric-a-brac, old doors, ancient wooden wine screws and even a wine press, barrels, an old donkey cart, and rather more bizarrely, a Messerschmidt bubble car and a motorcycle originally from a fairground ride.

Thirsty, he returned to the Bar Costa and the girl he loved, sitting down by her to watch the world go by. Across the road, an establishment promised a wonderful selection of 'tribal art', whilst on the far corner, nearest to the church, a further place of refreshment, the Es Canto bar also offered drinks and sustenance.

As their beers arrived, with their chosen tapas of simple pan y alioli and jamon serrano, the girl leaned across and whispered quietly, her accent indicating that she too hailed from the West Midlands, "That man on the next table keeps staring at us."

Doing his best to make it not obvious, Dave glanced at the person in question, and sure enough, he was certainly studying them intently. He was very tall, looked rather fit, and had a rugged sun-tanned face – partly hidden by the brim of his Australian Acubra hat.

"Anyone who wears an Acubra to show he's been on holiday downunder is only doing it for effect – who does he think he is, Crocodile Dundee?" the girl whispered.

Suspecting they were discussing him, the man smiled and raised the aforesaid Aussie symbol in polite acknowledgement, so they also had to smile, and nod their heads in greeting.

"I must go to the loo," the girl continued, "all that jiggling around on the scooter has made me want to wee. What do they call them – lavabos or servicios or something?" But the question was rhetorical, because without waiting for an answer, she disappeared into the establishment, a girl on a mission.

As she left, the man in the Acubra rose and approached Dave's table. "Good day, d'ya mind if I join you?"

"My God, you really are Australian!"

"'Struth – is it that obvious?"

For several weeks, Dave Walker had been pondering the big subject of proposing to his girl, and having just about come to the conclusion that he liked the idea, and really should propose, the next big decision was when and where. In fact he'd been wondering if this was the right moment – a sunny day in a pretty village on a holiday island. Then he thought a more romantic private location might be appropriate, perhaps with the two of them overlooked only by the moon and a starry night . . . .

But with the intrusion, the immediate decision was now taken from his hands, so he answered amiably enough, "Sure, help yourself," indicating a free chair.

The Australian sat down, and smiled. "You know, we Aussies are noted for our directness, so I'll come straight to the point – are you and the shelagh an item? You see," he added, "I watched as you walked across from the church, and was instantly attracted in a way I haven't been in a long time."

Despite his Birmingham panache, Dave was a bit taken aback. "Wow, that's certainly direct. But how did you know her name is Sheila?"

The Aussie laughed. "I didn't, it's what we call girls in Aus – shelaghs. I guess it's a sort of term of endearment," he added somewhat uncertainly. "But are you and, er, Sheila, an item?"

"Oh yes," Dave answered quickly, anxious to head him off, "we're definitely an item." He was beginning to wish he hadn't asked this tall rugged stranger to sit down, for no man likes competition.

"Such a pity – it's a long time since someone seemed so lovely to me at first sight. Still, I duly note the way the land lies, so no worries, mate."

"No worries," Dave was pleased to confirm, although at that moment he had plenty of worries, for he had long since come to the conclusion that he was not the most handsome bloke in the world, and knew he already showed signs of growing a beer belly. What would Sheila make of this hunky guy from downunder?

Biting the bullet, he extended his hand to the Australian, who shook it with a grin, just as the girl returned. "My name's Dave Walker," the Englishman said, and turning to the girl added, "Sheila, I'd like you to meet . . . ."

"Bruce Winters," the Aussie informed them.

The girl sat down, and reached across to shake hands with the big man, their eyes meeting for a moment. "Sheila Thompson," she said, "and you really are Australian?"

The man laughed. "Obviously a novelty, but I'm a dinky die, Australian born and bred."

"So what brought you to Ibiza?"

"A charter jet out of Gatwick – but that's an old John Lennon joke."

Nevertheless, the English couple laughed.

"What's it like – Australia?" Sheila asked.

"Don't you ever watch 'Neighbours'?"

"Of course," she replied.

"Well I reckon that's what Aus is like – all affluent bloody suburbia."

"Not more rough and tough outback – like a 'Town Called Alice'?"

"No – you were closer with 'Neighbours', though of course Alice exists alright. Why the interest?"

"This is our first time in a hot country, and we like it very much."

"Hot and dry is better than cold and damp," Dave added.

"And we were thinking, if we stay together," she glanced meaningfully at her boyfriend who to her intense irritation had not yet asked her to marry him, "we might consider emigrating to Australia."

"So you really do want to know what it's like?"

They confirmed they did.

He eased his hat backwards off his head, which he scratched contentedly as he searched for the right words. "Well Aus is beaut. To state the obvious, it's big – about three thousand pommie miles west to east. By English standards it ranges from hot through bloody hot to 'struth, mate! So much space, yet most of the population live within twenty miles of the coast, hence 'Neighbours' more than 'Alice Springs'. And wherever you go, we all speak with pretty much the same accent. Unlike the UK," he added, "where a few miles makes all the difference. For instance I would hazard a guess that you folk both come from at the most thirty miles from the Birmingham Bullring?"

Sheila laughed. "And we're not public school, either! But what's the standard of living like, in Aus?" she asked practically. Just for a moment her heart skipped a beat, as her eyes met those of the handsome Australian. Although she was sure Dave wanted to marry her, and had been expecting him to pop the question any time, could she really be sure he was the one – she hadn't been out with many other boys? Then her eyes moved from the Australian, and she glanced at her English boyfriend, and knew. Her heart told her he *was* the one. It wouldn't hurt to keep him on his toes with a bit of jealousy, though, so she decided to play up a little to their new friend, Bruce.

"After all, you all look so fit and healthy – as if you eat well and work out plenty," she added.

Dave gave her a sideways glance – did she fancy this Aussie guy?

"Yeah, I reckon across the board Aus has the highest standard of living in the world. I know in other countries – Germany, the South of France, California and even right here in Ibiza – there's plenty of wealth kicking about, but in Aus even a manual worker, if he really is prepared to work hard and not piss all his wages away on grog, can live in a very decent house on a quarter acre block. He'll probably drive a three litre car and the little lady will have her own wheels. They'll eat steak whenever they like, good healthy veggies, and yes, I reckon working out is a national pursuit, which is why we win all the gold medals, whilst you get your arses kicked if ever we meet at the mortal combat called cricket. But . . . ."

Sheila did her best to look at him rapturously. "But what?" she asked.

"But the currency's crap, so as soon as we leave Aus we feel poor."

Dave was feeling less pro-Australian by the minute; having increasing thoughts that his new mate Bruce might be harbouring his own thoughts of making his Sheila an Australian shelagh. And seeing the admiration in his girlfriend's eyes for the man from downunder, he thought it time to emphasise the negative.

"Why is that," he asked, "about your currency being crap – don't they think your country's trustworthy?"

"'Struth, I dunno, mate. Our sheep exports took a dive back when pommieland went into the EEC, and that probably started the whole anti-pom thing. So instead we now export live sheep out of Fremantle to the Arabs on container ships that look like tower blocks. If the poor bloody animals are lucky enough to survive the voyage – and a lot don't – their fate is to get ritually slaughtered rather than humanely killed, so there's more than a few Australians don't really like the practice.

"But Gawd knows, we're pretty self-sufficient in food and minerals – even oil. And our wine seems set to conquer the world, so you tell me why our currency's crap." Again he eased back his hat to scratch his head before continuing, "What line are you in, Dave?"

"I trained as a computer programmer, but now I'm an IT manager with my own department."

"Degree?"

"Mathematics," Dave confirmed.

"Sheila?" to the girl.

"Yes – in fact we met at uni. I got a B.A. in English, then did a PhD, and now I teach English to teenagers."

"Well believe me, I think you'd both walk into good jobs in Aus, and should you decide to emigrate, you'd lead the life of Riley, no worries."

"If that's so, why are you here, not there?"

"Here in Ibiza, you mean, Dave?" He paused, before going on to explain, "Look, I'm usually here from June through September; May and October I spend in pommieland, then back downunder for the Aussie summer.

"Chasing the sun – that's why you're here?" Sheila asked him.

"I reckon that's got a fair bit to do with it, but don't get me wrong, Aus isn't perfect. It can be quite old-fashioned in many ways, attitudes, prejudices etc . . . ."

"Do you have a place in Ibiza?" again from Sheila.

"Sure – a mate and I rent an apartment right here in Santa Gertrudis. But I also own an ancient Seat car, which another mate looks after for me when I'm not here, so I reckon I can make most any part of the island in fifteen minutes or so."

"How do you earn a living, or are you so rich you don't need to?" asked Dave.

"Me rich? No, you're wide of the mark there, Sport. Here in Ibiza I do mainly bar work, then at the weekend some promotional work for the clubs."

A waiter appeared, and Bruce called him over. "You blokes like another beer before I go?" They confirmed they would, and Bruce duly ordered them.

Sheila did her best to maintain a look of admiration as she asked, "Is there anywhere special we should go whilst we're here, anything we shouldn't miss?"

"First time in Ibiza?"

They nodded.

"Aw look, the whole bloody island's special. It's just magic, and you're best to find your own favourite places by exploring. Don't miss Es Vedra – the giant lump of rock sticking out of the sea at Cala d'Hort off the west coast – it definitely gives off some sort of vibes."

"I've heard of Es Vedra," the girl replied, "rumour has it that it was actually used to film Bali H'ai in South Pacific."

"That's right, Sheila. Rumour has it, like it has many things on this earth. Anyway, no doubt you'll want to do one or two of the clubs, but whatever you do, don't miss a late night meal at Sa Peña, the old town near the port. Saturday night's best, although Friday's also okay. Get there about ten-thirty for a bevvy at the Zoo Bar, then wander around and find a table to eat about midnight, whilst you watch the parade."

"Parade?" from Sheila.

"Yeah – there's a sort of circuit that the beautiful people do, and I guess some of them not so beautiful as well. It's all very informal, but très, très picturesque. And even the stalls and shops are open until well into the small hours."

Saying which he tossed some money onto the table to pay for the beers which had arrived whilst they were talking, and stood up.

"Anyway, nice meeting you guys, and enjoy Ibiza."

"We'll do our very best," Dave confirmed.

The Australian gave them a look, suddenly sad, before departing, saying half to them, half to himself, "Such a pity, so attractive. Really lovely, but you're too late, Brucey mate." Then a little louder, "See you later," saying which he was gone, round the corner into the little square.

Sheila watched him go. "You know, he was really gorgeous – so sexy," she said, much to Dave's annoyance. Then she added, "I bet he knows how to use it, too," which so shocked the Midlander that for a while, he was unable to speak.

That settled it – he was *definitely* not popping the question today . . . .

* * * * *

For the following few days, they took Bruce's advice, and explored Ibiza to their own ad hoc itinerary, with Sheila learning to sit easy on the scooter, and Dave to handle it with ever-growing confidence. They did indeed see Es Vedra, regarding it in awe as they enjoyed a coffee at the seafront restaurant at Cala d'Hort, although they both thought it looked even more spectacular from the mountain road from which they first spotted it.

They also checked out San Antonio, San Miguel, San Rafael, Portinatx and the incredible view from the cliff road looking down into Cala San Vicente. Then San Carlos, where they had a sherry and tapas sitting by the ancient numbered post-boxes in the vine-protected courtyard at the famous Anita's bar.

Afterwards, by recommendation from an elderly German gentleman whom they had met in Anita's, they found the beach cafe with wooden decking at Niu Blau, and seated at a table with a green check oilcloth under a bamboo cane awning, Sheila enjoyed a 'lenguado' (Dover sole) whilst to her disgust Dave tucked in happily to 'calamares' (squid), both dishes being cooked 'a la plancha' – on the griddle.

On another day, they strolled hand in hand along the stylish sea front promenade at Santa Eulalia del Rio, and visited the D'alt Vila in Ibiza, where they explored the tiny ancient streets and dined at the famous El Corsario – the supposed meeting place for artists of all kinds. And on consecutive nights they also did a couple of clubs – Space and Amnesia – both of which they enjoyed, but not the prices.

Then on Saturday evening at about ten-fifteen they parked their scooter on the dockside carpark in Ibiza for the short stroll across to Sa Peña, having decided to leave it there overnight whilst they caught a taxi, or if no taxies were available, walked back to their hotel at Figueretas.

Sa Peña on a Saturday night in summer is like nowhere else on earth. Close by the port, the old original part of Ibiza town is a unique combination of ancient buildings fronting directly onto streets and walkways, brightly lit and thronging with people intent on having a good time in a happy good-humoured way. Jostling each other contentedly, they stroll or loiter, stop and browse, whilst bars, cafés, ice cream parlours, market stalls and shops all vie for their business, the vendors, like their clients, coming from all parts of Europe, even Moors from North Africa joining in with cries of, "Looky looky here, missus – genuine copy watch, best native jewellery, lucky charm, potency bangle . . . ."

By about midnight, things gradually settle down from chaos to a sort of pattern, and it becomes apparent that an informal anti-clockwise parade is taking place. People strolling, looking, talking, laughing – tourists, locals, rich, poor, young, old are joined by the genuinely wealthy from the yachts, usually with a handful of film or TV stars inter-mingling with them.

Dave and Sheila had been lucky to find a table vacated by some early diners at the Restaurante Bahia, previously famous throughout the island for Juanito's 'pollo pages', country-style chicken, but now under new ownership still offering a wide selection of well-prepared dishes, including starters as varied as asparagus, fish soup, or cold hors d'oeuvres, and for the main course a choice of fish, steaks, spicy chicken and even rabbit. Bedazzled by the atmosphere and sights, they kissed, drank wine, ate an enjoyable meal, and watched the world go by.

And that was when she agreed to marry him, which of course called for a bottle of fizz – the Spanish sparkling wine called Cava, which slipped down very well as they celebrated their betrothal.

"That dark-skinned girl's wearing a daring costume," said Sheila, nodding her head in the direction of the parade, "or almost wearing it – she's really lovely."

Dave looked at the person indicated, and did a double take, before replying, "I think you'll find she's a he."

"Oh my God – you're right, but she's, that is he's, really beautiful!"

And so he, or she, was, and the young English couple looked on in amazement as a succession of beautiful transvestites strolled past wearing the most gorgeous outfits, proudly parading their glamour for all the world to see.

They relaxed even more after the Cava, drank some coffee, washed down by a local aniseed flavoured liquor called Hierbas Ibicencas, served over ice and provided with the compliments of the establishment, and felt all was well with the world.

Giggling a little, Sheila suddenly said, "One over there is looking at us – the tall pretty one in the gold lamé, showing a bare midriff and a tummy button bangle."

The tall pretty one with the bare midriff made his or her happy way towards them, and, to their acute embarrassment, and the great interest of the other diners, greeted them by name. "So, Dave and Sheila, I see my little pommie friends took my advice. Great isn't it?"

This time Bruce, the handsome rugged man from Santa Gertrudis, now not so much handsome and rugged as downright pretty, did not ask if he could join them, but just sat down at their table. Whilst the restaurant's other customers looked on with interest at the little cameo which was being performed for their benefit, their food temporarily forgotten.

To be fair to Dave, he did try to answer, tried to speak, but no sound came out. Sheila did manage a sort of squeaky, "Yes, great, er, Bruce."

Bruce laughed. "You seem surprised – but don't tell me you hadn't guessed. I thought I'd made it clear enough how much I fancied you, Dave – in fact I even asked you if you were available, or in a hetero relationship with the girl."

"You asked me what?" the Brummie asked incredulously, "but I thought you fancied the shelagh, that is, my Sheila!"

The Aussie again laughed as he stood up. "No, my little pommie friend, it was you. Such a shame, such a loss, for you and I could have made sweet music together – I had something for you that would have made your eyes water."

"Made my *mouth* water is the expression, I believe," Dave responded in something of a daze.

"Not in this case, dear, the Australian responded with a knowing smile. He opened his handbag, "Here, I hoped I'd find you, I've brought you a little present," saying which he placed a small envelope on the table.

Then very gently and lovingly he stroked Dave's cheek, "A great pity, yet another love not to be. But now I must away – I have work to do – tonight I'm promoting Pasha's."

Saying which, with a swirl of his dress and a sexy shake of his hips, he was gone.

Dave's hand was physically shaking as he opened the envelope and extracted the contents. "Good God – it's two VIP Gold Passes to Pasha's – free entry and free drinks all night. I bet they don't give many of those away."

But Sheila was not a happy bunny. "That's great, but you're sure there's not something you haven't told me, something I don't know about you?" she asked angrily. "You're not AC-DC, are you? God – what sort of a man have I agreed to marry?"

"Never mind what sort of a man – what sort of a question's that to ask? You're only mad because he fancied me more than you – in fact despite you being all droopy eyed and 'hey isn't he sexy' when you met at Santa Gertrudis, he wasn't even interested in you!"

"No – no, I guess he wasn't." Then she saw the absurdity of the situation, and burst out laughing. "Dave Walker, if ever you give me any trouble, just remember I know quite a few of your mates who'd be very interested to learn about your secret life – what sort of friends you like to make, and what sort of man you really are."

Dave grinned. "Later tonight I'll show you what sort of man I am, but meanwhile we've got a free night's clubbing to get through. Come on, Sheila, or I might just find another shelagh."

"Or another bloke," she grinned. They kissed, then she took her fiancée's hand as they set off, none too steadily, in the direction of Pasha's.

But to this day, Dave doesn't know whether to feel flattered or insulted that another man, an Australian called Bruce, really, really fancied him . . . .

The Three Tenners in Santa Eulalia

Luis Ramon was a nice man. His family thought so, his friends thought so, his fellow teachers thought so, and, somewhat unusually, even his pupils thought so, being honest about their liking for their short stocky teacher with the black curly hair. Thus when he retired from the school in the suburbs of Barcelona, where he'd held the position of Head of Modern Languages, to return to Ibiza and the ancient finca where he'd been born, there was sorrow for those who were about to lose him, but joy in Ibiza for the prodigal's return.

His wife, Elena, 'Señora Ramon', was also a nice person, possibly more practical and less of a dreamer than her husband, for her mind dwelt on matters such as the welfare of their now grown up children, and keeping a home that was worthy of the name. Slimmer than her husband, with the long black hair typical of her race, and a face, quite pale for a

Spanish woman, which switched regularly and easily from a seemingly serious look into a broad beaming smile. She and Luis had met when they first started at school (for Elena too was returning to the island of her birth), had become young school friends, then childhood sweethearts, then lovers, then man and wife.

A happy couple who had never accumulated great riches, but instead counted their wealth in kind friends, and, in the case of Luis, ex-pupils who had put his teaching to good use.

But Señor Ramon's greatest strength was also his greatest weakness, for Luis Ramon was an idealist. He believed not only in his God and the Catholic Church, but also in the basic goodness of people, and that an integrated Europe must, and would, succeed, not for economic reasons, but to avoid the wars which had so hurt and divided the continent for centuries.

Thus it was that his plan to augment his retirement income had a firm basis in his moral viewpoint, and in this it must be said he was fully supported by his wife, not because of her own personal beliefs, but because she believed in her husband, and if Luis thought so, then it must be right.

They were therefore happy, looking forwards to the future not back to the past as their little Renault Kangoo bounced up the track to Can Ramon. The surface of the track was a mixture of dirt, small stones and gravel, with a few larger stones nearly big enough to be boulders to make the journey interesting. To the left was an orange orchard, protected by dry stone walling, whilst to the right, the land could more honestly be described as only unproductive scrubby bush.

Luis loved the bumpy ride up to his childhood home, but nevertheless it would be odd to not find his elderly parents waiting to greet him with a smile and a hug at the door of the finca. His mother, Margarita, had died nearly four months ago at the age of eighty-six, whilst his father, the phlegmatic Pepe, who toiled so hard all his life and took everything it could throw at him in his stride, could not take the death of his beloved wife, and died just a month ago of a broken heart.

Somehow, to Luis, the coincidence of the death of his parents, thus vacating the finca, with his own retirement was as if God was pointing him to his own future, and this too had played a considerable part in his return to the island.

The property had in fact been in the family not just through his father's years, but for five generations, though throughout that time it had produced at best only a subsistence income to keep the family alive and decent in return for their very considerable labours. Just over ten hectares of stony ground was neatly terraced and mainly laid to citrus fruit – oranges and lemons – with also a few ancient olive trees. The farmhouse itself, although completely unmodernised, was actually in fairly good shape, as were the two smallish outbuildings. A deep well provided water for the house and to keep the bolsa – an open water storage area – topped up. From the bolsa, a primitive distribution system provided at least a modicum of irrigation to their land, to keep their trees healthy and fruit bearing.

Thus we have Can Ramon, situated on gently rising land about two kilometres from Cala Llonga on the road to the pretty but growing village of Jesús – pronounced by the Spanish as 'Hay-Zeus'.

In truth, Luis Ramon knew how much a wealthy German, Swiss or Dutch national might be willing to pay for a traditional and much coveted finca, knew that he could sell the old farm property for a small fortune and enjoy an affluent retirement on the proceeds, without the need to work. But he didn't want to sell his old family home, and instead had chosen to seek an income from his beliefs, whilst improving the property at the same time.

"You see," he'd explained to Elena on a rainy winter's night in Barcelona, "people in Northern Europe – France, Germany and especially England, have this weather all the time. So when they get old, the damp soaks into their bones, making them prone to rheumatism and arthritis."

"And my clever husband thinks he can change the weather?" Elena had asked him with a grin, her voice soft, gentle, and musical, like a Spanish guitar.

He'd laughed. "No, not the weather, but I can change where old people live – at least a few of them. We can bring them to a healthier climate to enjoy a happy retirement, and the money they pay for their board and lodgings will supplement our own retirement pension."

So their plans had developed. To preserve and improve the land for future generations, he would root out most of the uneconomic citrus trees, and replace them with slow growing but ultimately profitable olive trees, with also some vines to bring an earlier return, which, mindful of the resurgence in popularity of Ibicencan wine, he would also plant on the scrubland.

And to fulfil his belief in a cosmopolitan Europe, they would take only one retired person as a paying guest from each country, starting with Germany, France and Britain. These first three they could accommodate in spare rooms in the spacious finca, but later, as and when they were able to convert the outbuildings, they would have room for four more.

They decided to be a little selective in choosing their 'guests' by asking for written 'applications' to tell them at least a little about the person concerned. In this way, Luis and Elena Ramon would ensure pleasant company, providing them with stimulating conversations during cold winter nights and balmy summer evenings. In fact their first guest, an English lady, was due on the mid-day flight from Gatwick the next day, just six months after their own return to the island . . . .

* * * * *

Mary Tanner was not quite the lady Luis Ramon was expecting, for to say the least, she was neither smartly dressed and dignified, nor casually dressed as might be an intellectual. She was more, well, fat and scruffy. As they set off from the airport, where he had kindly been on hand to welcome her and explain who he was, her insistence in calling him 'cabbie' did not help.

In truth, Mary Tanner was not an introverted lady, and in fact the word 'lady' would not usually be even dreamed of as a description by the unfortunates who knew her. To be fair, she had led a very hard life, initially through sheer misfortune, then later because of her bitterness and abrasive character.

But as they bumped up the track to Can Ramon, and stopped in front of his lovely finca, her Cockney expletive, "Bleedin' hell – what sort of a fucking dump is this?" was not quite the comment he had hoped for from the first of his international guests . . . .

* * * * *

Thirteen is unlucky, a belief known to all, and accepted by many, if not most. Thought to have originated with the number of attendees at The Last Supper, there are numerous examples of the unlucky number playing its part in malfeasance – even entering the high-tech world of space travel, when it was Apollo Thirteen which suffered an explosion whilst en-route to the moon.

With regards to dates, the number thirteen is usually considered doubly unlucky if it falls on a Friday, and there are many intelligent people who will neither make a journey nor do anything of significance if it is Friday the thirteenth.

Mary Tanner was born Mary Smith on Friday 13th June, 1924. Even in birth she was unlucky, with her gin-soaked mother attended by an incompetent mid-wife in a small damp terraced house in London's East End, whilst her father languished in Wormwood Scrubs jail. To speed up the birth and hasten her own departure from the dank-smelling house, the mid-wife had used a clamp on the baby's head when none was necessary, let it slip as Mary plopped out from her mother's body, and left her with the ugly scar on the side of her forehead which she was to carry for the rest of her life.

In those days, life was hard for everyone in the East End of London, but doubly so for little Mary Smith. With most of the small amount of money her mother received from her job as a seamstress going to support her own gin drinking habit, Mary had learnt to steal, mainly from costermongers' carts, at a very young age. She had to, just to stay alive, for otherwise she would surely have starved.

Hope had dawned when her father, Alfie, was finally released from The Scrubs when she was six years old, but he was to contribute little to the family finances, and frequently beat his wife – sometimes so badly that the next day she was unable to go to work to earn her own pittance in wages. Just over a year after her father's release, his body was found floating face down in the Thames estuary. Cause of death was given as a blow to the side of the head, but it was probably well deserved, for Alfie Smith had been a violent man with few friends.

When Mary was fifteen, her country found itself at war with Germany, and when she was eighteen, the one good thing she was to experience in her life happened to her. She fell in love with a young soldier, who was training to be a new type of airborne commando, called a paratrooper. Like herself, little Bert Tanner with his blonde frizzy hair was a Cockney, 'born within the sound of Bow Bells', but he came from a supportive, happy family, which it should be said is more the East End norm. Bert himself was a happy, chirpy individual, who insisted on calling her 'Gel'. But, most importantly, although she was no raving beauty, she was *his* gel, and they were happy together.

Because of the pressures of war, it became the habit to marry young, and Mary Smith became Mary Tanner on March 26th 1944. They enjoyed a two day honeymoon in a hotel in the West End, before moving into Bert's old bedroom in his parents' house. Two weeks after their wedding, Corporal Bert Tanner was called away to join his unit.

On Mary's twentieth birthday, she received two pieces of news. In the morning she learnt that her husband had been killed in action during the early hours of D-Day 'somewhere in France'. Then in the afternoon she received confirmation that she was pregnant with his child. Her brief spell of happiness had come to an end.

* * * * *

That evening and the following two days were the worst of Luis Ramon's life. It wasn't so much that Señora Tanner was not quite what he had expected – she was truly *awful*. There was nothing in which she took an interest or pleasure – everything in the idyllic little spot he and his wife called home was 'naff' – whatever that meant. In fact she spoke a version of English he had never encountered in all his years teaching the subject, although he was sure most of her utterances were either slang or more likely profane swearing.

She expressed surprise that the 'effing telly' was rarely on, and incredibly surprise also that when it was they actually spoke Spanish. "What does she expect on a Spanish TV on a Spanish island," asked Elena, "that the whole country should change its language for her benefit?"

But Señora Tanner's stupidity over the TV was perhaps equalled by the 'bleedin' nonsense' that she couldn't have 'The Mirror' newspaper delivered to her door every day, or the 'News of the World' on Sundays.

She informed Luis that she had a great friendship with a person she assumed he knew called Eileen Fox, known as 'Foxy'. Foxy apparently called herself the Queen of Soho, wherever that was, but spent most of her time in Ibiza. "She's gorn on now, poor sod, but she reckoned it was bloomin' marvellous here. I reckon she was pulling my plonker."

Luis and Elena were so *unhappy*, it wasn't just that they had this ogre in their home, but their dream for retirement had so far become something of a nightmare. Luis again pored over the letter he had received from James Tanner, son of the ogre. He was clearly an educated man, and enclosed with the letter his cheque drawn on Coutts Bank (which Luis knew was a rather special bank for important people) for a whole year's advance fees. How could it be that such a woman could have such a son?

On the third day (and he was counting them by now) he received a phone call – his second guest would arrive tomorrow. This might be the answer, and it was therefore with a kindly smile that he broke the news to Señora Tanner as she was about to retire to her bed.

"'Ope she's not from Birmingham – I can't stand Brummies," was her only comment, as she exited the room and slammed the door.

* * * * *

Frau Eva Schulz was a tall, stern-looking woman who appeared unable to smile. She expressed no gratitude for being collected at the airport, but at least her appearance was an improvement on Mary Tanner. Although Luis Ramon spoke a little German, he was more at home with English, and to his surprise on their first meeting, his new guest confirmed she too spoke some English. However, the journey from the airport passed with no comment in either English or German from the back seat in which she insisted in sitting, even though he did his best to point out various local landmarks. The silence continued all the way up the track right to arrival at his home. Then it was broken.

"This looks very primitive – surely it is not where I am to live?" Her English was clipped and sharp, her voice harsh and guttural, not softened as it is with most modern Germans.

There was little that Luis could say other than to answer in the affirmative, before adding, "I'm sure you'll like it when you've lived here a while – come in and meet your fellow guest."

The introduction was not a success.

"A bloody German!"

"English! I hate the English. So violent and badly behaved, and, and this one is so *dirty*."

"Don't you call me dirty, you sausage sucker."

"I will call you what I like – *I'm* not frightened of English loud-mouths."

The introductory pleasantries went on in this vein until, with sinking heart, Luis brought them to an end by chaperoning Frau Schulz away to her room.

"There is no en-suite bathroom."

He had to agree, "But there is a wash-hand basin," he pointed out.

"I cannot shower or pass water in a wash-hand basin – this is unbelievable."

"I'll leave you to unpack," he replied, and bolted for the fresh air.

He found Elena picking the last crop of oranges before the trees were replaced by young olives.

"Our new guest has arrived."

"I hope she is more pleasant than Señora Tanner."

Luis' face said it all. "Do you know, I don't think she is. She's less uncouth, but I really believe we have another abrasive and unco-operative person on our hands."

And, sad that his dreams were turning to dust, instinctively he moved to his wife to give her a hug, as in moments of crisis people who have supported each other all their lives will.

"Why is God punishing us like this?" he asked her shoulder.

"Hush, Luis, we must not blame God. Perhaps the two ladies will come to like each other."

"They hate each other!"

"Oh." A pause, then, "When does Madame Paulette Dehez arrive?"

"Tomorrow."

"God has probably chosen her as the oil for troubled waters – let us hope that she will bring our English and German guests closer together."

* * * * *

"Frau Schulz, Mrs Tanner, I'd like to introduce our third guest, Madame Dehez."

"Frankzosin! – I do not like French people," was the welcoming phrase chosen by Eva Schulz.

"Can't trust the fucking Frogs – and they wouldn't even have their own country if it wasn't for the English."

The diminutive Paulette Dehez was thunderstruck as she spoke with an anguished voice to her host, "But Monsieur Ramon," she said in passable English, "I do not understand. I thought I was to share a home with *French* ladies – the English are so uncivilised and the Germans are so bourgeois. No, this cannot be. I cannot share a home with such people!" Like so many of her race, her hands, arms and whole body assisted her facial expressions in adding emphasis to her words, indicating that for her the matter was beyond question.

His heart in his boots, Luis answered, "I'll show you to your room – but I'm sure you'll all become friends."

"You're bloody joking!" said Mary Tanner, as Luis pushed his new guest from the room.

"Never – the French take all the German money and feed it to their inefficient farmers – they are bleeding my country dry."

But she was speaking to a closed door.

* * * * *

Twice in the ensuing days he took them to Santa Eulalia. "People who shop together, stay together," he reasoned to himself, and the beautiful promenade and characterful back streets of the small town were surely the ideal location to do it.

As a novelty, on the first occasion he chose for transport the water bus from Cala Llonga, but all they did was moan about the choppy ride on what was in reality a flat calm sea. The next visit was in the Renault Kangoo, when he was lucky to park only a few metres from the Paseo Maritimo at the bottom of the Rambla, outside the Restaurante Goya and close by the famous Owl and the Pussycat pub, with its round tables and Coca Cola Light sun brollies.

But when he dropped them off, the tree-lined Rambla, with its colourful stalls of artisans and traders, leather workers, woodworkers, silversmiths, cartoonists, sellers of costume jewellery, leather bags, hippy beads, children's' mini-toys, bamboo flutes and bongo drums, shawls and tapestries meant nothing to the three 'ladies', as they had all set off in different directions, only meeting up again, approximately on time, for their return journey to Can Ramon.

The happy atmosphere that Luis and Elena had created in their finca home had become like a morgue. No-one spoke, at least to each other. And when anyone spoke to Luis or Elena, it was only to complain. Mary Tanner would not shut-up about the lack of English telly and newspapers. Eva Schulz was clearly unhappy about the lack of facilities, and Paulette Dehez hated the food, together with the time and manner in which it was eaten. And they all hated each other.

Elena, always the cheerful one to hold a family together, was at a loss. "It really is hatred – not just prejudice," she said to her husband in bed one night. "Young people seem to get on well together, no matter where they're from. Why can't the old ones?"

But Luis was lost for an answer. "I must have displeased God in some awful way to be punished like this," he said, with a heavy heart.

* * * * *

"Forgive me, Father, for I have sinned." He spoke to the unseen person in the back of the confessional box.

"God knows your character and your love for Him, my son, I am sure your sin has not been a great one. Tell me about it." Unlike most of the priesthood, the speaker's voice betrayed his working class roots – friends for many years, Luis now sought out his favourite cleric, who he knew carried wisdom aplenty upon his person, and was often a good source of advice. Indeed, many years ago as a small penance, the priest had instructed him to learn the lines in Proverbs 4,7 'Wisdom is the principal thing, therefore get wisdom, and with all thy getting get understanding'. Luis had learnt the lines, and ever since had done his best to take the lesson to heart.

"I don't know what I've done, Father," the anguish in the voice palpable to hear, "but it must have been very bad, because He is punishing me cruelly."

"My son, you cannot place all bad things at God's door, nor should you assume you are being punished – although you might think you're being *tested*."

So Luis explained about his shattered dream to help others as he and his wife enjoyed their retirement, and the reality of the hatred his three guests had for each other.

"You use the word 'hatred', my son – do you not mean 'prejudice'?"

"No father, hatred is the correct word – surely that is such a sin?"

"Whilst it is true, my son, that much of the evil in our world is caused by hatred, it is not actually one of the listed deadly sins, nor is it one of the Commandments. 'Thou shalt not hate thy neighbour', even 'Thou shalt not dislike thy neighbour quite a lot' are both conspicuous by their absence. How have you sought to reduce this, er, hatred?"

"I try to pretend it doesn't exist, Father. When we're sitting in a group in the evenings, I speak to them each individually, and then ask one to comment on what another's said."

"And has this not worked?"

"No, Father, all it produces is abuse."

"Then we must try something else." (Luis thanked him silently for the 'we', for it meant his problem was now being shared.) "The problem must be confronted!"

"How, Father?"

And so the good priest explained what he must do.

* * * * *

The next evening Luis Ramon lit a mighty barbecue, one that would burn all night if it had to. Earlier in the day, he had prepared some jugs of what he called a 'Sangria Royale' – a sangria made from the finest ingredients, and left to steep in the flavours, but without the lemonade. Four bottles of Marques de Caceres red Rioja stood waiting and ready, as did white French Chablis, a selection of aperitifs, together with brandy, Tia Maria, Grand Marnier and Hierbas for later. He had truly taken the priest at his word.

All day long, Elena had been busy preparing the most delicious food, such a variety of tapas both ready to eat cold and for barbecuing – enough to feed the five of them for a week. Surely the old ladies would find something to like amongst such a wonderful selection?

* * * * *

"It's a lovely evening, I thought we'd eat outside, ladies. Also, to welcome you, Luis has made one of his special Sangria Royales," Elena informed her guests. Then, without waiting for answer or comment, she departed for the back porch and terrace area.

Thus she did not hear Mary Tanner's, "What the fuck is a Sangria Royale?"

But the Spanish couple did not have long to wait before curiosity got the better of their three 'curious cats', and one at a time, doing their best to look bored and uninterested, they presented themselves, each taking a seat in one of the very comfortable padded cane easy chairs.

The barbecue was already lit, as Luis added the Cordonui Brut Cava to a jug he had mixed earlier to form the first of the Sangria Royales. The large jug already consisted of fruit and alcohol, both in various forms – slices of apple, oranges and lemons were supplemented by green and black grapes, whilst red Valdepeñas wine was helped more than a little by an Amontillado sherry and Soberano brandy – before he added the sparkling wine.

Into the bottom of five quite large and ornate glasses, he put two chunks of Casa Montaña Ibiza Ice and a little fruit fished from the jug, then filled them with his wonderful aperitif, passing one to each guest.

Suspiciously, the three old ladies sipped from their glasses, and immediately they had a dilemma. For, wanting to be non-co-operative and complaining, the drink really was delicious. The flavour disguised the potency, and the first glass for each of them slipped down perhaps a bit quicker than it should.

Their drinks were replenished almost without them noticing, and quite soon the evening took on a warming glow. Elena produced a cold tapa of anchovies wrapped in jamón serrano – her version of surf and turf, followed by strips of peppers, softened by roasting and a marinade of spiced olive oil with balsamic vinegar.

For the first time since she'd arrived, Paulette Dehez started to relax. Even to her discerning French palate the nibbles were quite exquisite, and the drink, well, a most pleasing blend of a French kia and a fruit cup – though not as strong, of course.

Eva Schulz took another drink, and stretched her legs on the lounger, the tension of the last few days draining from her. And the views to the west over the pine wooded mountains were really quite enchanting.

The next tapa was produced by Luis, who unnoticed had been busy at the barbecue. "Sliced chorizos from Andalucia," he announced with pride. "They're a little spicy, ladies, and you may like to take some relish with them. A top up of their drink for anyone?"

Even Mary Tanner had to admit that the little strips of red sausage were tasty, and 'yes please, I will have another. And another drink'.

Unnoticed, Luis had moved on to the second jug, and decided he'd better slow the pace, for they were in for a long haul that evening.

Without comment, he produced the tiny duck kebabs, the strips of belly pork, and the other barbecued tapas, noting with pleasure that the ladies tucked into the delicious nibbles without further coaxing.

After another half hour or so, he surveyed the now contented faces of his guests, and decided the moment was right to confront their problem head on, trusting that the advice of the good priest was right.

"In vino veritas, my son," he'd said, "in wine we have truth. Arrange a special evening with plenty of alcohol – I have heard a spiked sangria is quite effective, or so it was once claimed by a young and very pregnant lady here in my confessional! Then, when your old ladies are well and truly tiddly, ask them to talk about themselves – at least that way we shall learn the reasons for their behaviour."

So Luis Ramon grasped the nettle. "Why do you hate each other so?" he asked.

Had he posed the question earlier, before the sangria, he would have been met by silence, but, possibly before she had time to think, Eva Schulz answered.

"That is easy to answer, though it does not reduce the pain. The reason I hate the English is because they killed my Hans, and the reason I hate the French is because they made his last months such a misery."

"Perhaps Hans deserved to be killed, unless he was in his own country defending it from invaders," Paulette commented. "My husband, Pierre, never hurt anyone. He was neither a collaborator or in the Maquis – the French Resistance. Yet between your two nations, you destroyed most of our family's wealth, and killed my husband in the process. To this day, I don't know whether it was a German or English bullet which took his life, but either way, he left me for ever."

"Can we sit at the table whilst Paulette tells us more?" Luis said gently, "the sardines are nearly ready."

With no complaints the ladies did as they were bid, whilst the delicious simple dish of barbecued sardines was served with 'los tomates y las cebollas' – sliced tomatoes and onions, all covered with the finest virgin olive oil, gently primed with garlic.

"Tell us about your husband," Elena prompted.

And the others listened, not only in silence, but also with interest.

"We lived in Normandy – in fact until I came here I still did. I had a small house where I took in what you call bed and breakfast guests – that's why I speak some English – though the income from a few guests who want low prices but have big appetites is not very great. Yet before the war, Pierre and I had a big farm house with some land, and a sizeable income from renting out houses we owned – mainly to fishermen and their families. When the Germans came they did not do so by invitation – instead they raced into France with their Tiger Tanks in their famous Blitzkrieg. And they took away our way of life, for their ways were not our ways."

She laughed a little cynically before continuing, "You know, as the war progressed, we actually thought we were lucky living in Normandy, rather than the Pas de Calais, where everyone knew the Allies were going to invade. Silly now, isn't it?" And unbidden a tear ran down her cheek.

"So what happened – how did you lose Pierre?" Elena asked, probing the hurt gently.

"I had gone to visit my aunt in Beauvais," Paulette said, "It was then that the madness erupted. I learnt later from a neighbour what had happened. It seems Pierre had loaded his bicycle with as many of our valuables and personal mementos as he felt he could carry, and was about to set off to pedal all the way to Beauvais to join me. But, but . . . ."

"But what?" Elena prompted.

"But before he could even mount his bike, a stray bullet killed him – whether it came from a British gun or a German gun the neighbour couldn't say."

Luis felt the time was right to move on. "Eva, tell us more of your life, and about Hans."

And the odd thing is that Eva felt she *wanted* to do so – *wanted* to unburden herself, and *wanted* to share her sadness.

"I was born in Koblenz," she said, "a lovely little city situated where the Mosel flows into the Rhine. When I was fifteen, I joined the Hitler Youth." Here, she held up her hand to prevent comment. "You must understand this was not a bad thing to do, it was what all good healthy young Germans did – just like in other countries they joined the Scouts or Guides."

Here she paused to pick at her sardines and take a drink of the Chablis which had been quietly placed before her. "It was during a summer camp in the Schwarzwald – the Black Forest, that I met Hans. He was an eighteen-year old boy from Berlin, so beautiful – tall and handsome, with blonde hair and the most piercing blue eyes I'd ever seen. He was our Gruppenführer, our group leader. We were so happy, Hans and I, so lucky to be young, and to be German, and to be so much in love. Two years later, we were married, and I moved to Berlin."

"What was Berlin like?" asked Elena.

Eva laughed, sadly. "It was wonderful, so exciting, so important – the most important city on earth. Hans joined the army of course, and because of his education and Hitler Youth Training was made an officer. He was part of General Rommel's Afrika Corps, and for a while wrote many wonderful letters home about their victories."

She paused for a moment, lost in thought, before continuing, "Then there was El Alamein, and he was lucky to escape without capture or losing his life. Because of his service record, he was not sent to the Russian Front, but instead joined the army of occupation in France. Somewhere," she said, wiping away a tear, "I have a photograph of Lieutenant Hans Schulz and his young wife just before he left for his new posting."

Again a pause before continuing, "You know, it was years later that I read a speech by Winston Churchill at that time. The British victory at El Alamein was the end of the beginning for Mr. Churchill, but for us it was the beginning of the end. Hans was so unhappy in France. He used to write how different it was from Afrika, where his war had been a warrior's war. But in France, he said it was different, somehow unmanly – a long way from what he had known as a soldier's life.

"Instead of fighting mighty battles, schoolchildren would chant rude songs at him and his comrades, and daub anti-German slogans on walls. They made it clear they hated the Germans, and the only fighting Hans did until the end was against the unseen shadows of the French resistance. But that was a dirty way of war, and he did not enjoy it."

Again the sad laugh before she concluded, "We too were glad he was not in the Pas de Calais, where we knew he would have to be prepared to lay down his life to repel the Allies when they invaded."

"And he was killed?"

"Oh yes, he was killed, fighting the British, doing his duty. Meanwhile," she added, "my glorious Berlin was crumbling into ruins from the British bombing. The whole world had gone crazy. I was pregnant of course, and had my baby all alone in the dark cellar of our ruined home. I was still living there when the Russians came five months later, as a result of which most of my life has been spent under their bovine bureaucracy – until the wall came down."

Then she sobbed, having run out of words.

"You have been quiet, Señora Tanner," Luis said softly, "What is your story?"

So Mary told them about her birth and childhood and marriage to her beloved Bert. "'E was one of the advance elite troops dropped early on D-Day," she said proudly, "though it was only later I learnt all about it. Their job was to secure a bridge over the River Orne, so when the main force landed they could break out from the coast. Although he was a paratrooper – he was in 'D' Division of the Oxford and Bucks regiment, and looked so smart in his red beret – they flew in by glider. They'd actually taken the bridge – its code name was Pegasus – and were starting to regroup in Ranville when he got shot."

"But Hans was stationed in Ranville," Eva said incredulously, "and he was killed on the morning of 6th June 1944!"

"It is hard to believe – but we also lived in Ranville," Paulette said quietly, "and the houses we owned were in Ouistream, though the Allies called it 'Sword Beach'. I lost my husband and our assets in one day of madness when the British and the Germans fought each other on French soil."

Whilst the ladies had been talking, they had quietly been served with and enjoyed the wonderful spicy chicken wings, followed by fillet steak, both accompanied by a change in wine to a Marques de Caceres Tinto Gran Reserva Rioja. Then Elena removed the empty plates and without speaking served her home-made graixonera pudding.

"It's almost as if," Luis said, "the three of you, who incredibly all lost your husbands on the same day at the same place, have been sent here. Perhaps you may wish to consider why?"

He turned to his wife, "Come, Elena, the ladies have much to talk about, let's leave them in peace." Saying which the two hosts crept quietly away to bed.

There are two types of silence, a stony silence – which their finca had suffered recently, and an amiable silence, which was what they now left behind them on their terrace. It was over an hour later that the three old ladies themselves retired to bed.

* * * * *

The following day, which had dawned unseasonably overcast, Luis again ran his three guests into Santa Eulalia, managing to find a parking spot in a blue zone by the Bistro T. Lautrec at the bottom of Mariano Riquer Wallis, the busy little road that runs from Calle San Jaime down past a palm-filled traffic island to the Paseo Maritimo – the promenade.

This time, to his great joy, the three of them set off in the same direction, towards the sea front. They weren't exactly holding hands, but at least they were together. Luis followed at a discreet distance to see what happened.

When they reached the Paseo, the three ladies walked across to lean on the black painted railings, surveying the peaceful scene of the beach and the sea, dotted here and there with a few boats, but on this cloudy day, with very few bathers braving its shallows. Nearby, easy access to the beach could be gained down a flight of steps, at the bottom of which was a free-to-use slimline stainless steel shower. To their right the Paseo opened out into a pretty area of palm trees, featuring a wooden water wheel actually flowing with water, whilst to their left, the Rambla itself was only about thirty metres or so away, past the elegance of the Atenea restaurante.

They did not stand really close together, but Luis was pleased to note that only a metre or so separated them. He watched as Paulette opened her bag to check her money – she had indicated she might have to go to the bank. Taking out three notes, each ten euros in value, she realised that she would indeed have to go to Banca March.

And that was the moment the peaceful scene was ruined, for suddenly a running youth, tall and rangy, dressed in jeans, dirty T-shirt and balaclava, hit her hard, knocking her to the ground. Not content with that, and with no thought for her fragility, for good measure as she fell he thumped her on the side of her head, before snatching the three ten euro notes from her hand.

But then something odd happened to him, for just as he was about to run off, he literally saw stars, and his legs turned to jelly. He was not to know he had been struck by Mary Tanner's weighty handbag, as with a sigh he sank to the ground and sweet oblivion, releasing the stolen notes – the three tenners – to flutter gently to the ground as he did so.

Mary and Eva each recovered one of the notes, and Paulette the third, as she was helped to her feet by the German.

"No bleedin' thug is going to rob one of my friends," Mary said vehemently, pausing only to aim a well-directed kick at the unconscious youth's genitals, as fortuitously for the young man a policeman arrived on the scene and unstrapped his revolver.

"Nor rob a friend of mine," Eva confirmed.

Saying which they joined hands and set off along the Paseo Maritimo towards the Rambla, leaving the policeman to deal with the prostate youth, who in recovering consciousness seemed uncertain whether to nurse his head or hold his crotch.

Satisfied and grateful that his prayers had been answered, Luis Ramon himself headed off in the direction of 'The Royalty' for a quiet celebratory drink.

As he did so, the sun peeped out from behind a cloud, and seemingly winked at him in cheeky contentment.

Taller Toni

The dark-haired mechanic in his mid-forties checked the short length of pipe for perhaps the tenth time. It had to be exactly right for its job. But the craftsman's eye which he ran over it told him little, for the secret was inside, hidden from view. From the outside, a perfectly standard Jaguar hydraulic brake pipe, but accurate drilling had made it so thin that under the high pressure of hard braking, the pipe would split apart like an over-inflated balloon.

When that happened, the fluid would not continue along the hydraulic system to the slave cylinders, there to ensure that the asbestos based pads gripped the hardened steel discs and hauled the big car down from whatever speed it was doing to a standstill. The fluid would instead squirt uselessly around the engine compartment – at least for the few seconds that the driver remained alive to keep the brake pedal depressed.

His skilled fingers now busy installing the pipe in Taft's car, Toni White smiled at the perfection of his plan – he'd even cover himself by writing on the invoice that a complete overhaul of the braking system was required . . . . That bitch, Taft, had it coming. Six months she'd given him, just for a little cut and shut job.

He was of course genuinely sorry, but sorry at being caught, not sorry at what he'd done, which like many others who live by crime, he somehow managed to rationalise as reasonable behaviour. It had started with 'clocking' cars – winding back the speedometer to show a lower mileage than the vehicle had actually covered. Although 'Tony' White, as he was then called, was of the opinion that a car which had covered a great distance in easy motorway cruising was likely to be in better condition than one used for low mileage inner-city work, and hence unfairly penalised in its re-sale value, the magistrate had not seen it like that, and had fined him five hundred pounds – a bit excessive for a first offence. Or at least, the first at which he'd been caught.

Then switching a car's ID to another. What harm did that do? A motor that matched one written off in a crash just happened to get stolen. All he did was take the VIN plates off the wreck and substitute them on the stolen motor, grinding out and replacing any stamped into the actual chassis. So who suffered? If it was properly insured, as it should be, the one with the nicked motor took the insurance money and bought a new one. And the insurers themselves were only doing what they took the suckers' premiums for. In any case, it's a well-known fact that there's nothing like a few claims to sell policies, so in a way he was even doing the insurance company a favour.

But what had happened? Some bastard had squealed, and he'd got a hundred hours community work, together with three months suspended sentence.

And so Tony White had progressed through the seedy lower echelons of crime to grime – the grime of the cut and shut. For that can endanger lives. The cut and shut is where two wrecks are cut apart and the best bits of each welded together into one vehicle. Superficially the result often looks okay, but the integral chassis of the modern car was not designed for such drastic adaptation, which lacks structural rigidity, or what a skilled driver would call integrity.

But was it his fault that the prat who had been only too pleased to buy a low priced motor, knowing it might be a bit 'dodgy', couldn't drive, and had to show his girlfriend what his new wheels could do on a country road when it was loaded with petrol and the driver loaded with 'pop'?

Although nearly two years had since passed, and the jail sentence was behind him, White remembered the moment like he remembered no other. The magistrate, Councillor Taft, looking down like she was God Almighty, her voice strong and confident as she gave her verdict, "The time has come to show you where your criminal exploits lead. A short, sharp shock is called for, and accordingly I sentence you to three months, to run consecutively with the three months suspended sentence already awarded to you . . . ."

At the memory, White's anger flowed easily and immediately into present-day violence, and he thumped the car he was working on with his fist. Again the memory – the previous suspended had been 'awarded to him', like it was a prize or something.

In jail, he had become determined to make a new start, to move to a location where his face was not associated with villainy. That was not to say he was determined to go straight, but rather not to be automatically a police suspect for any minor misdemeanour which took place.

Then one night, lying on his narrow cot in the confines of his prison cell, his mind had moved on, almost daydreamed . . . . If he was going to move, he might as well go somewhere pleasant, away altogether from Britain with its dirt and damp and police, somewhere the sun shone, and the booze was cheap. So in jail, at the tax-payers' expense, he had started to study Spanish.

If you do just one subject even for a short time you can become fairly proficient, and by directing the energy and intellect he used in his criminal career to that one subject, by the time of his release, Tony White was indeed proficient in his new language.

On release, his first port of call had naturally been the Costa del Sol, which just a few years before had been known as the Costa del Crime. But somehow it seemed to lack identity, the long main road which connected the various communities along its path failing to offer the spirit of community he'd enjoyed back home.

So he'd motored up to the Costa Blanca, which he preferred, and which seemed less frantic in the way it conducted itself. Then on a whim he'd put his 'S' Type Jag on the ferry from Denia to Ibiza. And that was it – immediately he felt he'd found his new home, enjoying the way in which ex-pats from various parts of Europe all integrated with the local Ibicencans and Spanish to form a community that actually worked.

After he'd found and rented a vacant workshop, and used the same contact to take a short-term rental on an apartment, he'd left the Jag in Ibiza and flown home to sell up his 'grease-monkey' garage to a small-time developer. A contact he'd made in Ibiza had recommended a firm in Southampton as being something of an authority on moving to Ibiza, and the company had indeed obliged with packing his tools and workbenches and personal effects in a very professional way, which seemed to indicate they knew what they were doing.

Tony White had so far never regretted chasing the sun to Ibiza. He'd rapidly built a decent social life, and even found work more pleasurable in his garage cum workshop on a small industrial estate, situated on the northern outskirts of Ibiza, to the west of the San An road. To pull in more punters, he'd changed his Christian name to the Spanish 'Toni' and also used the Spanish word 'Taller' (with 'Tall' pronounced as in 'pal' and an unseen 'y' introduced after 'Tall') meaning workshop or garage. Thus Taller Toni was born, specialising in British cars, but able to turn its hand to anything.

Then incredibly, just over a year ago at a bar in the Plaza del Parque in Ibiza, he'd met Sheila Taft. She'd recognised him immediately, and had no hesitation in making a beeline to speak to him. She seemed surprised but pleased that, like herself, he too had emigrated, was not just on holiday, and had laughed at what she called 'the coincidence' of them both choosing the same island. She'd also spoken of the other 'coincidence' of them both staying loyal to Jaguars, and could she bring her own thirty-year old Jag to him for servicing?

But he'd seen right through her, for it was obvious to him that, not content with the jail sentence she'd given him, Sheila Taft had actually followed him to Ibiza!

Her excuse was that she now ran an 'Inmobiliaria' – an estate agents – on the Rambla in Ibiza, but she seemed to find numerous excuses to keep an eye on him – there were always little niggling things wrong with her car, and she'd even discovered his favourite pub, where so often 'by coincidence' she contrived to drop by just as he was relaxing over a pint. To enable her to bloody gloat, more like.

"Well, we'll see who'll be gloating in a week's time, ex-Councillor bloody la-di-dah Sheila Taft," he said to himself in his East Midlands accent. "Any gloating you're doing then will be in the next world, not this." He sipped cold coffee from a mug made black by grease, then wiped his lips with his sleeve.

For a moment, just one brief moment, Toni White felt a twinge of conscience, for there might, of course, be others hurt in the eventual crash, *wherever* it happened. Wherever it was destined to be the fateful moment for *Mz* Taft, when she pressed the brake pedal that little extra hard . . . .

Then he laughed. If they were decent honest citizens, any others hurt would no doubt be insured, so someone would do well out of it. And if they weren't, they probably had it coming anyway.

He turned back to his task, nimble fingers fitting the pipe into place, or almost into place – it still needed a final little tweak to bend it to shape.

The original Jaguar XJ6 enjoyed a dual braking system. This ensured that if the pressure in any single part of it failed, a considerable amount of braking power would still remain. Toni White had taken care of this small problem by fitting not one, but two of his specially drilled-out pipes.

At least, he'd fitted one. But the second was proving a bit awkward . . . .

* * * * *

Smartly dressed in a skirted suit, Sheila Taft leaned back in her office chair, and looked without seeing at the book-lined walls, featuring numerous books in the Spanish language which she spoke so well, and even a few English titles such as Saunders' 'International Tax Systems and Planning Techniques', 'Land and Tax Planning' by Patrick Soares, or for light relief Patrick Way's 'BES and Assured Tenancies' to enable her to give advice for clients letting property back in the UK. She was slightly above average height for a woman, with a rather serious face which had only recently learned to smile in a relaxed natural way.

Her mind drifted to the reasons that had brought her to Ibiza. Still a spinster in her mid-fifties, that did not mean she had never been in love. But only the once, only with her lovely Brendan, and only when she was still in her teens. Brendan, gorgeous fun-loving extrovert Brendan, just three years older than her, when, at the age of twenty-one he'd been stabbed to death one Saturday night in a club having refused to hand over the wallet which contained the few pounds he had left from the hard-earned wages he'd received only the previous day.

She still thought of him. Was still in love with him thirty-six years later, and until recently despaired of ever finding another. Instead, she'd buried herself in her work, creating and building-up a successful estate agency. Parallel with that, she'd entered local politics, and served for nearly twenty years as a district councillor. And from her standing and contacts on the council, she'd become a magistrate. Then she'd started charity work . . . .

Sheila Taft had in fact led a full and useful life, but through it all had remained very firmly 'Miss Taft', with no hint of romance to lighten her existence. Her lifestyle had followed a distinct unchanging pattern until two years ago, when on a whim she'd agreed to holiday in Ibiza with a girlfriend.

And Ibiza showed her what she had been missing. A bit of fun on a daily basis, to mix with people being happy, laughing, intent on getting the best they could from their brief sojourn on earth. And of course the sun, and the sheer beauty of Ibiza which had taken her so much by surprise.

By the time she returned from their holiday, her mind was made up – she'd resign as a councillor and as a magistrate, sell her estate agency and emigrate. She, Sheila Taft, was going to kick over the traces and enjoy herself!

After the repayment of a bank loan and the building society mortgage, the sale of the estate agency and her house had produced nearly seven hundred thousand pounds, so that when she arrived in Ibiza, she was not urgently concerned with immediately creating an income. Really it had come about by chance, for the inmobiliaria through which she'd acquired her three-bedroomed villa was itself up for sale, due to the death of one of the partners.

So three months after selling her business in England, she was back in business in Ibiza. And for a while she loved it, loved it for the novelty.

But the other matter to do with love she herself couldn't quite believe. For about fourteen months ago, after a business call, early one evening she'd been walking through the Plaza del Parque, when she'd spotted and admired an English registered 'S-Type' Jaguar parked in the nearby blue zone. It had been a hot day, and feeling thirsty, on impulse she'd wandered over to a bar, intent on a refreshing shandy, with the beer to be mixed with her preferred 'Fanta Lemon' rather than lemonade. She would never have gone to a bar alone in England, but this was the 'new' fun-loving Sheila Taft – so she did, and found 'Toni' White.

Recognition was instant and mutual, and she thought she detected both respect and gratitude in the look she got from the man to whom she'd given 'a short sharp shock'. Yes, he was definitely one of her successes, and quietly she was rather pleased about it. Convinced that the chap was a basically good sort at heart, it seemed the brief spell inside had had the desired effect, for he proved good company, and had integrated rapidly into Ibiza ways, even changing the way he spelt his own name as a mark of respect for his new country.

It seemed that since his release, as she expected, he had made a good effort to pull himself together, and by incredible coincidence had chosen the same place as herself to enable him to start a new and decent life.

As they had chatted, seated in wicker chairs outside the tiny pub, it was with a shock she found herself 'interested' in him, his naturally extrovert personality reminding her, just a little, of her long lost Brendan.

And so they'd kept in contact, with Sheila becoming increasingly certain that the coincidence of them both moving to the same place, and of their meeting, was meant to be. Unbeknown to Toni White, it was through her contacts that, although newly established in Ibiza, he was a favoured call-out for accident wrecks. That gave him a good basic income, and to show the man that his debt to society was paid, she even entrusted him with her own car. A little gesture she was sure he appreciated, as she considered their relationship to be developing in the way she desired.

She consulted her watch. Would he have finished the Jag yet? It was a nuisance having to take it in today, but it had been mis-firing of late, and she had a long drive ahead that night. In reality, she was only fooling herself, for she'd have sold the Jag long ago had it not been the excuse to see Toni on a regular basis. For she had fallen full square head-over-heels in love, and was convinced he felt the same for her. But nevertheless, because of the cautious side of her nature, she had hidden her wealth from him, so that when the moment came and he popped the question – as she was sure he would – she would know it was love of her as a woman which had made him do it, and not affection for the life-style the two of them would henceforward lead. That would come as a lovely surprise to him.

She made up her mind – she'd walk up to Toni's garage – the long walk would do her good – collect the Jag, and head to the docks at San Antoni for a quick tapas before she caught the evening sailing to Denia. A quick word through the intercom, then out through the back door. Pleased the day at the desk was over.

Smiling ruefully, she reflected that in truth she had little interest in her inmobiliaria business these days, though at first the move to Ibiza had re-kindled her enthusiasm. She found her unpaid charity work far more fulfilling. Her mind moved on, to the rest of her day, for after landing at Denia, she had a long drive through the night to Madrid, where she had a nine o'clock meeting the following morning to learn how a project to involve young offenders in sporting activities had actually reduced their re-offending rate by a factor of three, to see whether the ideas would be of advantage for her own favourite charity's youth scheme.

Her no longer young legs aching a bit from the walk, she approached Taller Toni. She turned into the garage, and walked down the narrow drive at the side of the workshop, to the small yard at the back. Again she checked her watch – she *was* rather early, and suddenly panicked that her car might not be ready for her.

* * * * *

With a sigh of relief, Toni White tightened the last nut – the second piece of pipe was now in place. Just the engine timing to complete. Picking up the strobe light, he bent to the new task. But before he could even start, Taft called from the yard. What the hell? Sod the timing – once it got off the ferry at Denia, the car wasn't going far anyway. He threw down the strobe and went out to the yard.

"All ready, Miss Taft – runs like a dream."

* * * * *

With the briefest of comments about the brakes written upon the bill to cover him, 'but nothing really to worry about' he'd added verbally, and with conscience squashed into non-existence, he waved his customer 'Good-bye'.

Taft waved back cheerily – definitely one of her successes, and who knows where their relationship might be heading? She joined the main road and turned the nose of the Jag up the gentle hill towards San Antoni. But there was very little power, the engine missing badly. This was hopeless – the car seemed worse than before! It popped and banged its way to the top. She'd never reach Madrid like this.

* * * * *

Toni White watched the Jag disappear, then decided to lock up. It was very early, but he felt like a drink to celebrate, and already there'd be a few mates at his favourite bar to join him in an early pint. He turned the key in the door, and started to walk up the narrow side passage – he'd have to get it widened, there was only just enough room for cars like Jags and Range Rovers.

* * * * *

Ex-councillor Taft swung the Jag's nose onto the garage forecourt. There was probably still time to catch Toni. A fast and competent driver, she drove into the side passage at a speed approaching forty kilometres an hour – she could judge the width of her car to the inch, or in Ibiza, the centimetre. Good – there he was. But what a strange look on his face. Not so much surprise, as terror!

Distracted a little by this, Sheila Taft held her speed for a split second longer, until quite close to her beloved Toni.

Then she stamped on the brakes. Hard.

Sancho's Heart Attack

Like most Englishmen, I felt at something of a loss as the cricket season drew to a close, and indeed, it can only have been this that tempted me to leave my tranquil English South West, and, on no more than a whim, set off in the old MGA to meet a group of Yorkshiremen, together, I hoped, with a selection of their friends.

Yorkshire – even the name evokes sentiment, and not only amongst cricketers. Yorkshire, where men are men, and, until recently, any man who was a man spent his working hours down t'pit, and his playing hours swinging the willow or supping ale, and sometimes both together. The fact that, like my own Somerset, Yorkshire has a tranquil side, of moorland hills and quiet valleys and pretty villages may well be true, and was shown to the world to be so by the genius of James Herriot, but that is not the Yorkshire that is somehow evoked for me by the name.

No matter, it was not to the tranquil Yorkshire I was headed, or even to the industrial Yorkshire, for I was off a long way to the south of that largest of English Counties, chasing the sun to Ibiza and hoping to find a village where I could spend a few quiet days with like-minded people. As a bonus, I was on expenses, although my editor demanded what he called 'a human interest story' of no less than two and a half thousand words to justify matters. I suppose that in a way what follows are the background notes, together with a few confidential details, for the story I shall write for him when I get home.

Two of the greatest written works start with reference to 'The Beginning' – in the Bible, 'The first Book of Moses', called 'Genesis', starts with the words 'In the beginning', and more recently 'Under Milk Wood' written by the Welsh genius, Dylan Thomas, uses the slightly longer 'To begin at the beginning'.

This story saw its own beginnings some years before my involvement, not in Yorkshire, nor in Ibiza, but in Marbella. A group of ex-pat Yorkshiremen were one day enjoying their usual Sunday lunch-time pint, all sun-tanned, healthy and happy in their adopted country, but be-moaning the lack of hands-on cricket, especially for those 'of a certain age'. To cut that story short, for that story is not our story, they resolved to form the 'Ex-Pats Cricket League de España' to enable them to re-kindle their love of the evocative sound of a well-struck cricket ball – willow on leather – and enjoy some sociable company along the way. After considerable discussion, and due mainly to logistics, it was agreed to throw membership open not only to non-Yorkshiremen, but also to other nationalities, should they show any penchant for the noble art.

It was also decided to adopt the MCC's Official Laws of Cricket, although a lively discussion then ensued about additional 'special' rules that might be required for the better enjoyment of the game as played by unfit amateurs in a hot climate. It was therefore decided that a batsman could be brought a cold wet towel and a cold wet drink once an hour –

not that any expected to bat for that length of time. And that because of the fragile nature of the playing surfaces at most of the potential cricket grounds, to protect that surface from avoidable damage 'In all instances, rain shall stop play, and the match be declared a draw'.

With generous help from a sherry company in Jerez, the embryonic 'EPCLE' had gained a little sponsorship and a fair amount of publicity. Through this they had grown to eight teams, mainly throughout the south and east of Spain, with a couple in the Balearics, one of which was in Ibiza.

There is in fact more than one cricket team in Ibiza, but the ex-pats lot had the advantage of a rotund optimistic man called Charlie Crowther, by coincidence also a Yorkshire-man, who had moved to Ibiza in 1995 to open what he called an 'English style' country pub on the outskirts of Es Canar. Of course, Ibiza is not exactly short of English style pubs, and most of them are in far busier locations than that chosen by Charlie Crowther. He had to work hard to build his business, but in this he had a few advantages. The first being the truly enormous finca which he bought when such a property was still affordable, and which in the Spanish way was well-endowed with sabena beams, low ceilings and massive doors.

"Inside, there's not much difference between an old Spanish country house, and an English one," he said to his wife in his broad Yorkshire accent on the day they moved in. "Bung in the bar counters, nail up a few horse-brasses and a dartboard, and I reckon we can open for business."

Of course, it wasn't as easy as that – it never is – and it was nearly eleven months of bureaucracy and hard graft later that he and 'Flower' – his beloved wife Elsie – sold their first drink. To a Spaniard from the village, who introduced himself as 'Sancho', and congratulated them on creating such a typical Ibicencan establishment. Luckily, Sancho, who was a bit below average height but made up for it with his abundant energy, spoke very good English, which he put down to his job as a waiter, together with his interest in amateur dramatics and the Theatre Group. Just as he was about to explain to Charlie his part in their latest play, they were joined by another – their second customer.

"I hear you speak English," he said in a sort of Germanic English, "but this is such a wonderful German beerkeller – wooden beams and tables! It is just like Bavaria, like Munchen. What part of Germany are you from?"

Charlie explained that he wasn't, he was from a place called Bawtry in Yorkshire, but wisely refrained from pointing out that he thought he owned an English style pub, not a beerkeller. Remembering the hit-record eulogy, in a whispered aside to 'Flower' he said, "Like the deck of cards the soldier took to church, it seems we're all things to all men, but what does it matter as long as they spend their money?"

"Please, what does the name 'The Cricketers Arms' mean?" the German asked, as, a little sceptically, he sipped at his first glass of English beer. He was possibly in his early thirties, with blonde hair and a sort of healthy look about him, as if he exercised a fair amount. "I thought a cricket was like a cicada," he continued, "but surely they have only legs? Where are their arms?"

So Charlie did his best to explain that there are crickets, and there is cricket, and to be fair, the German, who introduced himself as 'Kurt', did show an intelligent interest in the English pastime.

* * * * *

The pub prospered, chiefly, but by no means only, supported by lovers of cricket and genuine wanabees from other nationalities. When the regulars heard of the creation of the 'EPCLE', with enthusiastic encouragement the land behind the old finca was flattened by the diminutive and enthusiastic Sancho, who borrowed his father's ancient JCB from the family farm, and a sort of cricket ground created, with the second hand wicket 'matting' being the most expensive item. Then they formed a 'sort of' team to join the new cricket league, and play commenced. Soon they grew in numbers enough to field a first and second eleven, with even then some 'spares' on the bench for substitutes. They were in truth a somewhat motley if enthusiastic selection of Yorkshiremen, Londoners, Brummies, Bristolians – even a Welshman and a chap who hailed from Bantry Bay, who was the life and soul of any party, together with Kurt and Sancho and friends from their respective countries.

Whether it was the cricket, the beer, the friendly atmosphere or whatever, Charlie Crowther and his 'Flower' found their pub prospered, and they considered they were ready to take the next step forward, that of taking paying guests. The Cricketers Arms was set to become an inn.

It was in fact their first advertisement in 'The Cricketer' together with a brief report in the Times about a club in Ibiza winning the Ex Pats' league which had enabled me to sell my idea for a human interest story to my editor, drive the old MGA onto the cross channel ferry, and head south down through France. I stuck mainly to 'D' roads, which, despite its age, the MG seemed content to lope along all day at 70 – 80 miles per hour, and with the wind blowing through my thinning hair, for a few precious hours I was able to pretend to myself I was rather younger than is actually the case.

Staying en-route at an auberge in the little hamlet of Camps-sur-l'Isle near Libourne, I again took out the leaflet which Elsie Crowther had sent me about their pub. "The Cricketers Arms near Es Canar – a haven for lovers of the noble art. The local team play on the ground behind this olde-worlde country pub, and the 'Cricketers Bar' serves as their club room. Five bedrooms, three en-suite, good English food, reasonable rates."

How could I possibly say no?

The following morning dawned as a sunny day in late September, a wonderful drive with the top down through Southern France and into Spain, and little traffic. Something just had to go wrong. Barcelona arrived without incident, and with time to spare, the MG bumped up the ramp for the overnight ferry to Ibiza.

But the next day, after exploring Ibiza town and the D'Alt Vila, where I had enjoyed a late and long lunch, as I motored through an astonishingly beautiful island and the reality of Es Canar grew closer, I became convinced the pub would be a dive, or overlooked by a derelict coal mine and an ominous slag heap. (I had not been to Ibiza before.)

Making a hash of the quite clear directions, I turned too early into Es Canar, entering the village from the south, or S'Argamassa end, instead of the north where my destination actually lay. After the ancient D'Alt Vila in Ibiza Town, Es Canar was not quite what I was expecting – the buildings were all new and clearly built to cater for the tourist trade. As I drove through, taking care to avoid the thronging multitudes of happy tourists, I spotted an Irish pub, called 'Murphy's', though confusingly advertising Guinness, an Aussie pub called 'The Outback', a Chinese restaurante, numerous bar-cafés, side by side sunbathers on the beach, and of course the package-tour type hotels which served as temporary homes for everyone.

I began to wonder whether 'The Cricketers Arms' would indeed be the 'olde-worlde country pub' I had seen advertised, or a modern take-off of one. And would it really be in the country, or in this busy, vibrant, and quite noisy village? Somewhat lost, I stopped to ask a cheerful looking chap for directions. He was both local and Spanish, and directed me in far better English than I spoke his language to take the road to Sant Carlos, then the third turning on the right, and a short way along a partly surfaced track I would find 'The Cricketers Arms'.

This time I did stick to directions, which were absolutely spot on. And to my great joy, when I got there, 'The Cricketers Arms' appeared exactly as it had been described in the advertisement. I parked the MG, and made my way inside, expecting my bubble of things going right to burst –

my booking would be for the wrong dates, or the Landlord would no doubt be a dour taciturn introvert, with a grudge against the world . . . .

"Welcome, sir. You must be Mr. Hunt from Somerset. Pleasant day for a drive, sir, I 'ope you enjoyed it." He wore an old-fashioned publican's apron, which somehow contrived to emphasis his ample belly, and the way he spoke could clearly have his roots in only one part of the world.

"'Er, yes, thank-you, very much."

"We had the windows open all day yesterday in your room – give it a good airing. Will you be dining with us tonight, sir?"

I nodded. "Yes, yes please."

He touched the side of his nose with the fore-finger of his right hand. "You might like to try the steak and ale pie, sir. The wife really makes it for ourselves, but a few of the locals get to enjoy some as well. You see, sir, she actually uses the thinner end of best rump, and, though I'll deny saying so if you ever repeat it" – he laughed at the confidence he was about to impart – "Theakston's Old Peculiar Ale."

I laughed with him, though not sure why, so asked why he should deny it.

"We don't sell it, you see, sir. But the missus, she reckons the particular taste and extra gravity helps bring out the flavour of the beef – we import the bottles specially for her cooking. Then, as well as the Theakstons, she adds a bit of grated horseradish – all makes that little difference, tha' sees."

I was convinced, and already looking forward to my meal. I told him so, and confirmed that as a temporary local, would he please put my name down for the steak and ale pie. My room proved to be homely and comfortable, with a low ceiling, wooden beams, and a small window affording a view of the cricket field behind the pub. A quick change into flannels and a T-shirt, and I was ready to inspect it – although it would be several months before the slap of willow on leather would be heard there again. I checked my watch before leaving – say a half hour's stroll to work up an appetite, then the bar should be open. One, or possibly two, pints before tackling the steak and ale pie.

Life was not all bad . . . .

* * * * *

And so it continued. To say the least, the cricket ground proved to have a rough outfield, but that was the case with most village grounds in England. And though certainly well worn, repairs to the artificial wicket showed that it had benefited from an amount of TLC – tender loving care – some of the local lads were obviously keen enough to put in the work. I hoped a few of them would be in the Cricketers Bar later – although the season was over, friendships made through the game have a habit of persevering for the rest of the year.

My stroll took me along some rough dirt tracks into rising hill land with neat terraces supported by dry stone walls, mostly given over to citrus orchards, and with just a few goats and sheep for company. Though wonderfully hot, warmed from the sun in a clear blue sky, the air was invigorating, less ozone than my native Somerset, but somehow with a cleanliness, a sparkle, to it. I breathed deep, and found myself walking a little more briskly than usual. Eventually, a narrow track off to the right, which was little wider than a footpath and may well have been on private land as a sign 'Coto Privado de Casa' must have meant something or other, took me on a circular route back to the pub. A quick shower and change, and I was ready for a beer.

The Cricketers Bar would not, I was told, be open until later, "but tha's find a reet good pint in public, Mr. Hunt." I did, it was Webster's, and I enjoyed it, or rather them. And the steak and ale pie was every bit as good as I had been promised. A small piece of imported Long Clawson Stilton with properly blanched celery followed it happily, and, refusing coffee, I headed for the now-open Cricketers Bar and yet more 'reet good ale'.

* * * * *

An open double door afforded entrance, and I immediately had a sensation of déja vu – I had been here before. But I hadn't, of course, it was just the cricketing memorabilia and the healthy rugged looks of the customers which made it seem so. Better furnished than most cricket clubs, it was nevertheless somewhere I felt instantly at home.

There were perhaps eleven or twelve folk seated in assorted groups around the room, mostly male, but including four girls varying in age from late teens to late forties, and presumably with their boyfriends or husbands. Girls no doubt happy to do the sandwiches or keep the score-book on match days – but in so doing clocking up brownie points to encourage their menfolk to go along with their own ideas on other occasions!

As I entered, I couldn't help noticing the variety of accents and even languages I could hear, and in this aspect this particular Cricketers Bar was far removed from the 'regional accent' sound of the conversation in most cricket clubs. I joined two chaps at the bar, as their pints were being pulled. They moved aside to make room for me, and nodded in a friendly way – it was that sort of a pub. "Sure, it's been powerful hot today," the shorter one said to me in an Irish accent, by way of a greeting. The barman passed him his pint, which he raised in a toast towards an impressive sporting cup, mounted in a place of honour behind the bar. "To Sancho's heart attack," he said.

I agreed with him about the day, as I ordered myself a pint from the pump, to be served in a jar with a handle, please.

"Tha's not from the Midlands, are tha'?" asked the Irishman's companion – like the landlord, clearly a Yorkshireman, in this case both a Freddie Trueman lookalike and soundalike. "That's for sure – more like a Devon accent."

I laughed – he'd a quick ear, but it's also funny how people north of Gloucester cannot separate the different west country dialects. Whereas we locals to the region would immediately recognise that if someone told you he had a 'good ideal', it was a Bristolian telling you he had a good idea, or if someone else was 'biding wom', it was a Somerset chap who intended to stay at home.

"Not far away," I congratulated him, "Somerset."

"Glory be, haven't we got a cyder walloper here?" joined in his pal, using a common nickname for the Somerset County side. "Do you follow them?"

I confirmed that I was a Somerset Vice-President, but a bit disappointed by their recent performance.

"I'll get that, Ernie," the Yorkshireman said to the barman, indicating that he would pay for my drink. He stuck out his hand to introduce himself. "Fred Scargill," he said.

I shook his hand, "Trev Hunt, sometimes called Taj, pleased to meet you."

His Irish companion also offered his hand, "Dave Letts." I shook it. "Taj – that's an Indian name, but to be sure, you don't look that sunburnt."

I laughed. "No, my real name's Trev, but to some of my older friends I'm known as Taj – a sort of family nickname."

Fred raised his glass towards the cup. "To Sancho's heart attack." He drank deep.

I raised my own glass, "Cheers, Fred," I said, acknowledging the kindness of the man who had paid for it.

"Cheers, Trev," he said. "Tha's play a bit, then?"

"I used to be first wicket down, but I've slipped to number seven over the past two seasons. Slow spinner as well – at least I roll out a few off-breaks occasionally – which might just help me keep my place for a few more years."

Fred and Dave nodded wisely – they were of a similar age to me, and no doubt also faced the dilemma of weighing their own desire to play against encouraging younger blood. "I bowl a bit meself," said Fred. The accent and the build was uncanny – it was as if the great Trueman himself had spoken. "But nothing subtle like spin – just knock the middle bloody stump out if I can."

We were joined by a newcomer, about ten years younger, who ordered a pint for himself, and a lager for his female companion. His lady smiled pleasantly towards us, as she seated herself at a small table a few yards away. The newcomer grinned towards me, as he indicated Fred with his thumb. "He used to knock out a few middle stumps, but it's mainly the dentist knocking his out these days." The accent this time definitely German.

"What do 'ya mean, you young loon – I'm still ten mile an hour faster than thee, aye, and always will be."

"No, Fred, not so – even being kind I would say no more than medium pace these days."

Fred had difficulty containing himself. "Call theeself a captain? Tha's should encourage bloody players – not put 'em down! Bloomin' German. Don't forget, it were Charlie Crowther and me who taught thee t' bloody game." But somehow it came through that the harsh words were spoken all in fun, and there was affection between the two men.

"But to be sure, Kurt, don't I still have trouble stopping Fred's balls – those that aren't clouted into the outfield, that is?" from Dave.

"To Sancho's heart attack," the newcomer raised his freshly pulled pint in the direction of the cup, and for the first time I spotted a colour photograph of a figure attired in white, situated also in a place of honour just below the cup. But this poor chap's whites were not Cricketers, they were bandages covering him from head to toe, making him look for all the world like an Egyptian mummy.

"Dave, thanks for the compliment, but tha's such a rotten wicket-keeper, tha's 'ave trouble stopping an underarm tennis ball these days – tha's more like Godfrey the 'Good Heavens' of Dad's Army than Godfrey the great Evans of Kent."

"Who's this, please – we have not been introduced?" the man with the German accent asked, indicating me.

"A cyder walloper, come to Ibiza to see 'ow it's done," grinned Fred, without malice. "Known as Trev."

The newcomer shook my proffered hand. "Kurt," he said, "very pleased to meet you – at least you look more refined than this uncouth Englishman and the wild Irishman." Kurt had obviously learnt the English humour of being rude to good friends.

I indicated the cup and the photograph. "So what's the story about Sancho?" I asked.

Fred laughed. "We owe t'cup to Sancho, an' no mistake," he said.

"Tha's reet there," confirmed Charlie, the Landlord, as he joined us for a social drink in his own bar. "Pint, please, Ernie," he asked the barman, before continuing, "and I'll tell thee summat else – Sancho Alonzo has been a wonderful servant of this club since he, I and Kurt first discussed forming it. It were he who did the spade work – literally – to make the wicket and the ground, although he had a bit of help from 'is Dad's JCB, I'll admit."

The others nodded wisely. "Reet enough," commented Fred, sagely, "best servant this club's ever 'ad."

It was so like listening to Trueman talking to Close, it was uncanny. I urged Fred to continue with the tale, but in truth he needed little prompting.

"It were last match of season," he explained. "We'd 'ad a good run, and only needed a draw to win cup."

"But it were that snooty lot from Andalucia . . . ."

"Puissance horses and fighting bulls," Kurt explained, or at least thought he did.

"Can I carry on?" said Fred.

"Anyway, weren't they only lying second, so we knew we were in for a terrible hard game, b'Jesus – they could still take the championship?" joined in Dave.

Fred glared at him, before continuing. "We batted first and 'ad a fair knock, at least *some* of us did," he added meaningfully, looking in Kurt's direction.

"I can't score a hundred every time I bat," Kurt retorted, as he left us for a few seconds to deliver his lady's lager.

"We set 'em 175 to draw, 176 if they wanted t'cup," Fred continued.

"And to be sure – didn't the beggars nearly get 'em?" cut in Dave. "Four overs to go, they only needed twenty-one, and weren't the batsmen hitting us all over the place?"

"But the storm clouds were gathering, and it was getting ready to rain cats and little doggies," Kurt explained, as he rejoined us. "It was then that Pete Barlow twisted his ankle and had to go off. It looked worse than ever, because our twelfth man was what I think you call a real joker."

"Who was that?" I asked.

"Why Sancho, of course, 'oo else does tha' think we're talking about?" from Fred.

I was going to explain that I had no way of knowing that Sancho was their twelfth man – the way they'd spoken of him I thought he was their opening bat – but I was too intrigued by the story to bother.

"It got worse after that, they wanted just nine off the last two overs, but the first drops of rain were falling. Then Sancho set off chasing a ball to try to save a two . . . ."

"When 'ee falls to the ground clutching 'is chest," joined in Fred. "Now back home, Pete Barlow used to be in the St. John's, and 'ee 'obbled out of the pavilion to look at Sancho, and proclaimed in a loud voice that 'ee were 'aving a 'eart attack – 'ee mustn't be moved until the ambulance arrived."

"So your man Pete limped off to his house – he lives only a few yards away down a side-track, or should that be metres in Ibiza? Anyway, Pete hobbled away saying he was going to phone for an ambulance," explained Dave.

"But before 'ee got back, the rain were coming down in sheets," continued Fred, "it were obviously in for night, the umpires 'ad 'ad enough, and declared rain stopped play – drawn game, as per the rules."

"So we won the cup," grinned Kurt.

"But the bandages," I asked, "what about the bandages – you don't get bandaged like that for a heart attack?"

"Well Pete came back driving the old van 'ee uses for the 'ippy markets – a Ford Transit," Fred explained. "He said there'd been a big accident on the Ibiza to San An road, and the ambulance would be at least an hour – we'd have to take Sancho to the hospital at C'an Misses ourselves. So we shoved Sancho in the back, and pretending it were like a real emergency, Pete sets off like a rocket in the old Trannie."

"But your man lost it leaving the ground, and the van rolled over – oh a terrible mess it was, to be sure," Dave interjected.

"And so were Sancho, rolling round in t'back," from Fred. They laughed, though for the life of me I couldn't think what was funny about a poor man who was having a heart attack bouncing round in the back of a van as it turned over.

Then I recalled Fred's previous words, 'pretending it were like a real emergency'. "And the heart attack?" I asked, suspecting I knew already.

At this all three burst out laughing. "There never were a 'eart attack, lad," Fred boomed, "that's why we couldn't have a real ambulance. Pete and Sancho 'ad cooked it up between themselves – they're both into amateur dramatics, and thought it might just slow things down 'til the rain came along. But 'ee finished up in 'ospital anyway."

"Sure didn't the poor fellah fracture his skull and break an arm, a leg and three ribs?" added Dave.

At this the three grown men and their host literally fell about laughing, so much so that I thought the one called Fred was in danger of having a heart attack himself. I thought of my own side, back in my village in Somerset. Sure, we indulge in a bit of gamesmanship from time to time, but would we stoop to such a tactic? Surely it wasn't, 'er, cricket? I'd like to think we wouldn't, but the more I imagined Sancho falling on the ground, giving his all for the club in the best way he could, the more I became uncertain.

Just then, a figure who could only be Sancho or the aforesaid Egyptian mummy hobbled into the bar, striving manfully to master a couple of old wooden crutches as he made his way to a group sitting at a small table by the empty fireplace. Obviously very popular, everyone in the room shouted a greeting to him, "Hola, Sancho," or "Buenas noches, mate, if it's thee in there," and other such welcoming calls.

"At least he'll be certain of a place next season!" I commented.

Fred and Dave and Kurt fell silent. "I don't know about that," said Kurt, "he might make twelfth man occasionally if he's lucky, but he's not really first team material. Never has been."

"Not got the big match temperament, tha' see," explained Fred.

"Never in a million years," confirmed Dave, as the three shook their heads in agreement, "never in a million years."

By then it was my turn to buy the beers. Somehow I felt honoured to join them in their usual toast, sparing a sympathetic though admiring glance for the mummified figure sitting on the other side of the room.

For much as I loved the game, I too was not first team material, you see, and never had been.

Never in a million years.

Once at San Vicente

Though blonde-haired, blue-eyed and pretty, with a naturally extrovert personality, Heike Schmidt had not enjoyed her teenage years. Her country, militant, successful and affluent had endured the most violent war in history, finally fought out on its own territory. Her own family's fortunes had in six short years commencing around the time of her thirteenth birthday, passed from decidedly affluent through belt-tightening to impoverished and homeless. Her father dead, killed 'somewhere in France' fighting for the fatherland, and she and her mother grateful to their country's vanquishers for the provision of a tent and basic food rations.

Chuck Williams, on the other hand, the crew-cut, tall and handsome 'all-American boy', had thoroughly enjoyed his teenage years – indeed, he had enjoyed all his life, raised as he was in the 'Land of the Free'. In the United States of America everyone was rich, at least compared to the rest of the world, but his family was rich above the average, rich with New England 'old money', and an indulgent father who was now a three-star general in the army of occupation in Germany.

General Patrick D. Williams had used his rank and wealth to bring his wife and son to Europe to see the suffering which was the reality of the aftermath of World War II. "And it will round off the boy's education perfectly – make him appreciate what he has back home," he'd confided in his Boston-Irish accent to his pleasant but strait-laced wife, Charlotte.

What he hadn't bargained for was good ol' Chuck, or rather good young Chuck, falling in love with a German girl, a one-hundred-percent dyed-in-the-wool impoverished fräulein – although he had to admit she was kinda cute. "Guess the boy's got good taste – like his pa," he grinned to Charlotte, when it finally became apparent to him that the couple had fallen deeply in love.

So when Chuck had asked if it would be okay for he and Heike to take off somewhere different, whilst he'd huffed and puffed a little, he hadn't really raised any objections. For after all, General Williams was armed with good ol' 'New England' common sense, and knew that a prolonged break with only themselves for company would either prove or break the youngsters' relationship.

"I've seen the good life back home, and God knows, pa, Heike's seen the bad one here – we thought we'd try somewhere backward, where nothin' ever happens. Sorta drop out for a while."

"Like where?"

"We were thinking of the Balearics – they're a group of islands where farmers and fishermen scrape a simple living under General Franco."

"He's a fascist, son."

"Yeah, Dad, but a benign one – and he sure helped plenty of British and American airmen who made it out of France into Spain to get back to Limeyland. He'd no time for Adolf, that's for sure."

"Okay son, but always carry your American passport with you."

"And Heike?"

The General thought for a while, and stroked his ample chin in contemplation before answering. "Guess she'll need one as well – okay, I'll fix it. But when you get back to the States, you start work – put those science qualifications to use, you hear?"

"Sure, Dad."

* * * * *

That conversation had taken place in May 1947, and just seven weeks later, on July Fourth, Chuck realised he was in love twice over. There was still, of course, Heike, but he had also fallen in love with the simple undeveloped island of Ibiza.

They watched a man, whose leathery face was burnt brown by salt and the Mediterranean sun, making him appear older than his actual years, beach his ancient rowboat, and helped him pull it onto the foreshore. The man was pleased when they bought two of his fish, over-size 'sardinas', and departed happily to show his wife his good fortune.

Hand in hand, and wrapped in happiness, the boy and his girl strolled along the now deserted beach at San Vicente. They'd first spotted the bay with awe, as they looked down the sheer drop from the precarious hillside dirt and gravel track along which they'd ridden from San Carlos on the pre-war Triumph motor-bike Chuck had bought in San Antonio. On an impulse, they decided to light a fire from pine twigs and brushwood, and grill the fish for lunch, washed down with San Miguel beers. With this simple meal they planned to celebrate the anniversary of Chuck's homeland gaining its independence from the Brits.

The dry twigs burst instantly into life, and soon the little fire was burning away merrily. It would need time to reduce to glowing embers for successful grilling, and, lifting her eyes from the flames, Heike looked longingly to the blue sea a few yards away, before her eyes turned higher to take in her surroundings. Quite simply she thought San Vicente to be the most beautiful place on earth – she herself had been to very few, but knew it just had to be. On both sides the sea was boarded by steeply rising cliffs – the one on the right with a background of pine trees, whilst its opposite neighbour was more rugged and bare. The sweep of the beach with its golden sands, fronted by the crystal clear blue of the Mediterranean lapping gently on the foreshore, and inland the hard-worked terraced fields, completed her idea of paradise – and incredibly they had it all to themselves.

They had taken to wearing what they called biblical type clothes – simple light one piece gowns which the German girl had created by sowing together some sarongs. Fifteen years later they would have been known as hippies, flower-power people, typical of a generation, but for now they were, unknowingly, merely forerunners of a new ideal.

Whilst the flames did their work, the young couple threw off their garments, and hand in hand ran into the sea for a refreshing dip. For about ten minutes, they frolicked and splashed each other before running back up the beach to cook their lunch.

The skills of summer camp not forgotten, Chuck speared the two fish on long sticks, which he stuck into the sand so the fish smoked and cooked gently over the now gently glowing fire. Contented, he lay back on the beach and shaded his eyes against the sun. High overhead, a flash of light appeared, moving quickly from west to east. Certainly not a shooting star, and long before the age of satellites, he was puzzled as to its origin. He laughed as Heike waved to it, "You think the Martians are coming, Honey?"

Then he too jumped to his feet, and laughing for love and happy, the two of them jumped up and down on the beach waving frantically at the flash of light – behaving nonsensically, as young people in love always have and always will.

"At least if they *are* Martians they will know that earth people are friendly!" Heike said, her English improving by the day, and, still laughing and waving, the two lovers again lay back onto the sandy beach.

* * * * *

As the rather extreme buffeting eased, the diminutive pilot switched off his auto-systems, preferring to take the controls himself for the last part of the long journey. He switched on his heat scanner, and the VDU picked out a small source on a little island. Selecting 'max zoom', he grinned as a young boy and girl appeared. Bizarrely, they were waving to him, and, equally bizarrely, he waved back.

Flying eastwards, he had passed over the big square peninsular and was heading now towards the south of the land he would always think of as a long boot, his beloved Mediterranean spread out before him. Gradually he lost height, and, approaching the island of cyprus fruit, where some thought mankind's sojourn on earth had begun, banked right to head south.

Soon, he would be home, landing alongside the great river which rose as a multitude of tiny streams far to the south. A buzz of excitement spread through him, coupled with the warm glow all travellers feel when they return home. His skilled hands eased back the giant engines, and his rate of descent increased.

But an icy fear replaced the warm glow, as his long-range sight detected a new river, cut through to the Gulf and the mighty ocean in the south. He had wondered whether the work on the pyramid would be well advanced, but saw to his astonishment not only that it was completed, but had been joined by two more, even larger ones. Descending lower, he spotted that the much talked about figure of a man's head on a lion's body had been actually constructed, and in the distance a new lake had grown.

He was returning home, yes, but this was not the home he knew. The friends to whom he had bidden goodbye with such sadness must have long since departed, for the works at which he looked had surely taken many generations to construct. And with this knowledge, the reality hit him. The new technique of placing people into a frozen suspended life-form, which had enabled his interstellar voyage to be launched with at least a possibility of success, was just that – a new technique, not an exact science. How long *had* he been away? He looked down at his little dark wrinkled body. He looked the same as his crew members, but were they the same as when they lifted off from earth? Had they aged, changed, but so slowly that none of them had noticed?

The icy fear increased, as he physically shivered with the realisation he could be over a hundred years old. If he proceeded with his landing, he might even be amongst enemies. With the ability for quick and cautious decisions which had first gained him his command, he flipped the intercom and spoke to his number two, the wonderful navigator who had nursed their craft with its sometimes ailing equipment through so many billions of leagues, his voice clipped, high-pitched, but nevertheless authoritive. "Rah, we are diverting to our friends at Takun. I have a concern about what has happened in our country, and wish to talk first with our Mayan cousins – I speak their Yucatec language."

"Certainly, Tac." A short pause, then, "It will take just under a twenty-fourth of an earth revolution."

The power of the engines pushed Tac back into his seat, as his craft headed back to the stratosphere for its short journey across the deserts of his own continent and then the calmer of the three big oceans to the land beyond.

* * * * *

On the beach at San Vicente, Heike and Chuck broke open their beers, and clinked bottles as Heike proposed a toast.

"To the Martians – we greet you in friendship!" and laughing, they slurped down the San Miguel.

"But seriously, Honey, I studied astro-physics on my college science course, and I'm damned if I know what it was. It flew far faster than any aircraft, yet it wasn't crashing to earth like it was an asteroid or meteor."

He moved to add a little wood to the fringes of the fire, ready to push it into position beneath the fish when it became hot ash. But a knife pushed into the fish told him that the extra wood might not be needed – the fish was nearly ready, and the last thing he wanted was for it to become so tender it fell off the spears into the ashes.

"Reckon we're nearly there, Honey," he said, "it sure smells good."

Heike smiled at him, and his heart missed a beat at her loveliness. Over the past weeks she had put on weight – nice weight, proper weight, to round out the wonderful curves that God had intended for her, but which her semi-starvation life in war-torn Germany had hitherto denied her.

"Can we come and live here, Chuck?" she asked him, "It's so lovely."

Chuck looked up at the cliffs which rose either side of them, the blue of the crystal clear sea matched by the blue of the sky, and grinned. "I guess that'd be kinda difficult, Honey – I'm going to be a scientist specialising in astro-physics, and whilst I might be wrong, I shouldn't think there's many vacancies for that sorta thing in San Vicente."

He reached forward to pull the fish kebab spears out of the sand, and passed one over to her, but as he did so, noting how crestfallen she looked, added, "Though we can keep in touch with the place, holidays and the like, then maybe one day, when I'm done with work, we'll make it back here . . . ."

* * * * *

Tac commenced his descent in the land to the north of the Mayas, intending a long glide as he turned left, southwards into the lands of his friends. But suddenly something felt wrong, his craft started bucking and shaking with a greater violence than could be caused by air turbulence, more akin to re-entry buffeting. But they were well down from the stratosphere, this should not be. He switched back to auto-pilot, considering it may be his own incompetence, long-unused to earth atmosphere, but the buffeting grew worse, and he was forced to return to manual control.

It was then, in the final moments of his great craft, that Tac showed his greatest skill, as he alternately fought and nursed it down towards the earth, near to what he took to be a small city alongside a river. The marvellous spacecraft, which had served them so wondrously well, was finally dying of old age as the pressures of its originating planet took their toll.

Tac held the controls sometimes lightly, sometimes firmly – he could surely not have travelled so far to fail in the last moments? All the way down, he held on, fighting, coaxing his craft, begging his crew to take up crash positions.

The landing when it came was even harder than he feared, the impact killing all on board, except, miraculously, himself. Shaken, dizzy, and with at least one limb broken, he dragged himself from the spacecraft. At last, in a manner of speaking, he had come home, and he fell upon the earth and wept.

He was not to know that nearly seven thousand earth years had elapsed since he had lifted off from the country now called Egypt, that the current year was called by a new system of counting 1947, or that he was about to pass into history in what would become known as 'The Roswell Incident'. He, who had so much to relate to the unthinking ones who now advanced towards him, with their guns at the ready . . . .

* * * * *

The following year, 1948, Chuck married Heike, and, putting his science training to good use as his father had bidden him, went to work first for Uncle Sam's Air Force, then for the embryonic NASA, where he played a key role in the moon landing program, and later in the initial planning for the space shuttle.

Three kids and a brilliant career behind him, in 1989 at the age of sixty-five, Chuck retired, and he and Heike achieved their life's ambition to live on Ibiza, an island with which as they promised themselves, they had never lost contact. They had indeed 'made it back', and moving now into old age, they still live there today, in a spacious villa in the hills behind San Vicente, where they'd laughed and cooked the fish all those years ago.

But often he lapses into deep thought, his scientific training merging with a memory, as he recalls the time, even the exact date, and remembers vividly the flash of light. In his mind, he puts two and two together, probably to umpteen places of decimals, and wonders. But for all his high level NASA security clearance, that clearance was never quite high enough for him to investigate the secret files on Roswell.

So he wonders and has his thoughts, but he will never know for certain what it was that he and Heike saw on that long ago day, on 4th July, 1947 . . . .

Spitfire!

Captain Jennifer Morton took pride in the landing as the Cessna Citation Excel executive jet kissed the runway – so gently that her VIP passengers would not be sure when they actually stopped flying and started high speed taxiing. Except of course for one, who however gentle the touch of the wheels on the tarmac, would feel it through the seat of his pants. He was the reason that good though she was, Jennifer always strived that little bit harder, so that her piloting skills showed continuous improvement. For she also took pride in the fact that it was he who'd actually appointed her, chosen her from over fifty applicants on the basis of her flying abilities, giving the lie to those who believed that his generation of men were all cut and dried male chauvinists.

The reverse thrust braking quickly slowed the private jet, and after a brief scan of the Honeywell and Primus CRT displays, she was able to take the first exit from the runway, to follow the little Seat airport control van to the executive aircraft parking area at 'Aeropuerto de Eivissa', the local name for Ibiza Airport, where she eased the Cessna into its allotted place amongst numerous other executive jets, bright yellow fire-fighting planes, helicopters and light aircraft, and braked gently to a stop. She commenced the closedown of the Pratt + Witney PW545A Turbofan engines, and pressed the button to open the bottom hinged passenger door – a clever device which was neatly curved on the outside to match the contours of the aircraft body shape, but as it folded outwards revealed a set of steps complete with handrail, to facilitate the exit of the important passengers.

A tall distinguished white-haired man wearing an expensive lightweight tropical suit was the first out. He was in his early sixties, and blinked in the Ibiza sun, as, unhappily, he looked across the parking apron to a World War II Spitfire. The aircraft was complete with original camouflage markings and RAF roundels, and sat glistening in the sunlight, its long proud nose pointing aggressively towards the sky where it believed it belonged, though revealing none of its secret – the great Rolls Royce Merlin engine beneath its nacelles.

But his Honour Judge Geoffrey Parker was not happy to be in Ibiza, or to see the Spitfire, however resplendent it looked.

Two other men followed, one middle-aged with long red hair, but a shortish body which was running slightly to fat, dressed casually in a T-shirt and jeans, the other standing nearly two metres, slim and dressed more formally with a jacket and tie.

They were followed by a fourth, of medium build and considerably older, though he carried his eighty plus years of age well as he bounced down the steps.

"See the old kite's there," he said chirpily.

"You've still time to call it off, Jack," Judge Parker said pointedly.

"If you did that, Jack," added the red-headed man, his accent, though not broad, nevertheless indicating his Yorkshire origins, "we could have a few pleasant days here at your expense, with no harm coming to anyone."

Jack Lee guffawed. "No harm's going to come to me, I can tell you, either in body or pocket. Why don't you address your comments to that silly young bugger sulking in the back of the plane?" The speaker's voice confident, not cultured, but certainly well-educated despite the chosen phraseology.

Next, the uniformed Captain Jennifer Morton descended from the aircraft, followed by a tousle-haired gangling slightly unco-ordinated youth, whose clothes looked as if they came from a second hand shop.

Judge Parker looked at the young man, for whom he had a considerable affection, and shook his head in despair. How on earth had it come to this stage? No wonder Brenda, Freddie's mother and Jack's wife, would have nothing to do with it, and was instead safely back in England, though no doubt worried silly at the stupidity of both her husband and son. Was it really three days ago the whole wretched affair had started – it was still so vivid in his mind?

.....They were at the golf club.....he remembered looking disapprovingly over the top of his half-frame glasses – he was simply not going to put up with the row any longer. Certainly the tall, slim and debonair Peter Montague, having recently taken silk, should know better. A damned sight better. Purposefully, he'd crossed the room to the participants.

"I say, you chaps, would you turn down the volume – this is the golf club, and not an East End boozer, you know," he'd said quietly, not used to raising his cultured voice to make his opinions known.

Peter Montague looked at his feet, embarrassed, shuffled them. He was, after all, a new silk, and knew full well that Geoffrey was a senior High Court judge. Also, of course, that Geoffrey was right – they were making too much noise.

And not pleasant noise, either, for it was clearly a particularly bad-tempered row.

But the youngest member of the group, armed with both the bravado of youth and the confidence inherent with the knowledge that his father was the wealthiest man in the district, if not the county, was not so easily over-awed, nor had he turned down the volume in his response. "Sorry Geoffrey, but this bloody Father of mine's gone too far this time – he's called me a coward."

"I did not call you a coward, Freddie, what I said was that when I was your age, instead of wasting my life away flying first class at my father's expense to the world's sunspots, I was flying Spitfires to defend my country, and you would have neither the ability or guts to do that." The speaker, a short stocky man in his early eighties, exuded power; a man to cross only with care and an understanding of the likely consequences – as those who had met him in aerial combat would have vouched. But the power came not just from his character, but from his wealth, for Jack Lee was the Lee of JLH Plc – Jack Lee Holdings, an empire he had built from a post war second-hand car lot to a conglomerate encompassing motor dealers, aircraft leasing and computers.

"But if I have neither the ability or, what was your word – 'guts' – then you're calling me a coward, right?"

The Judge remembered clearly that Jack Lee had then audibly sighed before replying. "Freddie, I didn't pick this fight, you did. But if you insist, then yes, you are a coward – for you certainly never seem to have the bottle to go out into the world and actually do or achieve anything. And to clarify, since you have never demonstrated any mechanical aptitude whatsoever, I believe also you do not have the ability to fly a Spitfire, or the co-ordination to learn how to fly it."

The other three members of the group all now looked embarrassed. "Steady on, Jack," Judge Parker recalled saying, trying to pour oil on troubled waters.

"I think you're too hard on the lad, he's a bit wild, Jack, but I bet you were at his age – or would have been if you weren't fighting a war." The red-haired Michael Measbamp was not only the Lee's family doctor, but despite the age difference, Jack Lee's closest friend.

"I bet I could!" Freddie Lee had almost screamed the words.

"Could what, Freddie?"

"Fly your bloody Spitfire!"

"Now you're being silly, Freddie," Peter Montague had interjected in his courtroom dominating barrister's voice. "Why don't you both shake hands and let the whole thing drop?"

But the madness was upon the twenty-one year old. "Well, is it a bet or not? Will you let me show you how easy it is to fly one of those old kites? Or daren't you let me prove it in that ancient museum piece you have?"

A rich man's whim, Jack Lee did indeed own his own Spitfire. Suddenly, his face had showed anger. "You really are a young idiot, Freddie. Yes, I'll bet you. I'll bet that you can't fly the Spitfire across the channel to France – you're my son, and I love you for that, but you're gutless and stupid, without the ability to safely drive a lawnmower, let alone fly an aircraft."

"Dad, I've told you you're going senile – you left the Spitfire in Ibiza to have the magnetos fixed – remember you were supposed to be flying it round Europe? Though I reckon you just found the whole thing too much."

"Don't be so childish, Freddie. Alright, so it's in Ibiza, and with all my work trying to control the company, I forgot where one of our assets is." He'd then paused, as a thought occurred to him, "You could still for instance fly it from Ibiza to Palma Mallorca. And to show you how childish you're being, I'll give you odds."

"Odds?" Freddie had responded craftily, "odds say of a hundred to one?"

"I'll give you odds of five hundred to one, if you like – you simply couldn't do it! Nor anything else that requires a bit of intelligence and bottle."

Freddie Lee's face had gone white, his father had called his bluff, and in front of witnesses.

"Well?" barked the older man.

Freddie appeared to have difficulty speaking, as if his throat were dry. "Well." A pause, then, "Well, I accept! I'll lay down that £100,000 that Aunt Marj gave me last birthday. And you will lay down . . . ."

"Fifty million, Jack? I think the young bugger's called your bluff!" The Judge could swear with the best of them when he had to, and had so desperately wanted to bring this unfortunate family row to an end.

But, "I accept," Jack Lee had replied quietly. "My fifty million to your hundred thousand that within the next seven days you don't fly Juliet Lima from Ibiza to Mallorca – weather permitting, of course. Furthermore, I'll place the company jet at your disposal for transport to Ibiza, and cover all your expenses – so you can't use that as an excuse."

* * * * *

Now they had actually landed in Ibiza, the group of four friends, together with Captain Morton and the tousle-haired Freddie Lee, were smoothly processed through Spanish entry procedures, and as they exited the front of the airport, a spotless cream stretch Cadillac glided to a halt in front of them. They were welcomed by a grinning chauffeur, "Buenos días, Señor Lee, Señors y Señora – ees good to see you!" The stockily built speaker showed a mouthful of gold teeth as his face split into a beaming smile.

Although he'd been given two full uniforms each comprising blazer and trousers, shirt, tie, peaked cap with the 'JLH' monogram, and even shoes, the Spaniard could never remember to wear all of them at the same time, thus today the resplendent shirt, blazer, tie and cap were complemented below the waist by jeans and sandals.

Nevertheless, his employer smiled indulgently at an employee he greatly liked. "Thanks, Pedro, good to see you as well." Jack Lee got into the back of the Cadillac, followed by the others, and the car pulled away, bound for the family's villa in the hills above San Mateo. From touchdown to leaving the airport had taken only fourteen minutes, part of the efficiency money can buy.

As they slipped silently onto the country roads of Ibiza for the short journey, the atmosphere in the big car was subdued, as far from a pleasant ambience as an atmosphere can be. But the judge, who was on his first visit to the island, noted with surprise the cleanliness, the pine woods and several pretty views as they climbed up into the hills en route.

The gates to the Lee's property swung open automatically, controlled by an unseen transmitter in the Cadillac, and three hundred metres later the big car glided to a halt by the main entrance to the house.

Jack Lee had imported some ideas from Australia to build his 'typical Ibiza villa' – for there is of course no such thing. But verandas on three sides allowed outside dining and relaxing in the shade as one followed the sun round throughout the day. The indoor swimming pool flowed over a waterfall into an outdoor pool, although not of course in the winter months. And surrounding it all, the natural Mediterranean style twelve hectares of grounds had been laid out by the Ibicencan specialists Noah's Gardens, with the line where garden finished and pine woods started intentionally blurred in a most skilful way.

Inside there was more Australian influence, for food and cooking and entertaining all played an important part in the Lee family's lifestyle. Thus the large kitchen was open plan to the dining area, which was also open plan to what the Aussies would call a 'family room' – an informal lounge area. And whilst there was a formal area, it was used mainly for business discussions, and rarely on a social occasion. There were only five bedrooms, although each enjoyed an en-suite bathroom, and, the villa being a bungalow, private access onto a terrace.

In the grounds were three other dwellings, each more the size of a French Gîte, and in the largest of these Pedro lived with his wife, Maria, a tubby lady who was both a brilliant cook and happy housekeeper.

On arrival, the visitors were shown to their rooms to unpack, following which they spent the afternoon lazing around the ornate pool, splashing under its waterfall, and doing their best to enjoy themselves.

But in truth, joy there was not.

In the evening, Maria produced a wonderful 'paletilla de cordero al horno' – shoulder of lamb cooked Ibicencan style in a traditional oven – which was served to the group by her husband, Pedro, who functioned as butler and gardener as well as chauffeur to the Lee family. Also as drinking companion to Jack Lee, if he happened to be in the mood and needed one.

About eleven o'clock Judge Parker suggested they all turn in, "A good night's sleep might put some sense into a couple of heads," he suggested determinedly.

But Freddie Lee laughed. "Not me, Geoffrey – I'm off clubbing to Amnesia. Don't worry – I don't need a lot of sleep, and a few cocktails will set me up right for tomorrow. Besides," he added with a wink, "I might get lucky – I could just make some girl's night, or even two girls' nights if I get really lucky."

"You know, Freddie," said Michael Meashamp, "Reluctantly, I think your Dad's probably right – you are a bloody fool. As they say, trust me mate, I'm a doctor, and I'm telling you, with what you have ahead of you tomorrow, you shouldn't drink at all, and you really do need your sleep."

But he was talking to a closing door, as Freddie exited the room. Shortly followed by the sound of a powerful car engine, and then squealing tyres on tarmac, as Freddie disappeared off to the nightspots of Ibiza.

"Hell, Jack, I don't like this, don't like it at all," from Peter Montague, "but I'm turning in." Saying which, he left the room, shortly followed by the others.

* * * * *

Early the following day, the Cadillac delivered the little group to the airport, and they received clearance to stroll across to the immaculate Spitfire, Juliet Lima, with the morning sunlight glinting off her wings.

Jack Lee scanned the skies with a practised eye. The weather was superb, of a brand usually pronounced CAV-OK by aviators – a symptom of high pressure, associated with 'nil' weather and good visibility – truly a pilot's dream.

He grinned to his companions, all witnesses to the bet, then turned to his son, "Freddie, if you apologise, we can call it off – we both got a bit hot and bothered at the golf club. What do you say, son?"

But his son responded to the olive branch only with anger. "I will *not* apologise! It's *you* who should apologise to me. The bet was that I can't today fly that ancient kite to Mallorca, weather permitting. Does the weather permit?"

His father looked briefly at the ground, and then at his son. There was to be no turning back. With a look of deep sadness, and a sudden determination, he nodded his head.

"The weather permits."

* * * * *

To be fair, Freddie tried to make the best of it. He swaggered confidently over to the Spitfire, climbed onto the wing, swung his leg over the rail and slipped into the cockpit. Next he started flipping switches on and off in an apparently random sort of fashion, before putting on a headset. But what happened then did surprise most of the onlookers, for with a groan from the heavy starter motor, the prop started to turn. Then, with a crackle of power, the mighty Derby built 27-litre Rolls Royce Merlin engine, which had played such a major roll in the battle of the few, roared into life. Only Jack Lee looked unsurprised, unperturbed.

After a few minutes, the ancient aeroplane eased into forward motion, and, zig-zagging from side to side, taxied towards the runway. Confidently, Jack Lee leaned towards Judge Parker. "He's only bluffing – I've just got to force him to a complete climb-down. I taught him how to start her and taxi her when he was fifteen years old, but not to fly her – he'll get out to the runway, then find some excuse to abort the flight, such as a dodgy oil pressure. Then he'll taxi back to us to call the bet off – wait and see."

"You didn't teach him very well, Jack," the Judge replied, "he's all over the place!"

The ex-fighter ace laughed. "No, he's doing that right. When you sit in a tail-dragger – an aircraft with a wheel at the tail instead of the nose – you can't see a damned thing forwards, so you have to zig-zag to see where you're going."

The Spitfire had reached the runway, lined up, and stopped. The engine revs screamed higher, then seemed to cough, then reduce. Then it started to taxi back, Jack Lee obviously having difficulty restraining his laughter. "What did I tell you?" he asked the Judge. "I *knew* he'd do that! Now for a bit of fun – he refused my peace offering to let him off with a simple apology, so I'll make the little sod crawl. It'll do him good in the long run."

The aircraft stopped in front of them, and the young man at the controls called them over. "I say," he shouted over the noise of the engine, "the right mag's a bit dodgy – are you sure you got it fixed? I could still go of course, but if you want to call the bet off, Dad, I'll agree."

Expectantly, the onlookers turned to the millionaire – would he let his son off the hook? Although he had loved her dearly, Jack Lee's first wife had given him no children, and after her death he was into his early sixties when God had finally answered his prayers and given him the son he always craved. Freddie, his gift from God and his lovely Angela – Freddie, who now looked down at him from the cockpit.

But despite that, he obviously wanted a greater humiliation of his son, and his reply showed the ruthless side of his nature, "There was only one condition to the bet, Freddie, and that was weather permitting. Juliet Lima is in tip-top condition, there's nothing wrong with the mags, whatever you say, and the weather does permit. Close her down and get out – you've lost the bet."

His son's face contorted with hate. "We'll see about that!" he screamed, and instead slammed the canopy shut.

This time he taxied out rather more quickly and entered the runway without pausing. Then, with a roar from the Merlin, the Spitfire accelerated. After a few hundred yards, the tail came up, a few hundred more and somewhat unsteadily the wonderful old machine eased off the ground. It was then that the engine seemed to hiccup, and the aircraft bounced crazily back onto the runway. But again the engine roared, and then she was airborne. Rolling frantically from side to side and climbing oh so slowly, her wheels just missed the landing approach lights, as she gradually climbed away over the Mediterranean, and turned to the left.

Northwards towards Mallorca.

* * * * *

It was fully half a minute before anyone spoke. "Bloody hell!" from Michael Meashamp.

"Oh, God, Jack, what have you done?" from Montague, the new silk.

"As good as killed his only son," from His Honour, Judge Parker. "I told you the whole thing had got out of hand – Jack Lee, you're a damned fool."

The man himself was lost for words, his face depicting the shock they all felt. A discreet cough from someone at his side brought him back to earth. “We could follow in the Citation, sir.” The speaker was of course Jennifer Morton.

“Yes, we’ll do that, Jennifer. Let’s follow.” But the words seemed to come from a man in a daze, not the Jack Lee they all knew.

Captain Morton, ever efficient, ran to the aircraft. “Come on, everyone, quickly now!” She pressed a button to open the cabin door to enable her boss and friends to enter. Once the ground crew had confirmed her requested urgent clearance for start-up, first one, then the other engine screamed into life, and shortly afterwards the small jet eased forwards, the engine checks being completed whilst taxiing to the runway.

Cleared to line-up and take-off, they were airborne just eighteen minutes after the Spitfire’s departure, climbing away at an impressive 3,790 feet per minute following a ground roll of just over a thousand metres. As they did so, it was the Judge who had the courage to speak the words they all feared, “Now, everyone, keep a good look-out in the sea for any wreckage on the way.”

“On the way?” from Michael Meashamp, “if he hasn’t crashed already, he’s probably well en-route for Algiers.”

“For God’s sake, Michael!” groaned Peter Montague. “Don’t talk like that. He did seem to set off to the north, so as Geoffrey said, can everyone keep their eyes peeled for signs of wreckage.”

Jack Lee slumped in his seat, refusing to look out, speaking to no-one.

At the controls, Captain Morton declined all air traffic control’s requests to climb to twenty-five thousand feet, and instead held a height of five thousand and a speed of three hundred knots to give them the best chance of a sighting.

But they saw no wreckage, and ‘el Aeropuerto de Palma Mallorca’ came up on the horizon only thirty minutes later. Captain Morton requested and was granted a straight-in approach at the Cessna’s preferred 118-knot approach speed, although quite why they were landing there she wasn’t certain

– they'd obviously missed the wreckage of the Spitfire, which was no doubt way off course anyway.

Then as she touched down, she saw it, they all saw it. Parked proudly and defiantly on the apron in front of the control tower stood Spitfire Juliet Lima.

"Jack, the young bugger's made it!" from the Judge. "You lost the bet."

A few minutes later, and the two generations of the Lee family faced each other. The one with a big grin, the other a face like thunder. The father angrily stabbed out his finger towards the son. "I want a word with you, in private." Saying which, he propelled the young man towards a door marked "Privado – Pilotos ".

"Now Jack," Michael Meashamp called after them, "it might be a lot of money, but you still have your son. You lost the bet, so be a good loser!"

But his last words were lost as the two men entered the Pilots' room. As soon as the door closed behind them, their attitude to each other changed, for, with a big grin, Freddie threw his arms round his fathers neck. "Oh Dad, I love you! It worked like a dream, just as you planned."

His father could hardly speak for laughing. "Fifty million passed on to you free of inheritance tax, son, and all witnessed by people of impeccable standing."

"Like you said Dad, Uncle Hank in Florida was a great instructor – although his Spitfire's not quite as tidy as yours – certainly in the victory roll I just did over the Med."

Jack Lee grinned. His American buddy, Hank Smedley, had been a fellow Flight Lieutenant in his war-time squadron, and in that terrible struggle between nations had also been the first to congratulate him when he'd been promoted Squadron Leader. Since the war, they had both become millionaires, and both, by coincidence, acquired their personal mementoes of those long ago days, with Hank using his as the flagship of his Florida based flying school.

"And the engine cough when you bounced – that really was the magnetos?"

"Sure Dad, a little icing on the cake courtesy of Uncle Hank. At the moment she became airborne, I flipped off one of the mags – though only for a second!"

This time Jack Lee's grin was worthy of the Cheshire Cat. "The old devil – I can tell you, it had me worried, Freddie. But what about clubbing last night – that really was stupid?"

Freddie Lee laughed. "I'm not that daft, Dad! – I'd given your pal at Figueretas a ring – he was pleased to give me a bed for the night. Though I suspect it was a bit late when he himself got in, *I* was sound out before midnight."

His father laughed. "Alright, I take it back – it was a nice little touch, son, going off like that – they were all convinced you're barmy. Anyway, now onto the second part."

"The slander action against you?"

His father nodded. "Plenty of witnesses for that, too. You must use the services of Peter Montague – he really is good despite his smooth manner. And go for a big pay-out – it's some years since Elton John won a whole million, and after all, your reputation should be proportionate to your new wealth and standing! Oh, and include the Judge as a witness – he'll be unimpeachable!"

"But how do we know the jury will agree with me?"

"Jury, what jury, son? We'll string it all out, create lots of paper work to back things up, then I suspect you'll find our side will settle on the steps of the court for say seventy percent of whatever figure you claim."

"Sounds good, Dad, very good! Although what I did to deserve you as a father, I'll never know."

"Become a chip off the old block, son, that's all you did. We're so alike I can live my life all over again through you. But now we must have another row, and appear to hate each other for a year or so. Are you ready?"

Freddie dumbly nodded his head, a tear starting to show in one eye.

"Ready Dad," he agreed, though appearing to hate the man he loved so much, the man he called 'Dad' really *would* be a hard act to follow through, whatever the tax saving involved . . . .

The Professor

It was a cold, black, wet, stay-at-home-and-sit-by-the-fireside night. And behind the tightly closed shutters of the Ibiza fincas – country cottages or farmhouses – that is precisely what folk were doing. Tonight was a night for the telly and for knitting; for warming your toes and drinking hot coffee, laced, for those who could afford it, with a touch of Soberano. Outside, in the blackness of the night, the howling rain rattled against the windows, hopped and skipped in the rapidly progressing puddles, flattened to the ground many a young plant, cut down before it could grow out of its childhood, and took the easy routes to the sea by becoming streams where no streams had flowed in Ibiza before. Tonight was a night to be indoors, and to be thankful that you were not outdoors.

Not surprisingly therefore, the ancient little Peugeot 205 cut a lonely path as it wound its uncertain way along narrow rutted tracks in the hills high above San Antonio. Its headlights, little more than two candles glowing through the storm, illuminated the road for only a little way ahead.

Inside the car, the tension between the occupants was increasing. James, Brian, and Annie, three different people from three different backgrounds, drawn together by a common duty, and the little car in which they travelled.

Variety there was, for certain. Compatibility, less certain. Not very easy, either. The swishy swashy thump thump noise of the windscreen wipers lost its monopoly over the silence inside the car, as James, the driver, small, dark-haired, neat, and public school spoke, "Just where the hell are we?"

Brian in the front passenger seat, was not in a helpful mood. "I don't even know where we've come from." His accent north country, Lancashire, somehow matching his large frame and beer belly. Although that might well be unfair to Lancastrians.

From the back seat, Annie chipped in, her Essex girl origins clear in the way she spoke, though not in the way she behaved, "Blowed if I can remember that, and I'm not at all certain where we're supposed to be going." As usual, she was wearing the garment which gave her the nickname of 'Annie the Anorac', sometimes used with malice, sometimes affection.

"We came up into the mountains from San Antonio, but that was ages ago – where's one of those maps?" from Brian.

James saw the opportunity to assert his authority, with that authority, or more accurately *desired* authority, apparent in his exaggerated public school accent, "Keep cool, Brian. Just remember, old chap, we *are* supposed to be the peoples' elected leaders, and be here to reach agreement well away from the media spotlight."

Brian looked up from his search for a map. "I am cool, thank you very much James." The anger in the voice gave the lie to the words. "I just think we should try to work together to get out of this mess." He turned round to glare at the shape huddled on the back seat. "You're no help, either, Annie."

In the darkness, Annie smiled an unseen smile, stretching her legs to make her stocky frame as comfortable as possible in the little car. Brian was quick to anger, and far more interesting company when he was roused. "But, Brian," she said smoothly, "I'm only a back-seat passenger. I didn't get us into the mess, and you've never wanted to work with us before. By the way, was that last turn-off we made on the map?"

Brian knew when he had met his match. He turned back to glare sullenly through the water-logged windscreen. "One of these days," he thought to himself, "I'll murder that snide bitch." He winced as his nails dug, a shade too deeply, into his own hands, and was able to reply with a bit of control, "The problem with this Ibiza map is that whilst nearly all the roads it shows do exist, there's a lot that exist which it doesn't show."

James didn't like the friction. Friction wasn't civilised. "I *think* I know what you mean. Anyway, cheer up – something's bound to turn up soon." This philosophy had carried James quite happily through life from an affluent childhood to a rich middle-age, and he saw no need to change it.

Brian suddenly leaned forward to wipe the mist from the inside of the windscreen. His eyes hadn't deceived him! "By heck, James, I think something has!"

The little car lost the few kilometres per hour it was doing, to stop outside a building. An oasis in the night, a monument to man's better thinking. It was a pub. High in the mountains above San Antonio, along a dirt road in the middle of nowhere, they found an olde-worlde-beer-and-skittles-one-hundred-percent-dyed-in-the-wool country pub. They could just make out the sign, illuminated in an eerie light, written both in Spanish and English, creaking and groaning as it swung backwards and forwards in the storm, 'La Taberna del Aquí y Ahora' – 'The Tavern of the Here and Now'.

"That's a new one on me," grunted Brian, "even in English."

Inside the one and only room that served as the Bar, Tap, Snug and Lounge, the two people had heard the car draw up.

Methuselah, an untidy and ancient be-whiskered man who would have looked more at home in the English West Country, moved from warming his backside, away from the roaring crackling logs in the inglenook fireplace, to perch on a stool at the bar. He looked at the door expectantly.

Behind the bar, Mary, the auburn haired landlady, fit, fat and forty, looked up from the newspaper which she had been reading. The door opened, and the three travellers entered, dripping, as if they had swum the short distance from the car. They shook themselves like collie dogs and grinned approvingly at the fire.

The landlady spoke, with no trace of a Spanish accent. "Good evening – what's it to be?" Her voice was warm and welcoming; the smile on her well-rounded face no less so.

Brian cast an inquiring glance at his companions. They nodded silently, eagerly even. "If you have it, two and a half pints of bitter, please, love," he said.

"I'd also like a pint, please Brian," Annie corrected him, "not a half".

Methusaleh watched with interest, but without comment. The three travellers looked around the room, in the manner people do in a strange pub. The black oak beams with gleaming horse brasses, the high backed wooden seats, made with care centuries ago to live in front of the fire and keep the heat from straying elsewhere, the stone-flagged floor where you could spill a drop of ale – not too much, of course – or in days gone by, spit, without causing palpitations or the price of beer to go up to cover the overheads, the nicotine stained ceiling, and the solid wood roughly hewn tables. But above all, the fire, its brightly burning logs scenting and warming the room – as much an English country pub as a Spanish taverna.

Brian moved across to warm his hands. "It's a cracking fire, is this." He turned his head to watch the landlady drawing the beer. She did it quickly, with no fuss, the beer, dispensed from measured quantity push button taps pouring without protest into the modern straight-sided sleever glasses.

Brian was disappointed. "I thought, you'd have real ale, drawn up from the cellar by a pump handle, like, in a place like this."

"Oh no, sir, we're right up to date in this pub." Her words though innocent enough, contrived to imply another meaning hidden behind them. Rather like a crossword clue.

Brian didn't do crosswords. He moved back to the bar to pick up his glass. James and Annie did likewise. They drank.

"Not bad ale, though," Brian commented, in case she had taken offence. And also because it was, after all, not bad ale.

"By Jove yes," agreed James readily. "I know a chap who started a campaign for modern ale. And he wanted it to be served in throw-away cardboard cups."

Brian looked at him, real ale was a subject close to his heart. Undeterred James continued. "He said it was more hygienic, and had accurate portion costings, with transfer of the critical overhead factor from human labour in loading and unloading the dishwasher to automated machine labour in manufacturing the cardboard cups."

Brian's concerned look had by now risen to one of horrified disbelief. "But he was a teetotal cost accountant, which I suppose explained it," James added. "The idea never got off the ground, anyway."

Brian relaxed, happier.

Annie laughed. With James you never knew whether he was being serious, or taking the, er, whatever they took out of you in Ibiza. It was therefore safer to laugh, as this covered all possibilities, and showed that she, at least, understood perfectly. "I agree," she said, turning to Brian, "It's not bad ale."

At this point, Methusaleh, the ancient yokel who looked as if he had slept in his clothes, could contain himself no longer. His voice was rolling and rich, the long 'r' of England's West Country very pronounced, softening his words, and making them sound, to a stranger, all the same. "Oi bin drinking it man and boy for the past several 'undred yrears, I'll tell 'ee, and 't 'asn't done I much 'arm. Changed a bit, though," he added.

The three looked at him in astonishment – what had brought *him* to Ibiza?

"*How* long do you say you've been drinking it?" asked Brian, convinced he was talking to a lunatic.

Methusaleh grinned, pleased at the effect his words had had. "Well I should reckon in this particular pub, the best part of two th . . . ."

He was interrupted by the landlady cutting in hastily. "Don't pay any attention to Methusaleh," she said, "he's always saying things like that." She sought to change the subject. "Might I ask what brings you three to 'The Tavern of The Here and Now'?"

James shot a puzzled look at Methusaleh as he answered. "You see, our being here is a bit confidential," he said, "but we're the leaders of the three main groups, which you may think of as Blue, Red, and Orange. In fact," he added proudly, "we were each chosen by several million people, and it's our job to plan the best way ahead."

Methusaleh was determined not to be left out of the conversation. "Like Moses, you mean?" he asked.

James was more than a bit taken aback. "Well yes, in a sort of way. But he was only a mythical figure – we're a bit more important than that."

Methusaleh spat on the floor, and took a swig from his glass. "Mythical, more important than Moses? Bah!"

Again the landlady hastily interrupted whatever else it was that Methusaleh might have been intending to say, "Are you going far?" she asked.

"Oh no, not really," from Annie, who thought that things were starting to get a little bit beyond her, "and we're almost there." She paused, before adding, "At least, I think we're almost there."

The landlady was relieved that her change of subject had been accepted. "Where is that?" she asked.

Annie grinned ruefully. "That's the problem. At least that's one of the problems." She took a drink of beer, before continuing. "You see, I want to go via a different route to a different place from my companions."

"And we've only got the one car," added Brian, as if that explained everything.

The landlady was puzzled. "But why can't you tour round and see everywhere – I assume you're in no hurry?" she asked.

Brian nearly choked on his beer. "Not likely, Love. When we get where I'm going, we're staying there."

James glared at him angrily. "Over my dead body."

"Mine too," Annie agreed.

"Very likely," from Brian.

Fearing for the sanctity of her pub, the landlady yet again tried to change the conversation. "Where have you come from, then?" she asked. "And what are you here for?"

The ploy worked, for the three travellers looked at each other sheepishly. "We don't know exactly," James eventually admitted.

The landlady was again puzzled. "Don't know where you've come from, or don't know what you're doing here?"

This time it was Annie's turn. "Well neither, actually."

"I thought 'ee said thee were chosen leaders," chortled Methusaleh.

If looks could kill, Methusaleh was dead, killed by a look from Brian. "We are, mate, we are."

"Well if you'm the leaders, why don't 'ee know where thee's come from, and what you'm doing 'ere?" from Methusaleh, triumphantly.

But before Brian could think of an answer, the door opened and a man entered. Most oddly for Ibiza, he wore a tweed country-style suit, which together with his well-groomed white hair, full-set beard, and general demeanour, lent him a distinguished air. He was absolutely bone dry. The newcomer greeted the landlady. "Hello, Mary," he said.

She was clearly pleased to see him, replying, "Good evening, Professor, I thought you'd be dropping in. The usual glass?"

"Yes, red wine, please, Mary," he confirmed, his voice cultured, articulate. "You have enough I take it?" he added with a grin, before turning to the ancient yokel. "Hello, Methusaleh."

Methusaleh greeted the Professor like an old friend, "How be on – good to see thee again."

Next, the Professor spoke to the three strangers. "Hello, and welcome to Ibiza." He nodded to them each in turn, speaking their names as he did so. "James, Brian, and Annie."

Annie was dumbfounded. Although the three of them were well known, she was sure she had never met the man before, and usually strangers were reticent, believing they had met a lookalike. "How on earth do you know who we . . . ."

She was interrupted by Brian, also speaking to the Professor. "It's stopped raining, then?" he asked.

The Professor smiled at him. "No, it's throwing it down," he said.

Brian looked at him in astonishment. "But you're bone dry!" he retorted, and walked across the flagstone floor to open the front door. The wind and rain poured in; he closed the door hastily, and turned to the landlady, baffled, "How come he's bone dry when it's raining cats and dogs out there?"

The landlady smiled a smile. "Oh, the Professor," she said, "he could walk on water if he wanted to. I shouldn't worry your head about him – he drops in the 'Here and Now' from time to time to see how things are going. Now he's the man who can help you find your way."

The Professor caught the end of the conversation. "Thank-you for your confidence, Mary, but do you really think they are ready to listen?"

The landlady nodded her head. "I think they might just be."

"Very well, then," the Professor agreed. He turned to the three travellers. "You have a problem," he said.

The three looked at each other, and nodded. Annie spoke, "Actually it's a bit of a long story. You see, I'm the Leader of Orange Group, Brian of Red Group, and James of Blue Group."

Methusaleh could not restrain himself. "Leaders – bah!" Not given to bad language, was Methusaleh. But explicit nevertheless.

"Yes, I know, and you're here incognito to try to reach agreement," the Professor answered smoothly.

This was more than Brian could stand. "Here just a minute, mate! I don't care if you are a bloody Professor, how do you know that – it's supposed to be top secret? And who are you, anyway?"

Methusaleh nearly fell off his stool with laughing. "Why, he's the Professor," he spluttered, "and 'tain't no use cussin', 'cos 'ee's never told a lie all the time I've known 'en."

James was a positive thinker, and rose above the situation. James rose above *any* situation. "I'll get the maps from the car," he said, "we'll see if he really can help."

The Professor picked up his glass of red wine, and moved to sit at a table near the fire, where he took a long drink. Annie and Brian sank their beer, and Annie asked the landlady if their glasses could be re-filled, although this time she did elect to only have a half. She turned to Methusaleh, "You having one?" she asked.

"Ar, don't mind if I do," confirmed the old yokel enthusiastically. They might not be the capable leaders they claimed to be, but that was no reason to refuse their hospitality.

Annie looked across to the Professor. "Another glass of wine, sir?" The 'sir' seemed appropriate, somehow.

The Professor smiled and raised his glass. It was still full to the brim. "That's very kind," he said, "but I'm alright for a while, thank-you."

This was too much for Annie. "You've already had several drinks from that glass – how can it still be full?"

"Don't worry about the Professor," the landlady said, "the one glass will see him through."

Just at that moment, the door opened, and James re-entered, absolutely drenched. He glared at the Professor. "I still don't know why you're not soaking wet," he commented, puzzled. Then he turned to his companions, "There's no other car outside, you know. He must have walked here." He looked at the beer glasses. "I'll have a pint please, whoever's buying,"

The landlady placed the re-filled beer glasses on the bar, and after paying for the drinks, Annie took the beers and went to sit by the Professor, who had already been joined by Brian and James. James spread out the maps on the table.

"Now then mate," from Brian, "since you seem to know everything, perhaps you could show us where we are – I think one of these is a map of Ibiza, and one of them probably isn't. But they don't make sense."

The Professor smiled, not put out by Brian's abrupt manner. He selected the smaller of the two maps, and neatly folded it. "This is a map of Ibiza, but you won't need it to get home tonight." He passed it to Brian, before turning to the other map, and immediately his smile became a grin. "I see your main problem straight away," he said. "As I expected, your map is too small – I mean it covers too small an area. It goes but a short way back along the road you have travelled, and the details are blurred."

This time Brian agreed. "You're telling me!" he said enthusiastically.

"And when you look to the way ahead," the Professor continued, "it shows so little of your journey." He leaned back in his chair, and took out an old cherrywood pipe. From another pocket he extracted a pouch, and as he continued, he filled the pipe with tobacco.

"You see," he explained patiently, as if talking to children, "the first thing you have to establish is exactly *where* you are and *why* you are. And to do that," his pipe full, he returned the pouch to his pocket, and extracted a box of matches. He lit the pipe, tapped down the tobacco, and drew contentedly upon it. "To do that", he repeated, "you have to learn where you've come from by separating the few grains of truth from the desert sands of fiction. Then, when you know these things, and you have discovered *why* you are, and *where* you are, then, and only then, will you be able to plan the road ahead. And I think you'll find the journey is far longer than you imagine."

The three leaders nodded their heads wisely, as if they understood. Which they didn't, quite. "That makes sense," said Annie doubtfully.

The Professor puffed on his pipe. "Although you think you have great differences, it appears you've all chosen virtually the same nearby destination – what I call 'The Mores'. And your differences are only in emphasis – choosing whether the More of this or More of that is the best place for your particular group to head for. You know, you really do have to look a lot further ahead!"

"But how far?" they asked in unison.

The Professor chuckled. "Don't you think you should have worked out the answer to that before departing, dragging millions along behind you?" He took a drink from his glass, and put it down. The glass was still full. Brian looked at it, fascinated.

The Professor paused to re-light his pipe. "You must always remember, good intentions are insufficient in themselves, and a good dose of realism is always required."

"But where on earth is our true road?" asked James in exasperation.

"Can't you give us a hint?" added Annie.

The Professor took another sip of his wine before answering. "I'm sorry, it really is for you to work out the answer to that, but I was intrigued you apparently limit your choices to 'on earth', James. I will give you one tip though – watch out for the stupidity and intolerance of those who hold strong beliefs built on myths and legends, for such closed minds only impede your true progress."

In somewhat of a daze from trying to de-cipher riddles, James collected the already-empty beer mugs. "Another drink, Professor?"

The Professor held up his glass – it was still full. "You're very kind, but I have plenty, thank-you, and I'm leaving soon."

James moved to the bar to order the beer. As the landlady bent to her task, he turned to Methusaleh. "Look, I'm sorry, I really am a bit confused – just who is the Professor?"

"Ar that'd be tellin'," the yokel replied, his eyes twinkling in the leathery old face. "But I'll tell 'ee this. He drops in the 'Here and Now' from time to time to help folks out. If you d'really think about what he said, I reckon he caught you three just in time, don't you?"

Just at that moment, the Professor tapped James on the shoulder. He was leaving. "Good-bye, James," he said. "best wishes for your journey. I think that now the three of you must all work together. And by the way, when you arrive at your destination, we'll need your help."

"What do you mean – you'll need our help?" asked Brian. But the Professor ignored him, and walked out through the door, closing it behind him.

Annie shouted after him. "Here, I say, wait a minute!" She ran to the door, and dashed outside. Methusaleh and the landlady exchanged grinning, knowing looks. A few seconds later, she returned.

"I don't understand it – there's nobody there!" she said, to no-one in particular.

Methusaleh and the landlady burst out laughing. James, his confidence shattered, picked up the three re-filled glasses and returned to the others.

"There was something distinctly weird about that chap," he said. James had a knack of noticing such things.

"I'm glad you mentioned that – I'd put it down to the beer," Annie commented.

"What on two pints!" from Brian. "And I'll tell you something else, old Methuselah's got more about him than you'd think – he seems to have known the Professor a very long time, as well."

James took a drink from his glass, before saying, "Yes, but what bothers me is how long." At this, they fell into what could euphemistically be called an animated conversation, which lasted for twenty more minutes, until they left the pub.

Outside it was a cold, black, wet, better-to-have-stayed-in-the-pub-and-sat-by-the-fireside night. The three of them squelched across to the small car, climbed in, and set off. Still the conversation and argument continued. Who was the Professor? How long had he known Methusaleh? Indeed, how long had Methusaleh been the local toper which he claimed? The questions ran like credits for next week's mystery thriller.

They had travelled only a kilometre or so when suddenly James could stand it no longer, and stood on the brakes. As the car was only travelling at twenty kilometres an hour, this in turn nearly stood it on its nose. "It's no use," he said. "I've got to go back to the pub to find out more about them."

For once in their life, the others agreed quite readily. In the black night the headlights gave barely enough illumination for him to turn round the little car, and peering through the misty windscreen, set off back down the narrow track.

A short while later, Brian spoke. "It was just around this corner."

And so it was.

Or rather, so it wasn't.

"I'm sure it was here," said James, puzzled.

But all there was was an olive orchard. A wet, muddy orchard, with rain from the olive trees dripping onto the ground, where it joined with dripping water from other trees to form into puddles. And though they searched for the rest of the night, it was as if 'The Tavern of The Here and Now' had never existed.

A Miracle at Sant' Llorenc

The old man raised himself upright on his knees and rubbed the lower part of his back with calloused rough hands – workman's hands. It seemed these days he was all aches and pains, but no matter, a coffee solo and small Soberano brandy would shortly ease his suffering. His weather-beaten face broke into a smile at the thought, and he returned to his task, tending lovingly to the memorial garden he had created in her favourite spot.

Lucia had been a good wife, and in the course of a long marriage they had loved and supported each other, and raised three happy children. Throughout all that time, they had respected their marriage vows and been faithful, one to the other.

Now she was gone, had left him six months before, and his mind drifted, for Manuel Ascensio was honest enough to admit to himself that although he had loved his wife, and she had been an agreeable companion to share his life, he had never been *in* love with her. For his heart had been lost to another, long before he knew Lucia, and ironically he had met her only a hundred metres from where he now knelt to his labours.

He was then a twenty-year old from Barcelona, where he was learning to work with wood – specifically to make high-quality bespoke furniture – when he had blown a whole years savings on a holiday to Ibiza.

He eased himself to his feet and moved to sit on a bench – one he himself had made and would shortly donate to the church in Lucia's memory – as his mind drifted back to Ibiza as it was back then. Francisco Franco ruled the island, as he did all of Spain, but 'el Caudillo' had mellowed, and in Ibiza especially, the atmosphere was relaxed and happy. The local Ibicencans – the farmers and fishermen – were poor but friendly, and learning to cope with the mystery of tourism. This was very low key, as the dirt strip that constituted an airfield could not take jets, but saw mainly the Douglas Dakotas of Spantax Airlines flying the short hop from the mainland or Mallorca.

Like the airfield, most of the roads on the island were surfaced only with dirt and gravel – with a few larger rocks to keep life interesting – and used mainly by donkeys pulling rustic carts. Never mind, the Vespa he had rented from Torres in Santa Eulalia had coped well with them, and with youthful red blood and adrenalin flowing he had wound open the throttle and leapt from rock to rock along the rural tracks as he searched out the secrets of the island.

He had come to Sant' Llorenc – it was then called San Lorenzo, a name he much preferred – to pursue his new hobby of photography, after a barman had told him it was the prettiest church on the island. The memory came back as vividly as if it were yesterday – he had parked his scooter alongside a similar one, and walked across to the church, which, as the barman had promised, was truly beautiful. Just as he was about to take a photograph with his elderly Kodak, a snub-nosed smiling young girl had emerged from under the arch, and greeted him.

"Hi – would you take my photograph?" she asked him, holding out her camera.

He had learnt a modicum of English at school, though the girl's accent made it unclear that was the language she spoke. But no matter, one look and he was hooked. She was in fact American, the first he had ever met, and spoke reasonable Spanish, picked up from her parents' Mexican maid back home in Texas. So Spanish was the language that Manuel and the pretty girl conversed in.

He took her photograph, she took his, and neither of them wanted to leave either the church or each other. When they did leave the village, they rode their scooters to Santa Eulalia, where she was staying at a smart hotel, and he in a humble hostel.

That night he spent some of his dwindling supply of pesetas treating the American girl to a steak at the Can Pere Celler, a restaurant which today remains pretty much as it was then, with enormous oak barrels a great feature of the dining room, as are the dark beamed rafters, chandeliers made from cart wheels, and even an ancient wine press. After an excellent meal, with their steak being preceded by a cold gazpacho soup, they went across the road to an open air nightclub called 'Ses Parres', where for part of the evening they enjoyed the company of Terry Thomas, the famous English comedy film star who lived on the island, and whom, whilst vaguely known to the American, was unheard of by the Spaniard.

Manuel and the girl fell in love, and spent the rest of their holidays in each other's company. They rolled in the surf, made love on the beach, and explored the mountains together.

So the devastation with which he received the news from the receptionist at her hotel that his American girl had left in a panic, following a phone message that her mother had been involved in a serious road accident, can be readily imagined.

"But she says don't worry," the receptionist said reassuringly, "she'll be in touch."

"But how," Manuel asked despairingly, "she doesn't even have my address?"

Two days later, he'd flown home to Barcelona in misery, resumed his work, and by the following year completed his training as a maker of wooden furniture.

The allure of Ibiza had not deserted him, however, and scraping together all his money, his possessions, and well-used bag of tools, he had caught the ferry to San Antonio. On a re-visit to San Lorenzo, he had taken the tenancy of a small finca, and received a tip where there was a run-down workshop available to rent cheap. It was just outside the village on the main road to San Juan, and he had taken it on first sight.

It had not been easy, but gradually Manuel Ascensio had prospered, for his work was of high quality, and his reputation grew steadily, with most of his new customers coming by recommendation. The finca became his own, he married a local girl, Lucia Mari, and the size of the finca grew to fit the family they created – three fine girls, though not the son he craved.

But he never re-found his American love, and a few months ago had also lost his wife. He sighed, and looked up towards the church. It seemed that God intended him to have a lonely old age.

* * * * *

The rented Mercedes glided to a halt, the driver leaving the engine running to power the air conditioning. He wore a T-shirt, had a crew cut, and was in his late thirties to mid forties. His female passenger was rather older, with blue rinse hair and designer label two-piece, her several rings and gold watch displaying her affluence in the American way.

"You're sure this is the place, Mom?" the driver asked.

"I'm sure, Elma, almost sure. Isn't that the most beautiful church you ever saw in your life?"

"Sure is, Mom, but you said it was along a small track, and the village was called San Lorenzo. We've driven along a metalled road, there's a proper carpark, an American style recreational area called 'Finca Can Pere Mosson' – and this village is called Sant Llorenc."

"I know, Elma, I know. It's all so, so different. But not the church – that's still the same, so beautiful. And I did hear that the local government had changed all the names back to what they were before Franco – like Ibiza becoming Eivissa."

"But that must be a bit confusing, Mom, if you think you've spent your life in San Lorenzo to be told you're wrong – it was Sant Llorenc."

"Guess you're right, son, but we do it with airports and things – even the Kennedy Space Center used to be Cape Canaveral."

"Tell me the story again, Mom, and now that we're here, swear that it's true."

"Oh it's true, Elma, it's true. And do you know, I'm not at all ashamed, because you were conceived with genuine love."

"I thought that was how all babies were conceived, Mom."

"No, son, most come after a session of alcohol induced lust, possibly with a complete stranger, at a party or on the back-seat of a car."

"So Dad was definitely not my Dad?"

"No. He was a good father to you, and a good husband to me – I never regret marrying him. I like to believe we made a happy home for you, and certainly your 'Dad' and I built a fair-sized business for you to take over."

"That's all so true, Mom, but why did you have to wait until Dad was dead before you told me the whole truth?"

"It just seemed right, son, that all the time you knew him, you believed he was your natural father." She paused for a moment, then continued with, "Elma, can we walk along the road for a little way, past that lovely little shrine? I'd like to see the pine woods again – we kinda went there a couple of times."

* * * * *

They walked along the high road from the carpark, to the left of the church, glistening white and resplendent in the sunlight, pausing for a while to look at the 'lovely little shrine'. Made of stone, with a domed top, it was also painted in pristine white. Set in the alcove was a hand-carved wooden cross, which bore an unexplained legend, 'Mision 1941', and to the left of the shrine, a flower bed separated it from a small white-painted stone pillar, which also bore a cross.

"It's all so different," she muttered, looking at the rising scrubby ground to the left, now part of the 'Area Recreativa', "but I'm sure it *was* here."

As they continued walking, the tarmac road became a dirt and gravel track, with the higher ground on the left held back by a dry stone wall.

"You keep saying it's different, Mom, but if the guy was so wonderful, how come you lost him?"

"It was all my fault," she said sadly. "When I got the message about your Grandma's accident, and that she only had hours to live, I panicked. I did make it back home before she slipped away, but it cost me my love. By then, although I didn't know at the time, you were already a little cookie starting to bake in my oven."

"Graphically put, Mom. But why didn't you contact him?"

"Because stupidly I did not have his address! We were going to exchange addresses and make plans on the last day of our holiday – but that day never came, at least as we expected."

"But surely you could have tracked him down?"

"I didn't even know his surname! Oh, he'd told me once, but I didn't really remember, and couldn't have spelt it if I had. If we used names at all, obviously they were our Christian names – and how many Manuels are there in Barcelona? He must have flown home hating me for treating him like that, after all we'd meant to each other, and all our promises." A short pause, then, "Damn!"

"Here, Mom, don't worry about the tears – this is an emotional time for you." He passed her his handkerchief.

* * * * *

The old man sighed as he lifted himself off the wooden bench, and decided the coffee and Soberano could wait – he wanted a few moments quiet reflection alone with his memories in the cool of the eighteenth century church.

It was locked against thieves, a sad reflection of modern times, but Manuel had a key. His gnarled old fingers inserted it into the lock, and he entered to the tranquillity which he sought.

As the door eased shut, Elma and his mother came to the front of the church. For a few minutes they admired the view across the valley, before moving to the wonderful arched entrance.

"Elma – let's get some photographs, so when we're back home, I can see where it all began."

Just as Elma took out his camera, his mobile rang. He answered it, and spoke to his mother. "Gee, Mom, I'm sorry, this is going to take some time – it's the office with a problem, and my notes are in the car. Can you take your own snaps – it's probably better you do that anyway?" he added, as he passed her the camera, and headed back to the Mercedes.

The old lady took her photographs, overwhelmed with nostalgia, and dearly wishing that someone could take one of her, under the arch of her beloved church.

Just then, an old man emerged.

"Hi – would you take my photograph?" she asked him, holding out her camera.

Cuth's Wine Tasting

by
Trev Hunt – known to Cuth as 'Taj'

The day was wet, the wind was cold,
When we visited Cuth's by invitation;
We tasted wine both young and old –
Cheeses so numerous to behold
(From cow and goat and lamb, we're told)
Each raised a glass in salutation,
A microcosm of our nation.

We chatted on, a merry band,
Warmed by the fire, watched the embers,
Enjoyed the wine from Cuth's generous hand,
Talked of friends from old England;
Of the summer to come, of sea and sand,
Of warm Julys and cold Decembers,
And anecdotes, as one remembers.

A knock on the door, a figure stood,
"I hope I'm not too bloody late,"
We sat as if each turned to wood –
It was 'Foxy', we understood;
I blew a kiss, as best I could,
She answered it, "Wotcha mate",
Then entered in with rolling gait.

Time moved on, the hours slipped by –
I tasted a '70 Rioja Reserva wine;
A little sip, good rounded taste, and fairly dry,
A damn good wine – "Here's mud in your eye !"
Alas, the clock told the story, we must say "Goodbye",
But 'twas a day to remember, for all that's fine,
When we visited Cuth, and tasted his wine.

12th March, 1985

Notes:-

This poem recalls an actual event I was privileged to attend – a private wine-tasting at the lovely home of Christopher 'Cuth' Adami. Cuth was one of the creators of the holiday village 'Pueblo Esparrogos' at Cala Llonga, and the original owner of the famous 'Wild Esparragos' restaurante.

Christopher 'Cuth' Adami

Scenes and Places

If you visit Ibiza, you may wish to explore the beauty of that magical island to enjoy many of the real scenes and locations described in this book. Such as:-

In Ibiza Town itself, the ancient citadel known as the D'alt Vila, or the old quarter called Sa Peña for its glamorous summer weekends night-life, or alternatively a quiet beer at one of the many bars in the picturesque Plaza del Parque.

In Santa Eulalia, take in the French-style chic of the promenade and the buzz of the yachting Marina, or a little to the north, detour to César's Beach Bar and Water Sports Centre at S'Argamassa for a simple but wholesome lunch - possibly preceded by aquatic excitement.

Opposite the lovely church in San Carlos, the centuries old Anita's Bar, famous for its shady courtyard and traditional tapas, or on a little further, the spectacular view of Cala San Vincente from the sheer-drop mountain road.

Over in the north east, the quiet peace of the terraced fields in the hills above San Antonio. And depending upon the month, you'll find San Antonio itself either a quiet pretty coastal town with docks and a marina, or a vibrant place full of young people enjoying themselves in noisy ecstasy, before moving on to one of the many island super-clubs, famous everywhere as the most fantastic night-life on planet earth.

South of San Antonio, discover the famous Pikes Hotel, set in an ancient finca and accessed via an unsurfaced track. A drink there will certainly cost you more than average, but you may well find you are sitting next to a film or rock star.

In the centre of the island, join the "in" crowd as they enjoy a drink and tapas in Santa Gertrudis – all this and much more you will find on a gentle tour of the Ibiza which the author knows and loves.

But please, don't waste your time looking for the following, ***which exist only in his imagination:-***

- All private houses, villas and fincas throughout the book.
- The 'Bar Don Quixote' in 'The San Rafael Kidnap'.
- 'La Cabeza del Toro' and Felix Gresham's shop in 'Fair Deal at La Cabeza del Toro'.
- The particular 'Astondoa' motor cruiser in 'Juan-Miguel and The Film Stars' – although Astondoa is a real builder of fine vessels.
- 'La Casagrande Bar-Restaurante', and all other bars, hotels and banks in 'A Victimless Crime'
- The small fishing boat 'el Rey del Mar', and the particular market stalls in 'An Ibicencan Meal' – although there are many excellent stalls at 'Es Marcat' in Santa Eulalia, which unlike our story, doubtless specialise in local meat, fish and produce.
- The San Antonio hotel and the seafront bar in 'The Teenage Pop Star of Figueretas'.
- The particular bar on the Plaza del Parque, Sheila Taft's 'Inmobiliaria' on The Rambla, and the garage 'Taller Toni' all in the story of that name.
- 'The Cricketer's Arms' outside Es Canar in 'Sancho's Heart Attack'.
- The 'Tavern of the Here and Now' in 'The Professor'.
- The 'Smart Hotel' and the 'Hostel' in 'A Miracle at San Llorenc'
- Back in the UK – the English golf club in 'Spitfire!'.